# The HUNTRESS of THORNBECK FOREST

# OTHER BOOKS BY MELANIE DICKERSON

## YOUNG ADULT

*The Princess Spy*

*The Captive Maiden*

*The Fairest Beauty*

*The Merchant's Daughter*

*The Healer's Apprentice*

*The Golden Braid* (Coming Fall 2015)

# The HUNTRESS of THORNBECK FOREST

*A Medieval Fairy Tale*

# MELANIE DICKERSON

**THOMAS NELSON**
*Since 1798*

NASHVILLE   MEXICO CITY   RIO DE JANEIRO

YA
DIC

Published in Nashville, Tennessee, by Thomas Nelson. Thomas Nelson is a registered trademark of HarperCollins Christian Publishing, Inc.

Thomas Nelson titles may be purchased in bulk for educational, business, fundraising, or sales promotional use. For information, please e-mail SpecialMarkets@ ThomasNelson.com.

Scripture quotations are from the KING JAMES VERSION and THE HOLY BIBLE, NEW INTERNATIONAL VERSION®, NIV® Copyright © 1973, 1978, 1984, 2011 by Biblica, Inc.® Used by permission. All rights reserved worldwide.

ISBN: 978-0-7180-3199-2 (HC Library Edition)

**Library of Congress Cataloging-in-Publication Data**
Dickerson, Melanie.
The huntress of Thornbeck Forest / Melanie Dickerson.
   pages cm.—(A medieval fairy tale romance; [1])
Summary:"Swan Lake meets Robin Hood when the beautiful daughter of a wealthy merchant by day becomes the region's most notorious poacher by night, and falls in love with the forester"—Provided by publisher.
ISBN 978-0-7180-2624-0 (paperback)
   [1. Love—Fiction. 2. Poaching—Fiction. 3. Middle Ages—Fiction. 4. Christian life—Fiction.] I. Title.
PZ7.D5575Hu 2015
[Fic]—dc23                                               2014046890

*Printed in the United States of America*
15 16 17 18 19 20 RRD 6 5 4 3 2 1

# 1

*The year 1363, in the northeast German reaches of the
Holy Roman Empire, the Margravate of Thornbeck*

THE TIP OF the arrow found its mark, a perfect shot through the deer's heart and lungs. The animal took two steps forward, then a side step, and fell over.

Odette's five men—more boys than men, as they were around thirteen or fourteen years old—darted out of the cover of the bushes and ran toward the animal that would feed at least four families. They began to cut it apart and prepared to carry it, and all evidence of it, away in their leather game bags.

But far more than four hungry families and many orphaned children inhabited the town of Thornbeck, so Odette motioned to the two boys looking to her. They set off deeper into the forest that was the margrave's game park. The only one reaping the good of Thornbeck Forest, rightfully, was the margrave. He could spare a few deer to feed the poor. He could spare them quite well.

Odette moved through the trees and undergrowth, trying to step as quietly as possible. The two boys stayed behind her. The moon was full, the night sky was clear of clouds, and enough light filtered through the trees to help her find her way to another of the harts' favorite feeding spots. Either a salt deposit was there or the grass was particularly sweet, because that was where she often found her most desired prey—fully grown red deer—with their necks bowed low as they ate.

Odette came within sight of the spot and crouched to wait, holding her longbow and an arrow at the ready. Soon, a hind moved soundlessly into the small clearing. Odette's fingers twitched in anticipation of the meat that would assuage the hunger of many people, but the twinge of pity that pinched her chest kept her from raising her bow and taking aim. It was summer, tomorrow being St. John the Baptist Day, and the hind no doubt had at least one newborn fawn, possibly two or three, hidden away somewhere, waiting for her to come back and nurse them.

Creating more orphans, even of the animal kind, went against everything Odette strove for, so she resisted taking the shot. Instead, she sat waiting and watching. After a few minutes, her breath stilled as a large stag with huge antlers stepped up beside the hind. He kept his head high as he seemed to be listening.

Odette swiftly raised her bow and pulled the arrow back. She pressed her cheek close to take aim and let the arrow fly.

Just at that moment, the stag must have caught wind of her or heard a noise because he turned and leapt away in one fluid movement, and the hind was less than a moment behind him. Odette's arrow missed them and disappeared in the night.

With the boys behind her, she went to search for the arrow. She did not want the margrave's forester finding it. She was careful to poach only one or two large animals a night, and it was important to take away all evidence that they had been there.

Where was that arrow? Odette went to the spot where it should have landed, beyond where the deer had been standing. She hunted around the bush, then parted the leaves to peer inside and underneath, searching for the white feather on the end. She felt around on the ground. No white feather and no arrow.

Her men were searching a little farther away. Suddenly, she heard laughter. She lifted her head, much like she had seen the deer do many times, and listened. Her two men looked at her, their eyes wide.

Voices drifted toward them, too far away for her to make out the words, but they seemed to be growing nearer. She clenched her teeth. Why couldn't she find that arrow? With reluctance, she motioned for the young men to follow her and moved away, back toward the town. She couldn't let anyone see her here, not with a longbow and a quiver of arrows on her back. The penalty for poaching was imprisonment, being fastened in the pillory in the town square, or having one's hand or ear cut off.

The voices likely belonged to people looking for special herbs and flowers to burn in the Midsummer bonfire the next night. Tomorrow even more people would be out in Thornbeck Forest, wandering into the margrave's game park. It would be too dangerous to go out hunting at all. If only she had not missed that stag.

She backtracked toward the three men she had left to take the hart she had killed earlier. They were hoisting the various pieces of meat over their shoulders and across their backs to carry out of the forest. They paused to kick the leaves and dirt over the bloody evidence of their kill.

As Odette approached, they turned and froze.

"It's me," she whispered. "We need to leave. People are coming this way."

They nodded as one of them dragged a tree limb over the ground to further disguise the evidence of their kill.

Just before they reached the edge of the forest, Odette pulled an old gray cloak out of her pouch and used it to cover her longbow and arrows, tucking them under her arm. She called to the young men, "Wait."

They stopped and looked at her.

"Give me one of those bags. I will deliver it."

They exchanged glances. Then the tallest boy said, "Rutger said we should deliver all the game to his storehouse, for him to distribute."

"I will tell him that I delivered this bag." She lifted a heavy haunch of venison off his shoulder. "He will not mind."

The boys continued on, but Odette, dressed as a boy with a long dark tunic and hose, her blond hair hidden inside her hood, went in a different direction.

She headed for the little hut just outside the town wall, a place where many of the poorest people lived in makeshift shelters. She knocked on the house that was leaning to one side and held up with sticks, and little Hanns opened the door, peeking around the side and rubbing his eyes with his fist.

"I'm sorry for waking you, Hanns."

"Odette!"

"Shh." She put her finger to her lips, then whispered, "I brought you something. In the morning you will have some fried venison for breakfast. How does that sound?"

Hanns stopped rubbing his face, his mouth fell open, and his eyes got round. As Odette held out the leather bag, the air rushed out of him with an excited, "Oh!"

"Don't wake your mother now. You can surprise her in the morning."

"I will!" Without closing the door, he turned and, straining to carry the heavy meat, disappeared inside the dark one-room, dirt-floor house.

Odette closed the door and turned to hasten home while it was still dark.

⁓

Jorgen Hartman knelt before the altar of Thornbeck Cathedral and bowed his head. As it was the feast day of St. John the Baptist, he and many other people from town had come to pray. Some of the townspeople had brought herbs to the church for the priest to bless, which should give the herbs special healing abilities. Others, like Jorgen, were there because they had missed the midday Mass and wanted to offer prayers on this holy day.

Jorgen finished praying and rose to his feet. As he did, a woman several feet away caught his eye as she lighted a candle. She was lovely, with long blond hair that fell in curls down her back from underneath her veil. In the candlelight, her face seemed to glow with piety and sweetness. He drank in the beauty of her facial features as she knelt, making the sign of the cross. But then she drew the veil over her face as she bowed in prayer.

Since he didn't want to stand and gawk at her profile, still visible beneath the veil, he made his way to the other end of the nave, perusing the stained glass windows depicting various stories and people of the Christian faith. He focused on the one where John the Baptist baptized his cousin Jesus and the Holy Spirit came down in the form of a dove. He'd always loved the brilliant colors of the windows and had often slipped into the nave as a boy, hiding in a corner to stare at the depictions and their bright reds and blues, greens and yellows.

The beautiful girl finally stood and was joined by a man. Was he her husband? *Holy saints, let him be her father.*

As they made their way toward the door, he tried not to stare.

She passed by him and out the cathedral door without ever looking his way.

Perhaps he would see her at the Midsummer festival in a few hours.

Jorgen went to visit his friend Paulin, who had broken his leg and was not able to go to the Midsummer festival. Afterward, Jorgen joined with the crowds who were flowing toward the sound of the *Minnesingers* in the town center. Young maidens skipped along in their flowing dresses, carrying bouquets of flowering herbs and wearing woven crowns of white wildflowers.

There would be a bonfire in the *Marktplatz* and dancing, and unmarried maidens would be alert to find their future husbands. Now that he was nearing five and twenty years, even his mother had approved of him coming to the Midsummer celebration.

Winking, she had said, "Perhaps if you dance with some pretty maidens, one of them will dream of you tonight."

He kissed her wrinkled cheek. "You should pray that whoever dreams of me tonight will be a good daughter to you."

"I will and do not doubt it." Her tone was gentler now. "She will be a good girl indeed to deserve you."

He touched her cheek and looked into her faded blue eyes. "Thank you, Mama."

Now he looked around and wondered which of the maidens, if any, his mother was praying for. Already he had seen a pretty red-haired maiden glancing back at him, and a raven-haired girl of perhaps sixteen smiling and waving at him.

As he drew nearer the center, moving slowly because of the dense crowd, the smell of fresh bread made him take a deep breath.

A baker stood outside his shop holding a tray of bread rolls. A small boy, perhaps six years old and dressed in rags, stood at the corner of the shop, his head peeking around from the alley where an even smaller girl stood behind him.

He caught his breath. It was little Helena.

No, Helena had been dead for more than fifteen years. The sight of her bloody body, lying in the street where the horse had trampled her, flashed through his mind like lightning. Her bright eyes stared up, and her mouth moved wordlessly as she fought to draw breath into her crushed chest. He could still feel her body growing cold in his arms while heartless, frowning faces stared down at him, and a man shouted at him to get out of the street.

The tiny girl who now stood in the narrow side street was not looking back at Jorgen. Instead, she was looking anxiously at the little boy peering at the baker and his bread. The look of desperation in the boy's face seemed familiar. Jorgen watched, knowing what the boy was about to do, but also knowing he would not be able to get through the people in time to stop him.

The boy darted around the corner and ran toward the baker, staying close to the wall of the shop. While the baker was handing two rolls to a woman who placed a coin on the baker's tray, the boy ran by and snatched a roll.

Perhaps he had not seen the woman on the other side of the baker, but she had seen him. She grabbed the back of the boy's neck with one hand and his arm with the other. "Thief!" she cried.

The boy dropped the bread and threw all his weight in the opposite direction, but the woman was too strong for him. Her grip held firm. The boy yelped.

From his view of the side street, Jorgen saw the girl child cover her face with her hands and her shoulders start to shake. Even though she couldn't see the boy from where she stood, she undoubtedly heard his pleading for the woman to let him go.

"A few hours in the pillory will do you good, you little knave."

The woman gave his ear a twist. Though his face twitched in pain, he did not cry out.

Jorgen broke away from the crowd and stepped in front of the woman and her captive.

"*Frau*, pardon me," Jorgen said, causing the woman to look up at him. "The child left home without his money. Will you accept this to pay for the bread he dropped on the ground?" He held out two coins to her, enough to pay for four of the baker's rolls.

The dark cloudiness of her expression changed as she looked at his money and then back at his face.

"I'm sure the child is sorry." He placed his hand on the boy's shoulder and stepped even closer.

"I suppose . . . but if he learns to steal now," she muttered, "he'll be a thief all his life . . . naught but a thief." She accepted the money, took three more rolls off her husband's tray, and handed the bread to Jorgen.

"I thank you." He nodded to her and nudged the boy as they backed away from her.

When they were a few steps away, with the boy staring up at the bread in Jorgen's hand, he pulled the boy aside and squatted so he could look the child in the eye. "Here is the bread, but do not steal. Next time you might be punished."

The little boy drew himself up, squaring his shoulders and lifting his chin, as if trying to look taller. "I am not afraid."

"Of course not. But your little sister would be very frightened if you were taken to the town square and fastened in the pillory."

The little boy glanced behind him at the girl who was standing at the corner of the alley, sniffling and staring at them both.

The little boy's shoulders slumped. "Can I go now?"

Jorgen's heart constricted at the look on the boy's face. "Do you have a mother or father?"

"I have a mother."

"Where do you live?"

He pointed in the direction of the alley. "With my mother's sister, but she says she cannot feed us."

"If you need food, go to the gamekeeper's cottage. Do you know where it is?"

"Outside the town gate, in the margrave's forest?"

"That is where I live. My mother will give you food if I am not there."

The expression in his eyes was much older than his years. Finally, the boy nodded. Jorgen walked him back to his sister, and the boy handed her a bread roll. They both put the bread in their mouths and bit into them. Then they turned and started down the alley side by side.

"Wait." He couldn't bear to let them leave with only a few small rolls. While he felt around in his pocket, he asked, "What is your name?"

"Martin."

"Martin, do not lose this." He handed him some coins. "Buy some food for yourself and your sister."

The whites of the boy's eyes flashed, as did his teeth, as he finally smiled. "Thank you." He grabbed his sister's hand and ran away.

Jorgen turned back in the direction of the town center and *Marktplatz*, blinking to try to erase the memory that the boy and his little sister had brought to the surface. The sounds of lute, hurdy-gurdy, and a *Minnesinger's* voice singing a familiar ballad lured him on toward the music and dancing, where he might forget that he was ever as poor, hungry, and desperate as the two children he had just seen.

# 2

ODETTE'S FRIEND ANNA held up a braided wildflower circlet and placed it on Odette's head. "Now you are ready for the Midsummer festival."

"Do you not think I'm getting too old to dress like the other unmarried maidens on Midsummer?"

"Of course not. You are unmarried, are you not? You'll be the fairest maiden in the town square."

Odette embraced her friend. "And you'll be the fairest married woman there."

Anna laughed. "And the sleepiest. The baby woke me up three times last night."

They stood admiring each other in the large ground-floor room of the half-timber house where Odette lived with her uncle. Odette wore the lightweight, white linen overdress that all the maidens wore on Midsummer's Eve, while Anna wore a beautiful blue cotehardie with cutaway sides and a decorative belt.

One of the maidservants came down the stairs with the cloths, brushes, and bucket she used for cleaning the upper floors.

Had Odette hidden her bow and arrows before going to bed just before dawn? The sick feeling in her stomach told her she had forgotten.

Trying to hold on to her smile, Odette squeezed her friend's arm. "Wait here while I go do something."

Odette rushed up the stairs to her bedchamber on the third floor and nearly ran into her uncle in the stairwell. "Uncle Rutger. I didn't see you. Did Heinke clean my chamber?"

He shrugged. "She may have. Did you need her to do something for you?"

"It's nothing. I just need to . . ." Odette hastened away without finishing her sentence. Inside her chamber, the flagstone floor was swept clean and the bedclothes were straightened. But the old cloak she used to cover her longbow and arrows was lying folded across her bed.

Odette scurried to her trunk against the wall. She yanked off the bear fur that lay over it and raised the lid. Her longbow and arrows were not inside.

Glancing around frantically, she caught sight of them leaning against the wall in the corner. How could she have left them in plain sight?

"Is that what I think it is?"

Odette spun around. Rutger stood in the doorway. Her uncle was only a bit taller than she was, and he was thin, with thinning brown hair.

"Oh. I didn't hear you there." Her heart thumped against her chest, and she hurried to grab the cloak off her bed, then to the corner where her weapons were resting against the wall. She wrapped the bow and arrows in the cloak.

"Did you not think it would be a good idea to hide that from view?" Rutger quirked up one side of his mouth.

"Of course. I never leave them out where anyone can see them. Last night I must have forgotten." She cringed as she placed them into the trunk and closed the lid, then drew the bearskin over it.

Odette closed her eyes and tried to take a deep breath. Heinke would not tell anyone that Odette owned a longbow and arrows, would she? And even if she did, they would never suspect the niece of a respectable merchant of poaching . . . would they?

"People will wonder what Odette Menkels is doing with a bow and arrows in her bedchamber. You could say you were hunting for a husband."

Odette rolled her eyes at him.

His dark eyebrows drew together. "But to be serious, if the margrave's forester were to discover . . ."

"I know," Odette said softly. She was in constant fear of the forester, whose job it was to capture poachers and bring them to the margrave to be punished.

She did not tell him she had lost an arrow in the margrave's forest last night.

Anna called to her from downstairs, and Rutger asked, "Do you need me to go to the festival to approve or disapprove of any young men wishing to dance with you?"

"Anna and Peter will be with me. Their mothers are staying home with the children."

"Very well."

"Perhaps you should come and find yourself a pretty wife." Odette raised her brows at him.

He shook his head. "I think not. My time is better spent planning how to make more money so that I can increase your dowry. But perhaps I should be trying to hunt down a husband that you will deem worthy." He shook his finger at her. "The men of Thornbeck have been clamoring at my door, begging to marry you for years. There is not another maiden in Thornbeck who is as picky as you. I have offered you every wealthy man in Thornbeck, and you have turned them all down."

Odette let her mouth drop open in what she hoped was an expression of shock. "Every ugly, fat, *old* "—she paused to emphasize the word further—"wealthy man. Are there any young men in Thornbeck who do not have a hairy wart on their nose and still have all their teeth who might be willing to marry me?"

"See how picky you are?" He gave a look of mock outrage. "I suppose you would be proud to have a handsome husband, even if he was also a poor peasant farmer living in a one-room hovel, but I happen to think you deserve better than that. You do not want your children begging for bread, do you?"

Odette frowned up at him, her hand on her hip. "Of course I don't want to marry a poor man, but are all the rich men ugly and old?" She tapped her finger against her chin, then held it up in the air. "I know! You should marry a rich widow. Then she could support all of us, and I would never have to marry at all."

"That is a very good idea. As soon as I find one, I will be sure to marry her as quickly as possible. And if she is unwilling to marry, I shall get her with child and then she will have no choice."

"You are incorrigible." She slapped playfully at his arm.

He winked and they parted. Odette headed down the stairs to her friend.

How fortunate she was to have an uncle like Rutger. Most guardians would have married her off years ago to the wealthiest man they could find and would not have allowed her any choice. But he had always asked her thoughts on the matter. If she were to marry, she could no longer do what she pleased—namely, hunt deer in the margrave's forest. Besides, those men had not held any appeal for her.

Odette joined Anna and they ventured back into the street. The crowds of people buzzed like bees as they made their way to the open space of the *Marktplatz*.

"Who do you think you will dream of tonight?" Anna asked as they walked arm in arm and passed the big cathedral, the tallest building in town, on their way to the festivities.

"I rarely ever dream of pleasant things."

Anna gave her a frown and raised her eyebrows.

"But tonight I shall pray to dream of a handsome husband."

Anna smiled her approval.

Already there was a large crowd of people dancing in the open plaza around the fountain where venders sold goods three days a week from portable booths. The weather was perfect as the sun sank behind the four-and five-story buildings that encircled the *Marktplatz*.

Jongleurs were throwing colorful balls in the air, keeping them moving in a continuous circle of three, while another young man played the flute and danced. Sellers shouted out various wares and foodstuffs for sale, but the bailiffs were forcing them to stay on the periphery to allow the people room to dance.

The *Minnesingers* and their accompanying musicians were set up at the head of the *Marktplatz* and were already singing an old familiar love ballad. One tenor voice rang out above the others as he sang:

*You are mine, I am yours,*
*Of that you may be sure.*
*You're safely locked away*
*Deep within my heart,*
*But lost is the key*
*And there you'll ever stay.*

The words made Odette wrinkle her nose. She did not like to admit it, but she did hope someday she might want to "lock someone away in her heart" and lose the key. But unless he was wealthy and willing to help the poor, she feared she might be destined to go on poaching deer until she grew too old to stretch a bowstring.

Straight ahead she caught sight of Anna's husband, Peter, waiting for them at the fountain in the middle of the cobblestone city center. The fountain was a popular meeting place, so the crowd grew even thicker as they drew closer.

Peter lifted his hand to wave at them just as a young man, dressed in the garb of a wealthy burgher, was pressing through the people toward them. Mathis Papendorp, the Burgomeister's son, was always smiling and bowing and kissing her hand. Rutger had long been speaking to her of his suitability as a husband.

The young man reached them and bowed. "Beautiful maidens, would you do me the honor of dancing with me this Midsummer's Eve?"

"I'm afraid we cannot both dance with you." Odette arched her brows at him. "At the same time, leastways. And although my friend is quite beautiful, she is also married."

Anna nodded. "It is true. And my husband is coming this way."

"I would dance with you anyway," he said, "but I would not want to offend your husband or expose a gentle lady to gossip."

Prettily spoken. His speech and manners were as smooth as she might have expected from the son of the mayor.

Mathis was somewhat handsome, she had to admit, with pale hair and blue-gray eyes. "But I should be glad of the chance to dance with this beautiful maiden." He bowed again to Odette.

She extended her hand toward him. "It is my pleasure to dance with you."

As Mathis took Odette's hand and whisked her into the crowd, she caught a glimpse of her uncle approaching Anna and Peter. All three were eyeing Mathis.

During the dance, he was polite, talking of the weather and asking her about herself. When the song was over, he escorted her to where Anna, Peter, and Rutger were standing but excused himself, saying, "I shall return in a moment."

Uncle Rutger leaned over and said, "I believe Mathis Papendorp is as taken with you as ever, Odette." He gave Odette a stealthy wink. "You could do much worse than the Burgomeister's oldest son."

"Ah yes. He is very wealthy." Peter nodded and raised his brows at Odette.

Soon Mathis returned. His eyes brightened as he turned to her. "Would you honor me with another dance?"

Odette placed her hand on his arm and allowed him to lead her to the area of the *Marktplatz* where the *Minnesingers* and musicians were playing and singing. Rutger would consider the mayor's son a worthy suitor. He was somewhat handsome, wealthy, and socially well placed. But as she glanced at Mathis's profile, Odette couldn't help wondering what sort of man he was.

As he lined up with her for the dance, she noticed a very handsome man coming toward them.

⁓

Jorgen made his way to the center of the *Marktplatz* when a beautiful maiden—the same young woman from the cathedral—caught his eye. She had the same golden hair hanging in ringlets down her back, unfettered by even a veil, and the same graceful profile and generous facial features. He was certain it was she—but she was dancing with Mathis Papendorp.

The good thing was that she wore the simple white dress and circlet of white wildflowers on her head that indicated she was a maiden and unmarried. How could such a beautiful woman, obviously older than sixteen or seventeen years, still be unmarried? Whatever the reason, his heart lightened.

Her face still glowed, even though it was now lit by the early-evening summer sun instead of the altar candlelight.

Mathis was obviously taken with her, with the way his gaze never left her. Would she dance all night with Mathis? Seeing her again in such a large crowd seemed like fate, and he could not let the opportunity escape him. But . . . the way she had been dressed at the cathedral earlier, she must be a wealthy burgher's daughter. She might not wish to dance with him, as he wasn't exactly part of the wealthy burgher class.

As the song ended, the dancers stopped. Mathis said something next to her ear. Whatever he said would be charming since Mathis was as good at making flattering little speeches as his father was.

Jorgen hung back as they walked past, wanting to approach her without Mathis around. Mathis bowed to the same man who had accompanied her in the cathedral and stood talking with him and the beautiful young woman.

Someone called his name, and Jorgen turned to see two maidens with flower circlets in their hair.

"Won't you dance with us?" the red-haired one said, smiling flirtatiously. "Someone told us that you are the margrave's forester. Is that true?"

He would have been pleased to dance with them—if not for the hope of meeting the blond maiden with the bright-blue eyes.

"I am the margrave's forester."

"Come, then." The brunette reached for his hand. "Dance this one with me and the next with my friend."

Jorgen allowed the bold girl to lead him to the group forming a circle for the carol.

As he danced to the lively music, he had to stop himself from searching the crowd for the beautiful maiden from the cathedral and to focus on his partner instead. When that dance concluded, he danced with her friend, the red-haired girl, who kept asking him questions while they danced. After the dances were over, he excused himself from them. But when he tried to find the mysterious blue-eyed girl, she was no longer standing where she had been before, and neither was the man he assumed was her father.

Then he spotted her with Mathis again.

Before he had time to think better of it, he walked forward and inserted himself in the circle of dancers just beside the beautiful maiden. As they spun around and clapped their hands above their heads, he caught her eye and smiled at her. A few moments later, she glanced in his direction, and when they had to turn all the way around again, she smiled back at him.

Out of the corner of his eye, he noted Mathis's look of warning but pretended not to see him.

When the music ceased, Jorgen placed himself in front of her. "Would you honor me with the next dance?"

She looked surprised but also a little pleased, if he read her smile correctly. "I will."

Mathis's face turned red, and he pressed his lips into a thin line. "Until later." He bowed to the maiden and walked away, glaring over his shoulder at Jorgen. But Jorgen kept his eyes focused on her. "I am Jorgen Hartman."

"Odette Menkels."

"A beautiful name, Odette." He let the name linger in his mind and on his tongue as he stared into her eyes.

The music started, and Jorgen's heart beat faster as everyone joined hands with the people beside them and formed a giant circle. He clasped his hand with Odette's smaller one on one side, and another maiden's on his other side.

The circle moved first to the right two steps, then to the left two steps, then forward two steps, clapping twice, then back two steps as they grasped each other's hands again. The steps repeated as the music grew faster and faster. The dancers shouted as they moved forward and clapped. His shoulder brushed Odette's. He tried not to stare at her. She kept glancing up at him, and by the end of the dance, the pace grew almost too fast for the dancers to keep up. She laughed.

When it was over, she said, "I should get back to my uncle."

So the man was her uncle. Jorgen wanted to dance with her again, but he didn't want to make her uncomfortable. "I will escort you." He held out his arm, and she placed her hand on his wrist.

As soon as they turned to move away from the dancing, Odette said, "This is my uncle, Rutger Menkels."

"Forgive my boldness in dancing with your niece." Jorgen bowed. "I am Jorgen Hartman, and I am honored to dance with the fair Odette."

"Indeed. I know of no other maiden in Thornbeck as fair as she." There was a challenging look in Rutger's crooked smile.

"Nor do I."

Rutger seemed to be sizing Jorgen up. But since her uncle said nothing to object to him, he turned to Odette. "I would be honored if you would dance with me again."

She smiled. "It would be my pleasure."

They moved back to where the dancers were readying themselves. But this time the music was slower and accompanied by a heavy drumbeat. They formed two lines, the men facing the women. Each man reached out and took the hand of his partner. Jorgen took Odette's soft hand in his as they stepped toward each other, passing and turning around as they exchanged places. The lines of dancers were quite close now as the *Marktplatz* became more crowded.

As they danced forward and back, he and Odette repeatedly brushed shoulders. They rose up on their toes, their hands meeting palm to palm just above their heads. Then they stepped back, then forward, again changing places as they twirled and faced each other. She was so close he could see her long eyelashes, which were darker than her hair, against her pale skin. Her cheeks were flushed in the warm Midsummer night air. She stole the breath right out of his throat, and he couldn't seem to take his eyes off her.

Perhaps his mother would get her wish, as this night did seem full of Midsummer night enchantment.

# 3

O<small>DETTE HAD NEVER</small> seen Jorgen Hartman before, and her uncle did not seem to know him. He did not look poor, but he also did not appear to be of the wealthier merchant class her uncle and Mathis were part of. Still, he was young and handsome, and she liked his courteous manner toward her. His dark-blond hair came almost to his shoulders and was thick and slightly wavy. His eyes were a mix of green and blue.

As much as she enjoyed Mathis Papendorp's attentions, she preferred the look in Jorgen's eyes.

They rose up on their toes, their faces drawing within a hand-breadth of each other, then falling back two steps. Could he see that her face was flushed? Would he realize it was not only from the heat or the dancing but from being so close to him?

His jaw hardened as he seemed to be looking at something behind her. He leapt toward her just before something slammed into her back. She stumbled into Jorgen's chest. He threw his arm between her and whatever had collided with her back, pulling her aside.

She watched over Jorgen's shoulder as a man with a torch passed them. He was waving the fire over his head, pushing his way through the crowded *Marktplatz* along with a small band of red-nosed, drunken men, shouting, "Light the bonfire!" Someone screamed, and another person fell to the ground, causing more screams as people scrambled out of the way.

Jorgen kept his body between her and the unruly men, shielding her until they had passed. His brow furrowed as he looked into her eyes. "Are you all right?"

"I am well. Thank you for protecting me." They were being pressed against each other by the people on either side of them as the music halted in the middle of the song. Some of the dancers loudly protested the shouting and pushing that was disrupting their dance.

Jorgen bent his head close to her ear. "Take my arm."

She complied, and he started making his way around the revelers. She smelled the wine and strong drink on the bodies passing in front of them. They were headed toward the other side of the fountain where the wood had been piled in readiness for the bonfire. But it was too early. They never started the fire until the Burgomeister had made a speech and darkness had fallen.

Odette and Jorgen moved at a slow pace, often forced to wait for a group to pass, many of them shouting and laughing and pushing. A particularly unruly group almost wrenched Odette's hand from Jorgen's arm, causing her to gasp and stumble. Jorgen turned his body so as to block them from her. Then he put his arm around her shoulders and maneuvered her beside him instead of behind him.

He kept his gaze on the crowd and on making a way out of the crush of people, which allowed Odette to study him covertly through her lashes.

He had a solid chin, a muscular jaw, and sturdy cheekbones that contrasted with a gentle look about his mouth and eyes. He clenched his jaw, his arm tightening about her when someone pushed against them.

Was he aware that she was watching him?

Soon they were free of the boisterous people heading for the bonfire. He loosened his arm around her as Rutger, Anna, and Peter approached them.

"There you are," Rutger said. "I was afraid you were caught in that crowd of ruffians."

"We were, but Jorgen kept me safe." She couldn't help glancing up at him. The way he gazed down at her made her heart trip and miss a beat.

Her uncle turned his attention to Jorgen. "I am grateful to you for protecting Odette. But now that the more unruly ones have gone to see to the bonfire, I hear the music starting."

"I believe it is my turn again." Mathis walked up behind them. "Odette, would you favor me with another dance? Jorgen is a handsome enough fellow. He will find another maiden to dance with him." Disdain dripped from his tone.

So Mathis and Jorgen knew each other?

Jorgen looked into her eyes, as though to see if that was what she wanted. Not wanting to slight either of them, she wasn't sure what to say.

"I thank you for dancing with me." Jorgen bowed to her. "Perhaps I will see you again." He smiled before walking away.

She bit her lip as she watched him go.

But when she turned, Anna gave Odette a wide-eyed look and raised her eyebrows. Anna seemed to be asking her what she thought of Mathis and Jorgen. Odette was under no illusion that Anna would let her go home without telling Odette her thoughts, and in great detail.

The section of the cobblestone town square devoted to dancing became less crowded as some moved closer to the bonfire. Odette danced with Mathis but found herself glancing over at Jorgen, who was dancing with a pretty red-haired girl.

When the song ended, Mathis leaned down and said with a grin, "You dance as gracefully as a swan."

"Thank you. You probably say that to every maiden who dances with you."

"Indeed, I do not." He feigned seriousness and leaned even closer. "You must come to my father's house when he gives his next party. As the most graceful woman in Thornbeck, you must come to all the mayor's gatherings."

She simply smiled back at him.

"I believe I should dance with Jorgen now." She turned away from Mathis before he could protest.

At seeing Jorgen talking with the red-haired maiden, Odette's heart sank. Would he want to dance with her again?

He seemed to be bidding the girl farewell and turning away. She caught his eye. He just stood there, looking at her, so she walked toward him.

One side of his mouth quirked up. "Would you like to dance?"

"*Ja.*" She tried not to exhale too loudly the breath she had been holding as she took Jorgen's hand. Never had she been so attracted to a man. Would her uncle deem him worthy? Not that Jorgen would ask her to marry him, but it was never too early to find out.

When the dance was over, Jorgen gave her hand a small squeeze and held on to it. "Are you thirsty?"

Odette nodded. "Let us go for water." She looked around Jorgen's shoulder at Anna and Peter. "We're going to the fountain for water. Do you want to come?" She didn't wait for their answer but turned and walked with Jorgen, her hand on his arm. She was too afraid to ask him his profession—afraid he would think she was using that to judge his acceptability—and afraid his profession would *not* be acceptable to Uncle Rutger. What could she ask him to make him talk about himself?

Peter and Anna caught up with them, and Peter said, "You may not remember me. I'm Peter Voreken. Do you live in town?"

"In Thornbeck Forest. The margrave has appointed me the new forester."

The new forester? Odette's heart sank into the pit of her stomach, then seeped all the way down to her toes. It was worse than she'd feared. Much worse.

This was the man who could send her to the margrave's dungeon.

It was as Jorgen had feared. Peter Voreken's smile faltered when Jorgen told him he was the forester. Peter's father was a wealthy merchant and a prominent person in Thornbeck. Jorgen was orphaned by the Great Pestilence of 1348 and left destitute. His adoptive father had taught him all about taking care of the game animals and all the duties of a gamekeeper, and although Jorgen still aspired to greater things, he was not ashamed of his position. But perhaps it had been a mistake to set his sights on Odette Menkels.

He dared a glance in her direction. A flicker of something akin to fear crossed her face, and her smile seemed frozen on her lips. Of course she thought his status too low, but she seemed afraid of him. Her fingers went loose on his arm. He should give her an easy way to excuse herself from his company, but . . . he wasn't ready to let her go. He would only go if she expressed her wish for him to go.

"Forester," Peter said. "That position is appointed by the margrave, is it not?"

"It is."

"Have you caught any poachers?"

"Not yet. But I consider capturing poachers my most important duty."

Why did Odette look pale?

"I've never spoken to the margrave," Peter went on. "I suppose you speak with him very often."

"I report to him once every week, sometimes more."

"You must be busy. Thornbeck Forest is very large."

"I am training two new gamekeepers now, so *ja*, I have a lot of work. What do you do?"

"I help my father with his merchant business, bringing goods here from the Orient and selling them."

The sun had gone down, and dusk settled around them as they stood with the others waiting to get a drink at the fountain. Some more people crowded in, causing a shift in their line, and Peter and Anna became separated from Jorgen and Odette. They seemed almost alone now in the middle of the crowd.

Odette appeared to have recovered from whatever had made her turn pale and look frightened. "What else do you do all day besides train gamekeepers?"

"You don't want to hear about my dull work—keeping track of the animals in Thornbeck Forest. I am interested to hear about you, though. What do you do when you're not attending Midsummer festivals and dancing in the town square?"

"I see. You want to turn the talk away from yourself and onto me now." She nodded and closed one eye, as if they were in on some secret. "You will probably think me strange, but I teach reading and writing lessons to the children who live outside the south wall of Thornbeck."

He turned his head to look full into her face. "That was you? I saw someone several days ago teaching the children outside the town gate. They were drawing in the dirt with sticks."

"I taught them their letters and now I'm teaching them words."

His heart thumped harder. There was more to this beautiful maiden than he could have imagined.

Odette admired the look in his blue-green eyes. He did not disapprove of her teaching poor orphans. She refrained from telling him that she also sometimes brought them food and fed them before the day's lesson, as she couldn't bear to think that some of them hadn't eaten all day. And she certainly couldn't tell him that she slept much of the day because she spent her nights poaching.

"I think that is . . ." His throat bobbed as he swallowed. "A very good thing."

One of the boys had told her that the new forester gave him food when he went and knocked on the door of the old game-keeper's cottage. Was that man Jorgen?

The mood had grown somber. Did the thought of the poor children make Jorgen sad? She decided to change the direction of their conversation. "How do you and Mathis know each other?"

"We attended the town school together when we were boys."

"I heard my name!" Mathis called from behind them.

Odette turned to include Mathis in the conversation, but Jorgen was slower to turn.

They were at the fountain now, and it was almost their turn to get water.

"We were talking about how you and Jorgen know each other."

"Oh, Jorgen and I knew each other as boys. We fought once, if I remember correctly, over something I said. Jorgen was serious and did not like my sense of humor, I am afraid."

"What did you say?" Odette wanted to know.

"It was many years ago," Mathis said. "I don't remember. Probably Ulrich Schinkel dared me to insult Jorgen."

"I remember." Jorgen had that somber expression again as he stepped forward and took the copper dipper that hung on the fountain, used it to catch the clear water pouring out, and handed it to Odette.

"Thank you." Their eyes met. Would he tell what he and Mathis had fought over? She kept her gaze on Jorgen over the rim of the dipper as she drank.

Mathis took another dipper and caught some water for himself.

When it seemed Jorgen would not tell what had happened, Mathis said, "We were both learning to read and write at the Thornbeck School for Boys, but with very different . . . childhood upbringings."

Jorgen shot Mathis a warning look, which made Mathis shake his head. "But Jorgen has done well for himself, much better than . . ."

Odette held her breath, waiting to see what Mathis would say. Finally, he ended the sentence with, "the old gamekeeper who raised him."

So the old gamekeeper raised him but was not his father? Jorgen's look turned even more hostile, and Mathis added, "And now here we are, dancing in the town square with beautiful maidens on this Midsummer night."

"Were you good students?" Odette asked.

Mathis turned his head to one side. "I was a good student."

Jorgen snorted.

Mathis laughed. "Very well. I was not a good student, nor was I well behaved. I wanted to be running in the sunshine and playing games. Jorgen was a much more attentive student than I."

Anna, who had been standing nearby listening, spoke up. "I was not a good student, either, though my mother forced me to attend the girls' school. Odette is quite a scholar, however." She nodded proudly at Odette. "She has a tutor, a monk who comes two days every week to teach her to read and write in Latin and French."

They all turned their attention to Odette. She shrugged. "My uncle humors me, even though he doesn't understand why I love to study. I enjoy learning languages and . . . other things." She decided not to reveal why she had not attended the town school for girls with Anna—or that Brother Philip was teaching her theology. He would only teach her theology if she vowed not to reveal it.

"Shall we dance some more?" Peter, who stood beside his wife, urged them all back toward the dancing and music. He could not know how frightened Odette was of the man she had felt such an attraction to only minutes before, frightened of what he could and would do to her if he discovered she was poaching the margrave's deer. Just thinking of him delivering her up to be thrown into the margrave's dungeon made her skin prickle.

She and Jorgen danced the next song together, and the next and the next. Perhaps she should have excused herself and danced with someone else, but Mathis did not return. The longer she danced with Jorgen, the more she was able to enjoy it and forget that he was the forester.

In fact, they danced until the *Minnesingers* began to play closer to the bonfire, now lit and starting to roar at the other end. They agreed they did not wish to join the drunken merrymaking around the fire. Jorgen kept hold of her hand a bit longer than was necessary. His touch made her heart flutter.

She caught her breath. How could she be foolish about this man she had just met? Had she forgotten what he could do to her? She must be a lack wit.

Uncle Rutger came toward them. "What a merry party you four make, dancing and laughing. Jorgen, you must come to our home for Odette's birthday feast in two nights. You will be most welcome. Peter and Anna will be there as well."

Oh, dear heavenly saints. Uncle Rutger must not know Jorgen was the forester.

Jorgen consented to come, and after the details were conveyed of the time and location of their house, Jorgen turned to Odette. "Until then."

Would he kiss her hand? But he only smiled, bowed, and walked away.

As Peter and Uncle Rutger escorted Anna and Odette home, Odette couldn't help but wonder what the reaction of Peter, Anna, and the handsome young forester would be if they ever discovered that she was poaching the margrave's deer and giving the meat to the poor. The fact that Jorgen's adoptive father, the old gamekeeper, was shot and killed by a poacher a few years ago would make Jorgen hate her.

Her heart constricted painfully in her chest. There was only one thing to do: never get caught.

# 4

Jorgen walked carefully through the thick undergrowth in the margrave's game park. He was sure the thicket where he had found the twin fawns was nearby. Curious to see if the twins were both thriving, he was also looking for signs of wolves and wild boar. None had been seen in Thornbeck Forest for many years, but it was always possible that they would wander in from the wilder areas nearby looking for food. The wild boar's favorite tree nuts grew here, and a baby deer would be easy prey for a wolf.

As he examined the undergrowth, the events of the night before were not far from his mind. He had danced with fair maidens before, but Odette was different. She was graceful and beautiful, but there was something in her eyes and in the things she said, an intelligence and a boldness that belied her quiet demeanor. He had been pleased—and surprised—to have been invited to her home for dinner.

If only Odette's uncle wasn't quite so rich.

When they were boys, Mathis Papendorp and Ulrich Schinkel, now the margrave's chancellor, had never let Jorgen forget that he was not as wealthy as they were. And now, to find that Odette had attracted the attention of Mathis . . . It seemed a bad omen. Mathis probably seemed the perfect person to marry someone like Odette.

Jorgen wanted to believe that the look he had seen in Odette's eyes and her manner toward him proved that she was as attracted to him as he was to her. He had believed he did see a preference in her reluctance to leave his side. But even if it were so, would she marry a forester?

Still, he remembered one particular moment when Odette had met his eye with such a sweet smile it had made his heart trip over itself. The memory of that smile warmed him so much, he halted. He had forgotten why he was there. Oh yes. The fawns.

As he pushed some brush aside, something on the ground caught his eye. He bent to look closer, then picked it up. An arrow.

The arrow did not appear to have been lying there long. It did not resemble the margrave's arrows, which were all made by the assistant gamekeepers with a distinctive feather at the butt, which they dyed bright red in order to be able to recover them. This arrow's fletching was snow white. Besides that, the margrave never went hunting without Jorgen, and he had not been hunting in weeks.

There was only one explanation: someone was poaching, or trying to poach, the animals in Thornbeck forest.

Jorgen stood and looked around, still holding the arrow. His whole body tensed as his heart beat faster.

His father had been shot by a poacher. Had it only been four years ago? It seemed like a long time, and yet he still sometimes would begin to go ask his father a question before realizing that he could never answer Jorgen's questions again. The memory of his death would flood him for the hundredth time.

After examining the woods that day, Jorgen believed the poacher had been discovered by his father. The poacher had shot at the gamekeeper and missed, then stalked him until he was able to kill him. It had been murder, plain and simple.

And that murderer's arrows had the same white feathers on the end.

The margrave's guards had searched for the killer, but they never found him. Jorgen had been preoccupied with comforting his grieving mother and seeing to his father's burial, not to mention his own grief and shock at his sudden death. He regretted being unable to hunt the poacher down himself. He hoped, with God's favor, someday he would find him and gain justice for his father.

This new poacher might not be new at all, but the same man who killed Jorgen's father.

He put the arrow in his own quiver for safekeeping. It was evidence and might help him find the murderer and prove him guilty. Even if this poacher was not the same one who had hunted down Jorgen's father and killed him, he must be punished. Poaching was dangerous and a serious offense against both the margrave and the king.

Jorgen would not tell his mother someone was poaching deer again. It would cause her to worry—another incentive to capture this poacher and make sure he never drew another bowstring.

⁓

ODETTE WAS WALKING *through the game park with her bow and arrows in the middle of the day. A large stag appeared and she shot it.*

*Suddenly, Jorgen jumped from behind a tree. She seemed rooted to the ground, as her legs refused to move. He grabbed her arms so tight her muscles ached.*

*"You will be sorry you crossed this margrave." He dragged her through the forest. She lost her shoes, and her feet raked over the sticks and rocks.*

*He took her to the margrave's castle, threw her into the dungeon underneath, and the metal key scraped against the lock as he trapped her inside.*

*She sat on the damp stone floor, and the cold wrapped around her body like icy claws. She was all alone and she was hungry, her stomach gnawing and cramping as it had after her mother and father died and she had no food. Nearly half the town of Thornbeck had perished in less than one year from the horrible sickness that ravaged its victims' bodies and left them dead, sometimes after only one day of being sick. She had been five years old, but being in the dungeon vividly brought back her terror at being left alone with no one to care for her.*

*Odette shivered and wrapped her arms around her empty stomach. "Jorgen?" she called, but there was no answer.*

She bolted upright in bed, a cold sweat on her brow and under her arms.

She had told Anna that she rarely had pleasant dreams, but one would have thought she could have dreamed something a bit less horrific on Midsummer night.

⁓

The next day Brother Philip came to tutor her. She usually relished her time with him and the opportunity to study, but today she could not concentrate. She could not stop thinking about Jorgen Hartman. She had not had a chance to tell Rutger who Jorgen was—that her uncle had invited the margrave's forester to her birthday dinner.

"Odette, are you listening to me?" Brother Philip was glaring at her.

"Oh, forgive me." Odette blinked hard and focused on Brother Philip's leathery face. "What did you say?"

"I brought you a Book of Hours I found at the monastery library. I am risking a lot by bringing it to you, so I would think you would at least be attentive when I tell you about it."

She would rather he just give it to her and let her read it. Must he always talk everything to death first?

He went on with his lecture on how various copies of the Book of Hours differed from each other, as well as how they differed from the breviary and the Psalter.

Brother Philip mentioned penitence, which brought once again to Odette's mind the dream she had had about Jorgen. It was the look on Jorgen's face she now could not get out of her mind. Anger, hurt, disappointment—she couldn't quite define it, but it haunted her.

Perhaps her poaching was not the right thing to do. When she was eight years old, she'd fashioned a crude bow and some arrows and shot her first pheasant. She remembered the pain of guilt she had felt. But when she had shared the meat with two other orphans who were starving, her guilt vanished.

But what she was doing violated forest law.

Still, the poor people would go hungry if she did not feed them. Her heart told her it was the right thing to do, that God would reward her for her kindness to the poor. Didn't the friars who wandered about preaching God's Word say the same? That it was the rich rulers, like the Margrave of Thornbeck, who oppressed the poor? And did the Bible not say God would carry out his vengeance on those who ignored the needs of the poor?

It was that silly superstition. Anna had insisted she place her flower circlet under her pillow, along with a bunch of calendula and St. John's wort, so she would dream of her future husband. But the only man she had dreamed of was Jorgen Hartman, the forester, throwing her into the dungeon. And even though his blue-green eyes made her heart thump hard against her chest, the dream had helped confirm her realization that she could never marry him.

Finally Brother Philip produced the Book of Hours. He made her rub her hands on a clean cloth before he would allow her to turn the pages, but it was worth it when she saw the beautiful illuminations on the pages. Colorful painted pictures of scenes from the Bible shone brightly. The margins of some of the pages were decorated with elaborately intricate flowers, leaves, and vines.

Perhaps the beautiful illuminations should have inspired her to appreciate God's creation and give thanks for it, but mostly they made her mind wander to when she was very small and her mother had kept a beautiful flower garden in their small courtyard behind their house.

Then her mind roamed to more immediate recollections. How many children would go hungry today because Odette had not been able to go hunting the night before, when there were too many people roaming the forest celebrating Midsummer? She had slept little, having awakened from her dream feeling cold, the pungent smell of calendula in her nostrils.

"Forgive me, Brother Philip, but I am too tired to study today."

He frowned at her. "No doubt you engaged in too much frivolity last night."

"If you are wondering if I went to the town center and danced with men I had never met before, you would be correct." Odette couldn't resist saying things she knew would evoke a look of shock on the monk's face.

His expression of horrified disappointment was a little more than she had been aiming for.

"My uncle Rutger and my friend Anna and her husband were with me the entire time, and nothing unseemly occurred. The two men who danced with me were very courteous, and my uncle approved of them."

"Humph." He scrunched his face. "Maidens of your age should be married or in a convent somewhere."

"How old do you think I am?"

"Your uncle told me you are twenty years."

"I will be one and twenty in two days. Does that make me scandalous, if I am walking the streets unmarried?" Odette laughed at the thought.

Brother Philip raised his eyebrows.

Odette suppressed a sigh, as she was often forced to do when she was with Brother Philip.

"Young women such as yourself never understand what a temptation you are," he muttered, looking down at the text he had been examining.

It wasn't the first time she had heard words to that effect, either from Brother Philip or from others, but it irked her nevertheless. "I shall endeavor to refrain from being a temptation, Brother Philip, but I rather think it is the men you should be warning. Shouldn't they shoulder most of the blame if they find me a temptation?" She almost asked him if she should sit at home and let her uncle arrange a marriage for her to a stranger, but he would say yes.

Brother Philip's leathery cheeks turned red. He took a deep breath, then quoted, "'Such is the way of the adulterous woman; she eateth, and wipeth her mouth, and saith, I have done no wickedness.'"

Odette answered, "'His own iniquities shall take the wicked himself, and he shall be holden with the cords of his sins.'"

His eyes narrowed and he growled, "'For the lips of a strange woman drop as an honeycomb, and her mouth is smoother than oil. But her end is bitter as wormwood, sharp as a two-edged sword.'"

Odette shot back, "'Unto the pure all things are pure: but unto them that are defiled and unbelieving is nothing pure; but even their mind and conscience is defiled.'" Odette couldn't hold back a smirk.

Brother Philip expelled a harsh breath and stood to his feet. "I see that I had better leave you now. Your scholarship is serving only to provide fodder for argument and the twisting of the holy Scripture." He reached across the table and slid the Book of Hours toward himself, then closed it with a dull snap.

Odette had been planning to ask if she could keep the beautiful book until he came back for their next tutoring session, but now she bit her lip to stop herself. He was in no mood to grant her such a favor.

Should she apologize? She had only refuted his warped opinion with Scripture. No, she was not sorry for what she had said, nor for anything she had done. Still, she wished her tutor would not go away angry.

She followed Brother Philip to the door, neither of them speaking. Then he turned to her. "I shall not return in two days. Your uncle will have to convince me that you are sorry for using Scripture to argue with me, and if he believes you will be able to concentrate and not allow your mind to wander aimlessly, I may return." He scowled at her.

Odette's cheeks burned. How ridiculous that he would take such offense at her besting him with Scripture! But she did want him to come back. She had no copy of the holy Writ, and he often brought his copy for her to read. She had to placate him if she wanted him to come back. So she bit the inside of her cheek and said, "Of course. Forgive me, Brother Philip." She bowed demurely.

He turned and left without another word. But he would be back. He was too fond of the food their cook fed him to stay away.

She would send Uncle Rutger to ask his forgiveness and pacify the friar's injured superiority.

~

"So . . . who is your future husband?" Anna asked late that afternoon.

Odette was baffled for a moment, then remembered she was supposed to dream of her future husband on Midsummer night. She didn't want to tell her friend that she had indeed dreamed of someone. "You know that does not work. Remember when Irmele dreamed of the swineherd on Midsummer night? And she married a wealthy merchant's son."

"Do you not think Jorgen is very handsome? Did you not dream of him?" Anna arched her brows suggestively. "Or did you dream of Mathis Papendorp?"

They sat in the first-floor room, eating ripe cherries. Anna leaned over and spit a cherry pit into the pottery bowl between them.

"You know Jorgen is a forester. I haven't told Uncle Rutger yet, but I do not believe he would approve. He wishes me to marry a wealthy man."

"But he is so handsome," Anna whispered. "And the way the two of you were looking into each other's eyes . . . I thought perhaps your uncle might set him up in business."

Was it true? Had they been staring into each other's eyes? "I do not think Uncle Rutger would do that. His last three cargos were lost, two at sea and the other to thieves. He is worried about his profits just now." Her stomach flipped. "Were we really looking into each other's eyes?"

"Do not worry. Probably no one noticed except me. And Peter."

"Did he say something?"

Anna nodded. "Even though Peter was taught at home by a

tutor, I think he must have known something about how the other boys treated Jorgen badly in school. He said several of the boys used to torment him because he was poor." Anna frowned.

Odette knew how it felt to be tormented for being poor. Her heart squeezed at the thought. But she couldn't let Anna think there was any possibility that she could marry Jorgen. If only Odette could acknowledge the real reason.

Anna nodded. "I was surprised your uncle allowed him to dance with you, even though he is not a gamekeeper anymore but the margrave's forester."

Odette did not contradict Anna's reasoning about why she could not think of Jorgen.

"I'm sorry if I misjudged your uncle," Anna said.

"No, you are right. It did seem strange that he would allow Jorgen to dance with me"—*especially since he would arrest me if he knew who I really was*—"and to invite him to dinner was even stranger."

"But there's something about him . . . He seemed gracious and humble, but humble in a . . . powerful way. That sounds foolish, doesn't it?"

"No, you describe him very well." Odette remembered how he had put his arm around her and guided her through the crowd of revelers, how he had made her feel so safe. She sighed.

"I must say, Odette"—Anna spit out another cherry pit—"I've never seen you look at a man the way you looked at Jorgen last night. I would not be surprised if you were falling in love with him."

"I barely know him. You should not suggest such a thing." Odette laughed to try to cover her discomfiture.

Jorgen was the last man she could ever allow herself to fall in love with.

# 5

JORGEN TREKKED UP the castle mount on the path that led to
Thornbeck Castle. The guard at the gatehouse waved him through.
At the front door, the servant said, "You are Jorgen Hartman, the
forester, are you not?"

"*Ja.*"

"The margrave is waiting for you in the library. Follow me."
The articulate servant turned and marched down the corridor.

Always a bit nervous when he spoke to the margrave, Jorgen
felt a trickle of sweat between his shoulder blades. He had to tell
the margrave that there was a poacher hunting deer in Thornbeck
Forest. He was certain to be displeased.

The servant motioned Jorgen into the room. The windows
were open, but as it was a cloudy, misty day, lit candles stood in
copper candlesticks on Margrave Reinhart's desk. He sat behind it,
staring down at some papers. Unfortunately, Ulrich Schinkel was
standing at his shoulder.

While the margrave seemed to like Jorgen, his new chancellor
did not, and the feeling was reciprocated. Jorgen could never forget
how arrogant Ulrich had been when they were boys because his
father was the margrave's chancellor, and Ulrich would often boast
that someday he would take his place. And now he had.

Jorgen strode forward as the margrave looked up at him.

Margrave Reinhart, or Lord Thornbeck as he was known, was not much older than Jorgen. He had become the new margrave when his older brother died in a fire in the west wing of the castle the year before. He had thick dark hair and eyebrows. He was just the sort one would want as a knight defender, broad and muscular shoulders and unusually tall. With the title of margrave, he was even more imposing.

The margrave's forehead was creased, as if he was concentrating. "Jorgen," he greeted and waved him forward.

Jorgen stepped up to the desk, doing his best to ignore Ulrich, but Jorgen could see out of the corner of his eye that Ulrich was sizing him up.

"As our forester," the margrave began, "tell me how the game is faring in the park. Any problems to report?"

"Lord Thornbeck." Jorgen bowed and decided to begin with the good news. "The mild weather has produced many new pheasant chicks, as well as many hares. In fact, it might be best, my lord, if you permitted the gamekeepers to snare some hares for your larder. Too many will cause the animals to be thin and sickly and might attract new predators, like wolves, to move into the game park."

"Please have your gamekeeper set some snares, then, as many as you think necessary." He turned to his chancellor. "Ulrich, tell the cook to prepare rabbit stews and pies for the next few days."

"For you, my lord, or for your servants?" Ulrich's pinched face looked even more pinched, as if he didn't look forward to eating rabbit stew.

"For both my table and the servants.'"

"Yes, my lord." His face took on a resigned expression. Then he scowled at Jorgen when he caught him staring at him.

The margrave was looking at Jorgen again, so he went on. "The hinds and their new offspring are mostly accounted for, my lord, but I believe some of the stags may be missing. I also found an arrow that does not bear your red feathers, as well as some evidence of blood on the ground that looks as if someone tried to brush over it with leaves. It appears there is a poacher afoot in Thornbeck Forest."

The look in the margrave's eyes sharpened. "A poacher?" He glowered.

"I believe so. If you wish, I can put up a notice in the town center. We can offer a reward to anyone who has information about the poacher."

The chancellor made a faint snorting sound. "A reward? Don't you think you are offering the margrave's money recklessly? You aren't even certain there is a poacher."

Jorgen's face burned. He didn't want the margrave to think him hasty about offering a reward.

"Perhaps we should wait before offering a bounty," Lord Thornbeck said. "I think a stray arrow is proof enough of a thief, but look around and see if you can discover any more information about this poacher. Poaching cannot be tolerated. The king's land, forests, and game in this region are entrusted to me, and it is my duty to see that they are maintained and protected." He gave Jorgen an intense look, and Jorgen could well imagine why he was renowned as a fierce fighter before he had been appointed the captain of the duke of Pomerania's guards, and later, Margrave of Thornbeck.

"I trust you to see that this poacher is caught."

"Yes, my lord. I shall find him and stop him."

While the maidservant hung the newly cleaned wall hangings, Odette glanced down at the guest list, which would have been impressive if she were looking for a wealthy husband. Her uncle wanted what was best for her. She suspected he wanted her to find a husband and cease poaching, although he had never said so.

The Burgomeister himself had declined Rutger's invitation due to another obligation, but his son would be there. The margrave's chancellor was also coming. And she wasn't sure if she was excited or terrified when she stared at Jorgen's name on the list.

But perhaps, if she were capable of being cold and calculating about it, she could see her friendship with the forester as a way to keep an eye on what he was doing and find out if—and what—he knew about her poaching.

Uncle Rutger appeared in the doorway.

Odette smiled as he came toward her. "I was just looking at the guest list. At first I thought you invited every wealthy merchant and important official in Thornbeck. But then I realized you only invited the unmarried ones."

He chuckled. "Odette, you are so fair of face and capable of every duty a wealthy official could want from his wife. I would invite the margrave himself and think he could not choose more wisely if he asked for your hand in marriage."

Now Odette laughed. "A very pretty speech indeed. I thank you."

"Are you eager for your birthday party tomorrow night?"

"Of course. But I have something I need to tell you."

"Yes?"

"Do you remember the man at the Midsummer night festival that you invited?"

"The one you danced with all night?" He raised a brow at her.

"I didn't dance with him all night. But yes, Jorgen Hartman. I think there is something you do not know about him." She glanced up at her uncle. How would he take the news? "Jorgen is . . . He is the margrave's forester."

Her uncle stared at her. "Did you say he is the forester?" He leaned down, and in a loud whisper asked, "Why were you dancing with the margrave's forester?"

"I didn't know he was the forester." She bit her lip.

"Odette, you've been dancing with the devil, and now I've invited him to our house." Even her normally jovial uncle, so full of jesting and humor, looked aghast. "But we cannot tell him not to come. We must be polite and hope he never finds out what a great marksman you are."

At least he wasn't too upset to make a jest about it.

"Do not fear, Odette." He shook his head. "He would never suspect you of anything. You are my niece, a beautiful, graceful young woman who receives at least three marriage offers every month."

"Not that many." She often had to rebuke Rutger for exaggerating.

"At least two every month." He made a gesture with his hand. "Do not worry. You are perfectly safe. You can enjoy his company for one more night and then you will probably never encounter him again."

She supposed that was true. "I must try not to be nervous around him." And try not to notice how beautiful his eyes were. Or how deep his voice was. Or how much she liked talking to him.

"The only reason I asked him was because of the way you were looking at him. I was hoping he might be wealthier than he appeared."

"What do you mean, the way I was looking at him?"

"The way you were looking at each other. But though he is

young and handsome, you are above his station in life. He is only the adopted son of the old gamekeeper."

"Do you know about him?"

"Why, yes. If the stories I've heard about the new forester are true, the old gamekeeper found him as a young boy in the *Marktplatz*, without parents or family, and took him home. He and his wife raised him. The old gamekeeper and his wife sent him to the town school, and Jorgen must have impressed the margrave because he appointed him the new forester. But after tomorrow night, I will not be asking him to any more parties, just to be safe."

That seemed the reasonable way to approach the situation.

"What did you think of Mathis Papendorp? He is also a hand-some man, is he not?"

"I suppose, though perhaps his status as the Burgomeister's son makes him a little more handsome?" She raised her eyebrows in challenge.

"Are you asking me or telling me?"

Odette laughed. "His manner is polished but . . ."

"You do not approve of him either? He is at least young! You cannot say I am foisting another old man on you with this one."

"I do not disapprove of him, but it is difficult to discern his true character after knowing him for so short a time."

"You have certainly known him longer than you've known Jorgen. But take your time learning his character. All I ask is that you do not reject him outright. After all, think of the influence he could have over the town ordinances and in your cause to help the poor of Thornbeck. Surely you can see the advantages of such an alliance. You could refrain from poaching and still feed the poor." He lifted his brows with a significant nod.

"I suppose." She hated to admit it, even to herself, but Rutger was probably right.

"You will not be going hunting tonight?"

"After missing two nights because of Midsummer, I don't want to miss another night."

"Sometimes I think you push yourself too hard."

"I am well and hearty. Do not worry."

The servant returned to hang another tapestry. Odette needed to prepare for the hunt, so she gave Rutger a quick kiss on the cheek and went upstairs.

Though her uncle was only fifteen years older, he was a good guardian. She couldn't imagine a better one. What need did she have of a husband? She was her own master, doing what she wished. Things like poaching that no husband would allow. As long as she avoided getting caught, she could see herself hunting and giving away the meat for a long time to come.

# 6

JORGEN MADE HIS way toward Rutger's house. The sun was still shedding its light across the sky, but the people on the street were heading home after their labors.

He was still surprised he had been invited to Odette's birthday feast. But unless Odette was a girl who cared naught for wealth, power, and status, she would never choose Jorgen over Mathis Papendorp. He would be foolish to get his hopes up about her.

A young man and woman were walking in Jorgen's direction. The man was smiling down at her, her face was upturned toward his, and she laughed. He smiled even wider and put his arm around her. She leaned her body into his, and he kissed her on the mouth before they continued down the street.

He had avoided thoughts of marriage as long as he was still a gamekeeper, but seeing that couple, he felt a slight ache in his chest. When he married, would he and his wife be in love like those two?

Now that Jorgen was the forester, he could afford to take a wife—a wife who was willing to live a less wealthy life than the one to which Odette was accustomed.

Rutger Menkels's house was a large four-story, half-timber structure not far from the *Marktplatz*. The lowest floor was made of stone and plastered white, and the upper floors jutted a little farther over the street with each higher level. Plaster was criss-crossed with wooden beams that gave it a decorative look, along with striped shutters on the bottom floor.

When he reached the house, the windows were open to the warm night air, and he could hear the voices inside. The door was also open, the servants nowhere in sight, so Jorgen walked in.

Odette stood in the large ground-floor room wearing a beautiful blue dress, her hair hanging across her shoulders and down her back, with a few tiny braids that were interwoven with matching blue ribbons. She was talking to Mathis—or, rather, listening to him.

"The old margrave was a great friend of my father, and his oldest son ran the region like his father had before him, but the new margrave . . ." Mathis shook his head. "A lot of people don't trust him."

Odette's gaze shifted to Jorgen standing just inside the doorway and her smile widened. "Jorgen! Come in."

She motioned for him to join their conversation, making room for him between her and Mathis.

"Jorgen would know something of the new margrave." Mathis turned toward Jorgen. "What do you think of him?"

Jorgen considered how to answer Mathis's question about the margrave, the man whose duty it was to protect all the people of the region, especially from invaders from outside the Holy Roman Empire, since they were so near the northeast border. "He is a good and competent leader, as much as his father and brother were before him."

Mathis raised his eyebrows. "My father says he's never done anything except train as a knight, and he had just started training the fighting men who protect the castle. He couldn't know anything about being a margrave."

Odette looked from Mathis to Jorgen.

"Lord Thornbeck is very capable. He has learned what he needed to know to execute his duties well."

"That is loyally spoken, Jorgen, but what makes you think so? Do you have that much confidence in his chancellor and chief advisor, our old friend Ulrich?"

Jorgen forced himself not to react to the jab Mathis aimed at him. Did he know that Jorgen feared the chancellor was trying to undermine the margrave's confidence in him? "Lord Thornbeck, as I said, is a competent leader."

"Competent." Mathis shrugged. "Perhaps, but some people still question if he had anything to do with his brother's death. A fire in the west wing? There's never been a fire in the castle that I can recall, and this one originated in the margrave's bedchamber."

Jorgen had heard the rumors. He wanted to upbraid Mathis for his insinuation, but he tamped down his anger. "How do you know it originated in the bedchamber? False rumors are started by people who enjoy gossiping."

Mathis shrugged again and smiled. "I cannot argue with that."

Jorgen added, "And the current margrave was injured trying to save his brother from the fire. The burning bed collapsed on his foot as he tried to drag his brother to safety. He still walks with a limp."

"*Ja.*" Mathis drew the word out, as though he doubted the truth of Jorgen's statement.

The margrave must now have help to mount his own horse. A fact that greatly annoyed the former knight.

"I believe the victuals are now prepared," Odette said cheerily. No doubt she was glad to end the uncomfortable conversation. "Shall we feast?"

When they reached the table laden with food of every kind,

Jorgen somehow ended up sitting beside Odette and across from Mathis, Peter, and Anna. While they ate, Odette seemed to purposely maneuver the conversation to more pleasant topics. She smiled frequently and laughed almost as much. Even the gossip about the margrave barely dampened his enjoyment of the evening.

Rutger stood and proposed to speak of Odette's virtues, and everyone grew quiet. "More than fifteen years ago, my beautiful niece's father and mother died in the Great Pestilence. As I had been in the Orient, it took four years for word to reach me." He looked down at Odette. "Bringing Odette to live with me here, in this house in Thornbeck, was the best thing I ever did. No man could ever ask for a better niece, and indeed, she is more like a daughter to me. She is kind, intelligent, and never idle, either in mind or in body. The man who can finally convince her to marry him will be a fortunate man indeed."

Everyone around the table murmured their approval. Odette's cheeks turned pink.

"For the joy that she gives to me and to everyone privileged to know her, please raise your goblets and drink to my niece, Odette Menkels."

Jorgen lifted his goblet with the rest of the guests. Odette was blushing redder now. She smiled and allowed her gaze to meet the eyes of the guests around the room. When the conversation started to rise again, she fidgeted with the cloth napkin across her lap.

"It is a lovely evening," Jorgen said. "Your uncle seems to think very well of you."

She looked up, a glint in her eyes. "I am blessed to have him as my guardian. I'm sure most would never allow me so much . . . freedom. And, *ja*, it is a lovely evening. I hope the sky is clear for your journey home tonight. How far is it?"

"Less than half an hour."

"Do you live alone?"

"My mother lives with me."

"I see. Is she in good health?"

"*Ja*, for a woman of her age." He smiled.

She smiled back. "And do you have brothers or sisters?"

"I had a sister. But she died. My adoptive mother was unable to have children. She often helped the poor children who came to her door looking for food. When I was ten years old, her husband, the old gamekeeper, brought me home and they adopted me as their own. I was also orphaned by the Great Pestilence."

Odette had been staring alternately at his eyes, then his lips, as he spoke. She seemed to listen intently.

Mathis's voice broke into their conversation. "I wondered if you would tell Odette how you spent your childhood on the streets, stealing from vendors and shopkeepers."

*Like a rat.* It was the taunt Mathis and his friends had used to plague Jorgen when he was a boy attending the town school. The priests who ran the school would sometimes scold the boys, but Jorgen had been forced, many times, to defend himself with his fists after lessons were finished. Mathis laughed as though it were all in jest.

"But that was a long time ago." Peter suddenly joined the conversation. "Jorgen is doing well for himself, impressing the margrave. As for Mathis and me, we have done little to distinguish ourselves besides go to parties in our fathers' stead."

No one spoke. Finally Odette broke the silence. "The gamekeeper and his wife sound like good people." She lifted her chin in Mathis's direction. "And I am sure they were blessed to have Jorgen for a son."

Mathis squirmed but was quick to say, "As your uncle has been telling me, you are a compassionate woman, very concerned for the poor. That is an admirable quality."

"Children deserve to be treated kindly, whether they are rich or poor. A child cannot control his own fate."

Mathis nodded meekly. He reminded Jorgen of one of those miracle players who performed on the church steps or in the *Marktplatz*, playing a part to elicit a reaction.

Some minstrels came into the room and began to play and sing a soft ballad, and the last course of the meal was brought in on platters—cake with apples and dates decorating the top, and a subtlety made in the shape of a swan. The guests all applauded the intricately devised bird made entirely of white almond paste, except for the black eyes, which appeared to be sultanas, and an orange beak, perhaps made of carrot. The feathers were quite detailed.

Odette clasped her hands and leaned toward him, her eyes sparkling. "My uncle knows I like swans. It is so beautiful." She smiled at Rutger and he winked at her.

A servant gave them each a large slice of cake. Odette did not even look at hers. She was staring at Jorgen's face. While the minstrels continued their song, she leaned even closer to him. "I hope Mathis did not make you feel uncomfortable. I realize you weren't the best of friends as children." Her eyes were so blue in the candle-lit room.

"We are older now. I can hope that he has changed."

A mischievous glint flickered in her eye. "You said you and Mathis fought. Did you fight a lot?"

"*Ja*, but he always had three or four of his friends jump in and save him."

Again the little mischievous smile graced her lips. "Did you ever beat him up?"

"The last time I fought him, he was alone and I left him with a black eye and a busted lip. After that, Mathis and his friends were a bit more . . . respectful."

She kept asking him about himself, but there were certain things he hoped she wouldn't ask, not wishing to tell her about some of the things he saw—and did—as a child.

As the margrave's forester, he was not in her social class. His mind told him that she should not be interested in him—as he noted the wealthier clothing worn by the other guests. But his heart saw only her compassionate eyes, her gentle features, and her incomparable beauty.

Perhaps if he did not allow himself to look into her blue eyes, his head would not be overpowered by his heart. It was worth a try, unless he wanted to be nursing his bruised pride—and a broken heart.

⁘

Odette gazed into Jorgen's blue-green eyes and imagined him as a child, alone and living on the streets, forced to defend himself against bullies. To see the confidence in his walk and the way he held his shoulders, the attractiveness of his dark-blond hair and features, she knew Peter was right. Jorgen had done well for himself. And since they had both been orphans, she felt a kinship with him.

But if he knew what she did every night, he would arrest her and have her thrown in the dungeon. Her Midsummer night's dream of him doing just that came vividly to mind.

She was about to ask him another question when the minstrels strolled closer, coming to stand just behind where they were seated, and it was no longer possible to be heard over their singing and playing.

Then she noticed Mathis with an exaggerated expression of hope on his face. He was the mayor's son, so she should make an effort to spend some time talking with him before the night was over.

When the minstrels finished their song, Rutger stood and announced that it was time for dancing. The guests began to speak in excited tones as they all rose, and the servants came to take away the trestle tables and benches where they had been eating.

"Odette," Mathis said, hovering over her shoulder and forcing her to turn around to face him. "I have been looking forward to dancing with you tonight. Would you dance the first dance with me?"

Mathis's pale skin, hair, and eyes contrasted well with his bright red, green, and pink robe. He took Odette's hand between both of his. "You are the most beautiful maiden I have ever beheld. You are like an ethereal creature, a pure maiden sent from heaven to earth."

Odette laughed. But when he did not seem pleased by her laughter, she forced the smile from her face and tried to look grateful. "I thank you for your kind words, Herr Papendorp. I was taken by surprise by your lavish praise. You are very poetic."

"Please, call me Mathis. And that was rather poetic, wasn't it? But I meant every word." He lifted her hand to his lips while staring into her eyes.

She pulled her hand from his grasp, hoping she didn't look repulsed.

The eager way he touched her hand was a bit disconcerting. She would much rather be dancing with Jorgen.

She had nothing against friendliness, but this man was looking at her as if he might ask her to marry him at any moment. Even if she wanted to marry Mathis, how could she be sure he would want to spend his money to help feed the poor?

"That is a sober expression for a woman who is dancing and enjoying herself." Mathis broke into her thoughts as the dance was ending.

"My mind tends to wander sometimes. It is a lively gathering, is it not? Do you see my friend Anna?" She looked around the room and spotted her standing next to her husband. She looked beautiful tonight.

"Ah yes. She is Peter Voreken's wife, is she not? I shall have to ask her to dance." Mathis leaned close to Odette's face, so close his breath brushed her cheek. "But first I would like to dance again with you, Odette."

A man approached them.

"Mathis, won't you introduce me to this beautiful young maiden?"

Mathis gave her an apologetic smile. "Odette, this is Ulrich Schinkel, the margrave's chancellor. Ulrich, this is Odette Menkels, the niece and ward of Rutger Menkels."

Without wasting any time, the stranger smirked and asked, "Would you do me the honor of dancing with me, fair maiden?"

He was a prominent person so Rutger would be pleased. "I will."

She danced with Ulrich, but there was an arrogant self-consciousness in his expression that Odette didn't like. When the dance was over, she said, "You may take me to my uncle. I am sure he would like to speak to you."

They made their way over to Rutger, who stood alone since Peter and Anna had gone to dance.

Ulrich greeted Rutger, then said, "If I am not asking too much, would you please allow me to dance again with your fair niece? I do believe she is the most graceful and beautiful maiden in Thornbeck."

The fact that he asked her uncle if he could dance with her

instead of asking her did not sit well with Odette. But Rutger smiled as though pleased and gave his consent. Odette allowed Ulrich to lead her back to the dance.

The dance with Ulrich seemed to take a long time.

When it was over, Ulrich opened his mouth, but Jorgen interrupted him. "Pardon me." Jorgen stepped quite close to them. "I would like to dance with the birthday maiden." He took her hand as if she had already accepted.

Ulrich looked daggers at him, but Jorgen kept his gaze on Odette. She nodded and he swept her away. They joined the circle that was snaking around the entire first floor.

"I am afraid that man, Ulrich, is angry with you."

Jorgen smiled. "He hasn't liked me since we were boys. I never mind it."

Odette was pleased to have been rescued from Ulrich, and she let herself enjoy the dance, turning and clapping, sidestepping and turning again.

She glanced around but didn't see the chancellor. She pictured Jorgen and Ulrich getting into a fight, like in their boyhood days. They were grown men now, and she did not wish to invoke jealousy or contention between them.

She couldn't seem to stop staring at Jorgen and his blue-green eyes. He made her feel so safe and protected. She couldn't ever remember feeling that way with anyone else. It seemed especially strange, considering his position.

When the dance ended, she turned to Jorgen. He stood very close to her side in the crowded room, which made him seem even taller. She could see the stubble on his jaw and the small dent in the center of his chin. The tilt of his head as he bent to hear what she was saying made her heart alternately skip a beat and thump against her chest. "I will sit down for a while now."

"Are you well?"

"Only a little tired." She still had to go hunting tonight, and she needed to conserve her strength. "You may dance if you like while I rest." She moved toward an unoccupied bench against the wall.

Jorgen walked with her to the bench, then was called away by Rutger and a couple of other men who seemed to want to talk to him.

Odette sat and watched as Peter whisked Anna onto the floor. Several other couples were taking advantage of the musicians and dancing every dance. Perhaps she should have continued dancing, for now she was watching everyone else enjoying themselves. Who could she talk to? She glanced around. Where was Jorgen?

There. He was sitting with one of Rutger's friends, a man with a bulbous nose who seemed to be telling Jorgen a story. His eyes were locked on Jorgen's face, and he was leaning forward, hugging a goblet of wine to his chest.

She caught Jorgen's eye. He looked restless, and she motioned with her hand for him to come and sit with her.

Just then, the older man who was talking to him sat back and yelled at a passing servant, thrusting his goblet at him. Jorgen took the opportunity to excuse himself and strode over to Odette.

"Sit and talk with me. I'm rather tired of dancing. And now that I think about it . . ." She probably shouldn't, but, "Would you accompany me to our little garden? It would be so much easier to talk out there, without the noise."

He held his arm out to her and she took it, allowing him to lead her out the back door. She hoped no one would gossip about them being alone in the garden together.

# 7

The night sky was clear, and the sun's rays had not completely disappeared from overhead. Fortunately, they were not alone, as a few other people were strolling in the garden or sitting on one of the benches.

"I hope you are enjoying your birthday."

"Oh *ja*, I am." She walked over to the iron bench and sat down, leaving plenty of room for Jorgen. "It was so loud inside. I thought we could continue our conversation better out here."

He did not sit beside her but continued to stand.

Perhaps this was a mistake. She had not thought this through. If she did not want to be alone with him—and she should not—or to make him think she was showing a preference for him, then she should not have asked him to come out to the garden.

"Do you want to go back inside?" she asked.

"Are you cold?"

She shook her head.

He sat down at the other side of the bench, leaving two feet between them. "Tell me about you. I know you like to teach the poor children to read and write. What else do you like to do?" A thick lock of his blond hair fell across his right eyebrow, and the dimple in his chin was accentuated by the shadows of the falling twilight.

"I . . ." *I like to hunt.* She couldn't tell him that. "I like to study."

"Your friend Anna mentioned that you like to study and that you have a tutor. What do you study?" He reached out and picked a leaf off the bush behind them and stared down at it in his hands.

"Brother Philip mostly brings me theology books. We have some lively debates sometimes, but I don't tell anyone about that." She bit her lip. Would Jorgen disapprove? Her heart seemed to stop beating as she waited to see what he would say.

He barely glanced up at her. "Why do you keep that a secret?"

"Some people might not approve."

"I wouldn't think you would care what some people think. Some people are lack wits and do not treat women very well, but I suppose you would not tolerate anyone like that for long."

They smiled at each other. "No, I do not suppose I would."

"I have a Psalter and two of the Gospel books," he said.

"You have the Gospel books? All your own?" Odette's mouth fell open.

"You can come and read them sometime, if you wish."

"I would love to own the entire holy Writ. I have a Psalter, and sometimes Brother Philip brings a copy of the Gospels and other books of the Bible for me to read. Do you read them often?"

He nodded. "I like to read. I nearly have the book of Luke memorized."

"What else do you like to do?"

He seemed about to say something, then halted and stared down at his leaf.

"What? I told you my secret." *One of them.* "Now you must tell me yours."

Jorgen expelled a breath as though he was laughing at himself. Then he turned and pointed a finger at her. "You must vow not to tell anyone."

"I will not reveal it. Tell me." She leaned toward him, in case he wanted to whisper.

"I like to write . . . things."

"What kind of things?" She held her breath.

"Many kinds of things."

"Tell me!"

"Tales. Verses. Rhymes." He still would not look at her.

"Oh, I would love to read them! Won't you show them to me?"

"Some are for children. I have never let anyone read them."

"You should come and read them to my children! To the poor children who come to my classes, I mean." She lowered her voice. "Truly, you must. They would love it above anything. I know they would."

He shrugged and turned his head. "I don't know."

"You must. Tomorrow after midday, at the south wall. Please do, Jorgen." She liked the sound of his name coming from her lips. It sounded friendly and familiar, as if they were old friends.

He didn't answer.

"You aren't afraid, are you?" Men hated anyone to think they were afraid.

"Truthfully? *Ja*, I am afraid."

Odette laughed at his unexpected answer. "But why?"

"Perhaps I will. As long as it is only children who are listening."

"Only children. And me."

"And only if you vow not to laugh."

"I would not laugh."

"You would if the rhymes were very bad."

"If they were very bad, I might laugh. But they won't be bad."

"Now you have to tell me an embarrassing secret, since I told you one of mine." He glanced at her out of the corner of his eye, still cradling the leaf in his hands.

"An embarrassing secret? I don't know if it is embarrassing, but . . . since Mathis said what he did about your childhood, I can tell you that after my mother and father died, I was destitute. I was five years old and a neighbor took me in, but she made me sweep and scrub her floors and barely fed me. Four years went by before my uncle Rutger came to fetch me. And I was never allowed to go to school when I lived with them."

She decided not to tell him that she had spent a lot of her time scrounging for food, until a peasant boy around her own age had taken pity on her and showed her how to make a bow and some arrows. She'd taught herself how to shoot pheasants and discovered she was quite good at it. Being able to provide food for herself and some of the other poor orphans in town had made her feel powerful, and powerful was not something she had ever felt.

After she went to live with her uncle, he gave her a lot of freedom, and she often amused herself by hunting. Once, when she was twelve, Jorgen's father caught her killing pheasants in Thornbeck Forest. She had been terrified he would put her in the pillory or turn her over to the margrave. But he only scolded her—and offered her food if she was hungry and would come to his cottage. She ran away instead.

But she could never tell Jorgen that story.

"How did you learn to read?"

"Uncle Rutger hired a tutor to teach me. He said a wealthy merchant's wife must not be ignorant." She blushed, realizing she had admitted to Jorgen that her uncle expected her to marry a wealthy merchant.

But Jorgen didn't seem to notice. "You are no ordinary maiden."

"Perhaps. But I am determined that you will not change your mind about tomorrow. You must come to read your verses and stories to the children."

He shook his head and chuckled, a deep, throaty sound, cascading over her like a warm waterfall. "Does anyone ever say no to you?"

"Not often."

"But I cannot stay long."

"Why not? Are you so busy?"

"I usually am not, but something has just happened that I must look into."

"Oh?" She sat up straighter. "What has happened?"

"I believe someone is poaching deer in Thornbeck Forest."

"Why would you think that?" Her voice sounded breathless. She swallowed, trying to force her racing heart to calm down.

"I found an arrow."

"Is it not the margrave's arrow? He hunts there sometimes."

"*Nein*, it is not."

She was about to ask him how the arrow was different from the margrave's. Such information would have been quite helpful, but he went on.

"I should not be talking about that. You couldn't possibly be interested in such a thing."

*You would be surprised at how interested I am.* "I hope the poacher will not cause you much difficulty. Perhaps it was only a child trying out a new bow and arrow his father made for him, for play."

"Perhaps. But some of the stags are missing."

"Stags are skilled at hiding themselves, are they not?"

He stared at her. By now it was completely dark, except for the bit of light shining through the house windows and the partial moon in the sky.

She shrugged. "Or so I have heard." Wanting to change the subject, she crossed her arms and said, "I had asked you into the garden so I could hear more about you, but we have mostly talked about me. Didn't you say you had a sister who died?"

A strange look came over his face. If only she could see him better, could read his features. Once again he bent his head to stare down at the leaf.

He nodded. "My adoptive parents never had children. Sometimes different boys would stay with us for a while, sleeping on a pallet on the floor. There were two brothers, older than I, who stayed for about two years before they started working in the margrave's stables."

Even though she sensed he did not want to talk about his sister or his childhood before he was adopted by the gamekeeper and his wife, she felt that he had had a good life after he went to live with them. Gratitude toward his adoptive parents welled up inside her.

"I always wished I had a sister," Odette confessed. "I had an imaginary sister when I was very young. I think the family who took me in thought I was daft when I would talk to my sister, Sophie. I rather enjoyed shocking them."

"I could see that about you." Jorgen nodded, an amused smile gracing his masculine lips.

"Odette?" Rutger's voice called to her. She stood quickly. Her uncle's outline was lit by the open back door. "Are you out here?"

"*Ja*, I am here."

"You must come and join the festivities. I want to introduce you to some people."

Jorgen stood, too, and escorted her to the house. "I hope you won't be scolded," he whispered to her.

"Oh *nein*. Uncle Rutger never scolds me. I am an adult, after all."

"Ah, Jorgen. I see you are with my niece. Taking in the night air?"

Odette interjected, "I couldn't hear well inside, with the music, and asked him to come into the garden so we could speak without shouting."

"Of course." Rutger smiled, but she saw the surprised look in his eyes—surprised she would be spending time talking to the forester.

She was a little surprised herself.

Once inside, Rutger introduced her to a man and his son—no doubt another marriage prospect for her—and then some other guests. One of them was an old man with saggy jowls who eyed her lecherously. He made sure to tell her his wife had died recently and he was looking for a new one. Odette cringed and excused herself from him as quickly as she could.

"There you are!" Mathis caught her hand. "Come and dance with me."

A new song was beginning, and they joined the other dancers. But many people were beginning to leave, and the dance floor was less crowded than before. When the dance was over, she saw Jorgen was heading toward the front door. She started to go toward him, but Mathis pulled her back with a hand on her arm.

"Odette, I think you are the fairest maiden in Thornbeck. What do you think of me?" A pleading look flared in his eyes.

"I think you are . . . a very complimentary gentleman." She laughed a little, hoping to lighten the moment and break away from him to say farewell to Jorgen. "I shall be back in a moment."

She pulled out of Mathis's grasp and reached Jorgen just before he passed through the small entryway between the main room and the front door. Others were standing nearby, including Rutger, and she felt his eyes on her.

As she rushed forward, Jorgen turned. She found herself face-to-face with him. "Don't forget. The children and . . . the verses." She hoped she had kept her words vague enough that she had not revealed their rendezvous to Rutger.

He gazed intently into her eyes. "I won't forget." His crooked smile stole her breath.

Rutger gave her a weighty look, but Anna and Peter were also waiting to say farewell. She embraced her friend, who whispered in her ear, "I shall come tomorrow. I want to know where you and Jorgen went."

Odette ignored Rutger's look of suspicion and went back to Mathis. "Forgive me, but I am so exhausted. I do not wish to dance anymore."

He did not protest, probably because the minstrels were playing their last song and everyone was leaving.

"Good night, my fair Odette." Mathis kissed her hand.

"*Gute Nacht,*" Odette answered, trying to look kind but not flirtatious. Thankfully, Rutger was standing nearby. She had a nervous feeling that Mathis might have told her he wished to marry her if her uncle had not been there.

When all the guests were gone, Odette squeezed her uncle's arm. "Thank you for the party."

"Did you have a pleasant birthday?"

"Oh *ja,* very pleasant."

"It gives me joy to hear it."

Perhaps she didn't thank him enough. Her conversation with Jorgen tonight had reminded her how her uncle had saved her from crushing lack, loneliness, and mistreatment at the hands of people who did not love her. She owed him so much.

Tomorrow she would tell him about the arrow and about Jorgen's realization that there was a poacher about, killing stags. For now she had to prepare herself for the hunt. She didn't want anyone to go hungry tomorrow because she had danced too much and was too tired.

And she had tomorrow afternoon with Jorgen and the children to look forward to.

# 8

ODETTE YAWNED AS she walked to the place outside the town wall on the south side where she taught the poorest children to read and write. Most of them lived in rickety shacks propped against the brick wall of the town. The little hovels were made of cast-off materials—wood, tree limbs, blankets, and whatever else they could find to keep out the wind and rain. Some of them were orphans and lived with older siblings, and some lived with parents who couldn't work due to sickness or infirmity and couldn't provide a better place to live.

These children were too embarrassed by their shabby clothing to attend the town school. The other children would tease them mercilessly. She suspected that if it were not for her, the children would not care enough to learn their letters and numbers, or how to read and write, add and subtract, which she also planned to teach them.

As she drew nearer the patch of bare ground where the children played and where they practiced making letters by drawing them with sticks in the dirt, she heard Jorgen's voice.

He was standing, and the children were sitting in a semicircle in front of him. They were gazing up at him in rapt attention.

". . . and when the rabbit hopped, the wolf leapt and landed on the grass. But there was no hare beneath his paws. His dinner had disappeared."

The children began to ask questions in hushed tones, and he answered them patiently, glancing at Odette every so often as she was standing behind the children. Finally he announced, "Your teacher is here, so listen to her now."

Odette came forward while he took a step back. "You are not leaving yet," she warned him before turning and facing the children.

She spoke to them for a moment before asking, "Wouldn't you like to hear some more of Forester Jorgen's verses and tales?"

The children cheered and shouted their assent.

Jorgen half smiled before pulling some folded sheets of parchment from the pocket inside his hip-length leather tunic. Although up to now she had seen him wearing the style of dress of a middle-class burgher, today he wore the type of clothing one might expect of a forester going about his duties in the woods: A brown linen shirt covered his neck and arms, and over it was a green, sleeveless, leather cotehardie that buttoned down the front. A dagger hung from the belt around his waist.

He looked just as handsome as he had the night before, only more rugged and more sure of himself—a combination that made her heart beat like the *Minnesingers'* drums at the Midsummer festival.

He first recited a poem about a magpie and a grasshopper that made the children laugh. Then he read them a tale about a baker and a starving raven that stole one of his pies. By the end of the story, the baker had made two pies for the bird and her baby birds. Of course, it was a children's story in which the bird could talk, but it made tears come into Odette's eyes. When he finished, she applauded along with the children.

After each poem or rhyme or story, the children all begged

him to read another. He spread his hands wide. "There are no more. I have read them all."

"Read them again!" the children shouted.

Odette and Jorgen both laughed. He shook his head. "Not today."

Odette gave a short lesson, then dismissed the children to play. Jorgen walked her back toward the town gate.

"Your tales and poems were delightful." She probably sounded like the children as they had hopped up and down, squealing at him when he was done. But she didn't care. He deserved the praise.

He gazed down at her. Could he tell that she had slept very little the night before?

She had been out hunting all night but only managed to shoot one pheasant. Anna woke her up early and called her "lazy head" for still being in bed. They had talked for hours about her party the night before.

"It is true Jorgen is not rich." Anna had frowned. "It is a pity because he is very handsome, and he seems to like you. But what man wouldn't adore you? You are beautiful and will make someone a very good wife. Odette, why don't you marry?"

"And whom do you suggest?" Odette feigned a flippancy she did not feel.

Anna sighed and shook her head. "That is the trouble. There is no one worthy of you."

Odette snorted.

"Truly, if I had to pick someone, I do not know anyone I think is good enough for you. They are all either too old or too ugly or too . . . something."

Would Anna have felt the same way if she knew the secret Odette was keeping from her? She hated hiding things from Anna. Now she was even hiding something from her uncle, for when Rutger had confronted her about spending so much time with Jorgen at her party, she had not had the courage to tell him that Jorgen knew there was a poacher killing the deer in the forest, and that the reason he knew was he had found one of her arrows.

She and Jorgen reached the gate, and he halted. "I must get back to my duties, but I want to thank you for asking me to come and read my writings to the children."

"They loved it so much. Your tales and verses were wonderful. I could see on the boys' faces that you are now their model of a perfect man, and they will be talking about you and your stories for a long time. I do hope you will come again soon."

"I will." He grew almost somber as he said softly, "You are their model of a perfect woman, and I can see why. Thank you for being so kind to them. You are probably the only kind person in most of their lives. They adore you."

Her heart did another strange leap inside her chest. "I adore them too." Dirty, often reeking, sometimes crying, and sometimes cursing at one another—she dearly loved them.

"Will you come again in two days? I teach them every Monday, Wednesday, and Friday."

He stared at her a moment, as if his eyes were seeking something in hers. He seemed to find what he was looking for and nodded.

~

Odette's heart beat quick and her hands shook that night as she clutched her bow and arrows to her chest underneath the black cloak she used to conceal them. She would never be able to keep her aim steady if she didn't control her nervousness. Why *was* she so afraid?

It was that foolish dream. She had dozed off after the evening meal, so tired after sleeping so little the last day and night, and dreamed once again that Jorgen was dragging her off to Thornbeck Castle's dungeon and locking her inside. His reproachful stare had sent a physical pain through her chest. How he would despise her for deceiving him, for making him think she was a merchant's daughter instead of a law-breaking poacher. How he would hate her for letting him tell her about the stags going missing, and all the while she was the one who had stolen them.

But it was only a dream. Only a dream, she chanted to herself.

Besides, who would help the starving children if she didn't? The margrave sat inside his majestic castle enjoying every luxury, while not far from his castle, beside the wall of the very city he proposed to protect, children were going hungry. Was he trying to feed them? No.

But Jorgen might not see this with the same view that she did. In fact, he seemed quite loyal to the margrave. Foolish men were always loyal to the wealthy and powerful, but was Jorgen foolish?

She and the young men made their way toward the cover of the trees. She would feel better when she was in the dense darkness of the forest. Jorgen would be asleep in his bed right now, not looking for poachers. But what if he was not in bed? What if he was indeed out looking for poachers—looking for her?

She had to cease this kind of thinking. It was making her hands shake.

They made it to the cover of the trees. Odette hid her old cloak in a bush and slung her quiver of arrows over her shoulder. She moved with stealth through the leaves toward one of her favored hunting sites. Squatting and peering through the leaves, she nocked an arrow to her bowstring and waited. Several deep breaths later, her hands were steady when a large stag with enormous antlers moved into view.

She wasted no time but raised the bow, pulled back on the string, and sent the arrow flying toward the buck. But as soon as the arrow left her fingers, the hart moved. Then it jerked sideways and leapt away, disappearing as the normally silent creature crashed through the bushes.

Odette gasped and almost dropped her bow. Had the animal been wounded? Or had she missed him?

She ran forward, still hearing the animal crashing through the undergrowth. She tried to follow him, but the sound was growing faint. He was gone.

She arrived at the place where the hart had been when she shot her arrow. There was no sign of it. She walked farther away, searching the ground, inside and under the bushes, kicking the leaves, but she still did not see the arrow.

Getting down on her hands and knees, with the three young men also searching near her, she combed through the thick layer of cool, loamy, decomposing leaves.

*God, help me. I have to find that arrow.* Her hands were shaking again. She couldn't give Jorgen more evidence of her poaching.

She went on searching until her hand touched something warm and wet and sticky on the leaves. She raised it to her face and sniffed. The coppery smell of blood. Her arrow must have wounded him.

Her stomach churned. Bad enough to injure the animal without killing it, but now he would be carrying the evidence of her poaching with him.

Feeling sick, her stomach threatening to throw up her dinner on the forest floor, she sucked in one deep breath after another. *I must stay calm.* She was sorry for the deer, but there was naught she could do for him. She must not think about his suffering.

Odette forced her mind to conjure up the faces of the children she fed with her poached meat. Most of them did not know the meat came from her, or because of her, but they were the same children who attended her reading lessons, who gazed up at her with gratitude. How could she let them down? Would she now become squeamish and weak because she had injured the deer instead of killing him and let the children starve?

And then there was the evidence of her arrow that was possibly still in the deer, more evidence of her crime. But no one would ever know the arrow was hers.

One of the young men held out his hand to her. She grasped it and let him help her to her feet. She motioned for them to follow her and headed in the opposite direction the big buck had gone.

"My dear." Rutger found Odette in the kitchen the next day gathering some bread, cheese, and dried fruit to break her fast after waking from sleep. "Young Mathis Papendorp is proving to be a valuable acquaintance. It seems his father has invited us to his home for a dinner three days hence. Are you not happy to be invited to the home of Thornbeck's Burgomeister?"

Odette tried to muster a smile. She had dreamed of Jorgen again, and this time he had clamped her in the pillory in the town center and marketplace. He had lifted the wooden board, made her put her head and hands inside, and secured it. She was trapped, unable to move. People came to laugh and point at her. They threw rotten fruit at her face. They even approached and smeared mud and filth in her hair.

Her stomach clenched. The dream had seemed so real. Not only could she smell the rotten fruit and feel it hitting her face, she had felt the hard wooden pillory around her neck, choking her if she didn't hold her head a certain way, the wood biting into her wrists. Jorgen seemed to have vanished after placing her there. And Rutger had stood nearby, his arms folded across his chest as he refused to help her.

She had woken herself up, thrashing her head to the side to avoid getting hit with a rotten egg. After that, she had another dream, no better than the first. A large stag with red eyes tried to gore her with his antlers out of revenge for what she had done to his brothers.

"Odette, are you unwell? You look pale."

"Only a little tired. I am well." She needed to put the ghastly dreams out of her thoughts. She would ask her uncle about something else that had been bothering her. "I have been thinking about what Mathis said about the margrave at my birthday feast."

"Oh? What did he say?"

"He said there were rumors that the margrave set the fire in Thornbeck Castle deliberately and that he had wanted his brother to die so he could be margrave." And if it was true, if the man could do something so ruthless to his own brother, what might he do to her if she was caught poaching?

"It is only a rumor."

"Do you think the rumor is true?"

Rutger shrugged. "No one knows, I suppose. Although it does seem likely. With his brother out of the way, with no heir and no wife, his younger brother would inherit everything. Otherwise, the younger brother would never be anything more than the captain of his brother's guard."

When thinking about it like that, it did seem likely.

"But I was speaking to you about the Burgomeister inviting us to his home for dinner. I thought you would be excited about seeing Mathis again. You seemed to enjoy dancing with him at your birthday dinner."

"I do enjoy dancing."

"I could imagine him asking you to marry him soon."

Odette shook her head. "I do not believe I would ever marry Mathis."

A look of disappointment flickered across his face. "I suspected as much."

"I am sorry, Uncle Rutger. You have been so good to me, and I'm sure my marriage to Mathis could advance your interests." She waited for him to confirm or deny the truth of her statement.

He shrugged. "While it is true that Mathis and his father could help my interests a great deal, I would not have you marry against your will."

She felt a tinge of guilt. Was she being selfish? Some people would say she was—selfish, foolish, and oblivious to her own interests.

"I cannot marry anyway. Neither Mathis Papendorp nor any other man in Thornbeck would allow his wife to poach deer to feed the poor."

Rutger smiled, but there was a solemnity in his eyes that belied his amusement. Then he shifted his head as he seemed to have a new thought. "Of course you would not poach deer." He turned partially away from her and fingered a beautiful vase from the Orient that sat on a small table. "You could influence the mayor and others of the wealthiest people in Thornbeck to form a special society to help the poor. You would no longer be forced to go out hunting every night."

It did sound appealing. She might stop dreaming these horrible dreams and finally be able to sleep.

"You don't want to hunt deer every night for the rest of your life, do you?"

"No." As she was realizing more and more. She couldn't do it forever, and she was bound to get caught sooner or later.

"Then why not marry Mathis?"

Odette was silent for a few moments. "It is something to think about." And another reason why she could never, ever marry Jorgen. He was not rich enough to help feed the poor. She might ask her uncle to help feed them, but because of his recent setbacks in losing his last three shipments of goods, she knew he was unable.

"You look sad, my dear."

"I am not sad." She shook her head, but even as she did, she had to blink away tears. *How foolish.* It was only because she was so tired, and exhaustion made her susceptible to tears.

"There is a reason why I am mentioning all of this." He stared at the colorful vase. "I am worried about the forester discovering that you are the one poaching the margrave's deer."

"Why do you say that?" A fist squeezed her stomach.

"The men told me how you lost an arrow a few nights ago."

"I know. Both very careless mistakes." Her breath shallowed.

"These sorts of things will happen, no matter how careful you try to be."

She supposed that was true. It did seem as though her only choice was to marry someone rich who would not mind helping the poor.

He said nothing for a moment. "Mathis Papendorp adores you. I think he would be easy to persuade. He would hardly miss the amount of money it would take to feed those children you teach. Unlike Jorgen Hartman."

"I have not decided to marry either man. Nor have they asked me."

"Forgive me. I have upset you with all this talk of marriage. You do not have to marry anyone, not as long as I am alive." Uncle Rutger did not speak again for several moments while Odette's thoughts churned. "But that is another thing to consider. I will not live forever, my dear. And if something unexpected were to happen to me, you could not go on as you have been. You would need to marry."

Rutger glanced down at the food she still clutched in her hands. "Go on and eat. I will leave you in peace." He touched her cheek affectionately before leaving the room.

Odette nibbled her bread as she sat at the kitchen table. Cook came bustling in from the cellar carrying potatoes and carrots.

"Your uncle wants what is best for you," Cook said in her usual grumbling tone of voice.

"Did you hear our conversation?"

"I may have heard some of it." Her tone dared Odette to complain. "He has been so good, giving you everything a father might have given his own child. And then, when he should have made you see your duty was to marry, he never forced you, and you rejected every good and wealthy man he paraded in front of you. Well, it is not my place to criticize, but I have an opinion, I have. If Herr Menkels wants you to marry Mathis Papendorp, then I am sure it is the best thing for you, and if you were the dutiful niece you should be, you would not tell him no."

Odette's cheeks grew hotter the longer Cook talked.

"You are right." Odette stood to her full height and smoothed her skirt. "It is not your place to criticize." She gathered her food into a cloth and trudged up the stairs to her bedchamber on the third floor. But before she even reached her door, a coldness filled her insides.

If Cook had overheard their conversation, then she had heard what Rutger said about her poaching. Would Cook tell anyone her secret?

# 9

JORGEN HAD BEEN busy for days helping the gamekeeper set snares for the rabbits to control their numbers. It seemed a shame that some of the ones they had caught could not be shared with the poor, particularly the children Odette had been helping. He would suggest it to the margrave at their next meeting.

As he knelt to set the snare that was big enough to catch a hare but too small to harm a deer, he heard a rustling nearby, followed by the snort of a large animal.

He stood, moving as quietly as he could in the direction of the sounds. He could tell he was getting closer, as the labored breathing was getting louder.

He paused. If the large animal was human, he might be about to interrupt a young couple from Thornbeck doing things they could not get away with in town. But no. The blowing noise sounded like a deer in distress, and not a sound any human could make.

He stepped closer, entering a dense thicket of bushes and vines and small trees. Finally he saw it: a large hart lying on its side. He wasn't moving, except for the heaving of his sides as he struggled to breathe. An arrow stuck out from his back haunch, with both dried and fresh blood around the wound. And the feathers on the arrow were white, just like the one he had found earlier.

Heat rose from his neck to his brow. Someone *was* poaching deer in Thornbeck Forest. This could well be the same poacher who stalked Jorgen's father and then killed him.

The deer was dying. The kindest thing would be to dispatch him and put the poor creature out of its pain. He drew an arrow from his quiver and the bow from across his back and aimed for the spot behind its skull and from the angle that would kill the animal instantly. He released the arrow, and the hart's heaving sides stilled.

Jorgen's own breath was coming hard as he clenched his teeth and stared down at the poor dead deer and the arrow protruding from its flesh.

Who was poaching in Thornbeck Forest? If it was only an occasional deer to feed a man's family, Jorgen might never catch him, but with as many deer as Jorgen suspected were missing, he must be selling the meat.

Anyone caught selling deer meat in the town center on market day or any butcher selling it from his shop would be arrested. This poacher was probably selling it secretly—which meant he was operating a black market.

But this could work in Jorgen's favor, since the black-market selling would give him another way to find this poacher.

This was Jorgen's chance to avenge his father's death. No matter what Jorgen had to do, he would capture this poacher. And he would make sure the margrave did not let him off easy. However, he had a hunch that he needn't worry about that. Lord Thornbeck would be inclined to punish this poacher to the full extent of the law.

Although Jorgen's new job as forester was not well known inside the walls of the town of Thornbeck, he needed to make sure no one would recognize him today.

Jorgen donned a long dark-blue surcoat that reached to his ankles. The air was still moist and cool from the heavy rain of the early morning, so he would not appear quite so strange as he pulled the hood over his head to partially obscure his face.

He set out from his home in the forest. Once inside the city, he headed toward the town square. As it was Tuesday, the market would be underway, with sellers and buyers crowding the circular cobblestoned area. Even the rain earlier would not stop most of the sellers. But first he went inside a shop on Butcher's Guild Strasse, the street where nearly every shop sold meat of various kinds.

He asked the shopkeeper, a plump woman old enough to be his mother and who was probably the butcher's wife, to tell him what kind of meat she sold.

"What kind do you want?"

"I want something that tastes of the wild."

"Tastes of the wild?" She scrunched her face at him. "What do you mean? All our meat was raised in the meadows surrounding Thornbeck. We don't sell wild meat here."

"Do you know anyone who does? I would pay a lot of money for some deer meat." He watched her for her reaction.

"I know not where you can get such meat." She huffed and turned on her heel and went into the back room. When she returned, she laid a large goose, all plucked and ready to be cooked, across the counter. "That's as wild as we sell here, and it was raised at the old Schindler farm north of town. They clip their wings when they're young, so their meat is as tender and tasty as any you will find." She fixed him with a narrowed stare. "If you find deer meat, that'll be poached from the margrave's own land, and we would never sell poached meat here. The margrave would have our heads. Unless you are daft, you should know that."

"I see you are an honest woman. That is admirable. Perhaps I will come back for the goose on my way home."

Jorgen left the shop, joined the crowd on their way to the market, and looked around. Sellers of every description had their booths set up and their wares on display, and Jorgen saw nothing out of the ordinary. No one looked as if he was selling venison. No one even looked suspicious.

He would not find the black-market seller in the open market. He must look elsewhere or find someone who knew where this seller was located. The seller could be anywhere, but it seemed advantageous for him to be near the market.

Who should Jorgen ask? He had already raised the suspicions of the woman at the butcher shop.

Glancing around him, he saw women with large baskets on their arms as they did their shopping. Some were servants, and others were middle-aged or older women shopping for their families. Most of the sellers were busy and did not have time for a private chat. But as he drew closer to the side of the marketplace that was flanked by the massive town hall building, he saw a young man. He was lounging against the side of the *Rathous*, watching passersby. He looked fully grown but younger than twenty. Would he know anything?

Jorgen approached him. "Do you know where I might buy some deer meat?"

"Why do you want to know?" He looked lazily back at Jorgen from half-closed eyes.

"I want to buy some venison. Is that so strange?"

"Not strange at all." The young man pushed himself away from the stone wall and turned to go around the corner.

Jorgen waited a few moments, then followed him down a narrow alley between two buildings facing the marketplace. Could he have found a person who could lead him to the black market? Or was Jorgen about to get a rude greeting from brigands?

The doorways on either side of him along the alley were too shadowy for him to see if they were open or closed. Hardly any sunlight came through the narrow alley, and a large tree at the end further shaded the street. Jorgen made sure he could reach his knife, letting his hand rest on it in its sheath underneath his surcoat.

The young man reached the end of the narrow alley and glanced back at Jorgen. He then turned to the left and disappeared.

Jorgen followed, looking first to the right and then the left. No one was lurking behind the buildings, and the residents were obviously using this back side to dump their chamber pots. The smell made it difficult to breathe, mingling with the summer heat like a stifling fog.

The young man was several feet ahead of him and motioned for him to catch up. Jorgen proceeded, alert for any motion in the dark back street. His boots squished through filth. They turned right when they came to another back alleyway that led behind a row of houses. A woman stood in the first doorway. Her hair was red and wiry, somehow managing to stick out in all directions even though it was braided down her back. A couple of her teeth were missing in front.

"What do we have here?" She let her gaze linger on Jorgen's face.

"I want to buy some venison."

"Why did you come here? You don't think we have that here, do you?" She kept one hand on her hip, and she used her other hand to wave around when she talked, as though she were spreading out the words. She gave him a provocative half smile. "You do look like a man who knows what he wants, I admit."

He suspected he was standing behind the house of prostitution called The Red House, which faced *Waschefrau Strasse.*

"He only wants venison," the young man said. "Give him what he wants."

She reached out and slapped the young man on the side of the head.

"Ow!"

"Who do you think you are? You do not tell me what's what and who's who. Do you know this man?"

*"Nein."* He sounded petulant, more boy than man.

She turned her gaze back on Jorgen.

"I want to purchase some venison for my aged mother. The barber said the red meat would strengthen her blood."

She stared at him, then stepped back. "Come in."

He went inside the dimly lit back room and followed the woman down a corridor and into a small kitchen. Slabs of fresh deer meat were laid out on the tables.

"Is this what you were looking for?"

*"Ja."* Jorgen examined the meat, skinned and readied for cooking. He was certain this was venison. He pretended to look it over, selecting what he wanted. The only other person in the room was a boy about fourteen years old who stood and offered him a hemp cloth to wrap his selection in.

Jorgen did choose a slab of venison, wrapped it in the cloth, and handed over the money to the woman. She stuffed the coins in a purse that hung from a belt around her waist, then escorted him back to the door in the alleyway.

As she opened the door to let him out, two people were standing there waiting. One was a servant from a wealthy household, if he read her tidy appearance and clothing correctly, and the other was a young man, also with the appearance of a servant.

Did the wealthy people of Thornbeck know about this black market of poached deer? If only he could find out who was behind it.

Perhaps he could find out who owned this building.

When he was back on the street and unescorted, he circled around to the front. It was the brothel as he had suspected. As much as this house of prostitution had been spoken of by all the boys his age when he was growing up, he couldn't recall anyone saying who owned it.

Nevertheless, he had discovered the black market the poacher was using to sell his meat.

The margrave invited Jorgen into his library. Lord Thornbeck looked preoccupied, his face drawn and somber as he stared down at the papers on his desk. His chancellor stood just behind him, glaring at Jorgen.

"Jorgen, do you have news for me?"

"Lord Thornbeck, thank you for seeing me. I do have news. I have discovered that there is a place in town where people are going to buy venison, and I believe it is deer that have been poached from Thornbeck Forest."

The margrave's brows lowered, giving him an even darker look. He stood, then limped while leaning on a walking stick as he moved toward the tall windows overlooking the steep, wooded ravines behind the castle. The sun had not yet broken through the clouds, even though it was almost midday, and he stopped and gazed out.

"Tell me everything you know," Lord Thornbeck said without looking at Jorgen.

Jorgen began by telling him about the deer he had found with the arrow sticking out of his side and the white feathers that matched the other arrow he had found. He described the situation in the back alleyway behind the *Rathous*, not far from the market-place, the meat, the buyers, and the sellers.

"In which house was it located?"

"The house of prostitution everyone calls The Red House."

"I will have my steward find out who owns it." He turned back to Jorgen. "I thank you for your diligence in finding out about the black market and poaching problem. That was very good work."

"It was my duty and honor, my lord. I intend to capture this poacher." Jorgen bowed.

"Please do keep me informed if you discover anything new."

"I do have one other matter to ask you about, my lord, if I may."

"Of course."

"Since we are snaring so many hares this week, would you like to donate some of them to the poor?"

He stared, as though the question surprised him.

"Donate them to the poor?" Contempt oozed from Ulrich's voice. The chancellor stepped forward to glance at the margrave's face. "My lord, I have never heard of previous margraves doing that."

"I do not do the things the previous margraves did, Ulrich." Lord Thornbeck cleared his throat. "I think it is a good idea, Jorgen. Besides, I do believe my cook is ready to start tossing hares in the rubbish heap. Therefore, you may give all the hares you snare, from this point on, to the poor. You will take charge of it."

"Yes, my lord."

"Ulrich." The margrave glanced at his chancellor. "Send for my steward. I have a matter to discuss with him. And you may show Jorgen out."

Jorgen bowed one last time to the margrave, then followed

Ulrich, whose face was red and pinched, as if he were tasting something bitter.

At least Odette would be pleased when she learned that the poor would receive a great bounty of hares in the next few days.

# 10

ODETTE ARRIVED AT the dinner party with Peter and Anna. She was awed upon entering the Burgomeister's home to find it even larger and more luxuriously furnished than Rutger's.

At one point Odette noticed Rutger and Mathis's father speaking to each other in a corner by themselves. Then Herr Papendorp led Rutger out the back door, and they disappeared.

"Odette," Mathis said, brushing against her arm as he appeared at her side. "You don't seem to be enjoying this party as much as the last one. I am so sorry there is no music. My father says he cannot hear what anyone is saying if musicians are playing, so he never has dancing at his parties." Mathis quirked an eyebrow at his father's failure as a host. "Can I get you anything? Anna? Something to drink?"

Before they could answer, Mathis motioned for a servant carrying goblets of wine on a tray. He took two and gave them to Odette and Anna.

While Mathis talked, Odette sipped her wine. She remembered the cutting words of the woman who had been their cook for the past ten years. Would she be wrong to reject Mathis if he should ask her to marry him? *Could* she marry Mathis? He was charming and young. Cook thought she was selfish not to marry someone rich. Perhaps Rutger would finally marry if Odette was out of the way. He was thirty-five years old, not too old to get a desirable wife.

But should she allow their cook to influence her thoughts about something as serious as marriage? Cook would not have to live Odette's life if she pushed her into making a poor choice of husband. Only Odette would have to face the consequences.

"It's a pity," Mathis went on, "we don't have any music. I would love to dance with you again." He drew closer, and she noticed the gray flecks in his light-blue eyes. Certainly, he was not unattractive. Most women would think him handsome.

"Mathis! Come here and tell this man what you said about the mules and horses my men brought from Spain." An older man motioned him over to where he stood with two other men, all elaborately dressed in the latest fashions—brightly colored robes with fur trim and long liripipes hanging from their hats and hoods.

"Excuse me." Mathis looked reluctant but moved away from Odette and Anna and joined the three men across the room.

Peter drew near. "Anna, darling, come and meet someone. It will not take long." And then Odette was left alone with her thoughts.

Unlike Mathis, she would rather talk than dance, knowing she would soon be out on her nightly hunt—or perhaps it was because Jorgen was not here to dance with her. But she should not be thinking about him like that. Sleeping in the daytime was difficult, and she had not been sleeping well, plagued with bad dreams. Besides, talking with Jorgen had been even more pleasant than dancing. Her mind so often went back to their conversation in the tiny garden behind her house. She would see him tomorrow.

"What is going on inside that fair head, Odette?" Mathis had gotten rid of the interloper and was leaning close to her again.

She laughed, a nervous sound. "Nothing very noteworthy."

"I am sure that cannot be true. You must have many noteworthy thoughts." He grinned. "Since we cannot dance, I would wish you to come with me to the inner courtyard. I have something to show you there." Without waiting for her answer, he took her hand and slipped it into the crook of his arm and led her out of the large room and down a short corridor and into the twilight of the open courtyard.

Perhaps Odette should have refused to go with him, as she was very aware that she was leaving the safety of the crowd. Even though she and Jorgen had gone out into the garden at her birthday dinner, other people had been in the garden as well, and she was not sure she trusted Mathis as much as she trusted Jorgen.

Mathis pulled her into the relative darkness. "Our gardener plants beautiful flowers out here."

She glimpsed a few men standing around a small pony penned at the other end of the courtyard. They appeared to be discussing the animal. Seeing other people made her breathe more freely.

Mathis led her to some large pots overflowing with flowers. One pot was filled with red geraniums that shone bright in the nearly dark courtyard. Another pot was home to a rosebush with several pink flowers.

"My mother loves roses, and my father likes to indulge her." He was looking at her and not the flowers. "Do you like them?"

"They are very beautiful." Odette touched a petal with her fingertip.

Mathis broke one off and held it out to her. "For you."

"Thank you." Odette brought the flower to her nose. "It smells wonderful."

He led her to a fresco painted on the wall facing the courtyard, a scene of two lovers embracing in a garden of flowers.

"It is well done and looks quite real. The artist is very talented."

"My mother loves color. Father commissioned the artist to come all the way from Heidelberg to paint it. My father loves my mother very much." Mathis leaned closer. "I would like to make a love match when I marry. I do not care so much about a dowry, as long as the woman is able to love me, and I her."

Odette placed her hand to her chest and cleared her throat. "That is very commendable."

"I believe I could love you, Odette, the way my father loves my mother." He moved even closer, his voice a hoarse whisper.

"Oh." She leaned back. "Your feelings do you credit, and I thank you for the honor of expressing the thoughts of your heart to me, but—"

"Do you think you could love me, Odette?" His eyes were large and round, and he seemed to be holding his breath.

"I do not know. This is very sudden for me, and I am not as sure about my feelings as you seem to be."

He nodded and backed away a few inches. "I understand. So does that mean you *may* feel . . . something for me? Perhaps?"

"I cannot tell you anything of my feelings, as I am unsure of them myself." Jorgen's face flashed through her mind like a bolt of lightning. But she could not be thinking of him. She cleared her throat again as she tried to clear her mind.

"I can give you time." He touched her arm, staring into her eyes. "You are the most beautiful and sought-after maiden in all of Thornbeck. If you will promise to think of me, to consider me, I will wait for you." The breathlessness of his voice seemed to prove his sincerity.

Odette couldn't block the stirring inside her at the fervency in his manner, but she suspected it was more pity than anything else. "Very well. I promise to think of you."

"As a possible husband?"

"Yes." But even as she said the word, the stirring became more of a churning in her stomach.

The men who had been examining the pony were walking toward them. "I believe that is my uncle." She was uncertain who the men were, but it was the first thing that came into her mind to say to distract Mathis. "We had better go back inside, I suppose."

"*Ja.*" His tone seemed a bit deflated, but he smiled.

Mathis took her elbow, and they walked back toward the door while the men walked several feet behind them. When they reached the narrow corridor that led inside the house, Mathis whispered, "May I kiss you?"

Her heart began to beat so rapidly she felt dizzy. "Not tonight. I need time to think."

As he led her the rest of the way inside, he said, "A maiden has a right to choose when she wishes to be kissed."

Odette quickened her step as she heard the voices of the people again. She entered and went to stand beside Anna. Mathis did not join them.

She stayed near Peter and Anna the rest of the night. She spoke with other people, including a few that Rutger introduced her to, until he was ready to go home. Mathis kept his distance, only once bringing her a goblet of wine when he saw that she had misplaced hers when they had gone into the courtyard.

Rutger said his farewell to Mathis and his father, while Odette nodded politely to Mathis and allowed him to take her hand and lift it to his lips for a brief kiss.

Once they were on the street, she let out a long breath. She was not quite ready to tell Anna what had happened. She let her jumbled thoughts keep her company while Rutger chatted with Peter and Anna all the way home.

Odette stood at her upper-floor window. When she saw Brother Philip walking toward her home with a cloth-covered bundle hugged to his chest, she hurried down the stairs, holding up her skirts and taking the steps two at a time.

Rutger had sent a note to her monk–tutor offering his favorite treat to entice him to return. He had not been to tutor her since she had argued with him by quoting Scriptures. She guessed by the bundle in his arms that he must be bringing her a new book to read. Her heart beat fast at what it might be.

She opened the door for him herself and ushered him into the large open room. Then she pulled the table out from the wall and provided a stool for each of them.

"I brought the Old Testament books of First and Second Chronicles." Brother Philip unwrapped the bundle and laid the parchments reverently on the table.

"Oh, I have not read these." Odette sat down eagerly. But Brother Philip was still standing. "Why don't you go into the kitchen, Brother Philip? Cook has made a nice pork roast with spicy plum sauce especially for you, and I believe she has just taken a loaf of bread from the oven. I can smell it from here."

He kept his eyelids half closed, as if uninterested. "I suppose I cannot disappoint her."

"Indeed not. You must go and sample it or she will be grumpy for the rest of the week."

Brother Philip needed no further encouragement. He headed out the back door for the kitchen.

Odette sighed and set about to read the new treasure.

The Chronicles were familiar, as she had read similar accounts in the books of First and Second Kings, and in her studies with

Brother Philip she had learned that they both chronicled the same period of time and the same kings. But she relished the very real stories of human mistakes, failures, and sometimes triumphs. The triumphs mostly came because the kings were obeying God, and failures came when they ignored God.

How wonderful it would be if God spoke directly to her the way He had spoken to the prophets. The kings of old simply had to inquire of God and He would tell them what to do. When she came to the story of Jehoshaphat in Second Chronicles, she was struck by how many times he was reminded to "seek God." When he had sought God, things went smoothly and God worked everything out, but when he had not sought God, disaster threatened.

Brother Philip strolled into the room, moving slowly and rubbing his belly. "Your cook is the best in Thornbeck, certainly better than my fellow monks who take turns cooking at the abbey."

"Brother Philip." Odette stared down at the text before her. "Why did God say that His wrath was on Jehoshaphat when all he had done was try to help King Ahab?" She had her own idea about the answer to that question, but she knew it would flatter Brother Philip to be asked.

"Let me read it again."

Odette pointed out the passages. Brother Philip sat and read it over silently. "King Jehoshaphat must have known that King Ahab was wicked and did not follow God. He was foolish to follow King Ahab into battle with his enemies. The conclusion we can draw is that we must never be loyal to a wicked person."

Odette nodded, thinking of Jorgen. Was he doing what Jehoshaphat had done? Was Jorgen being loyal to a wicked person—Lord Thornbeck?

But she also couldn't cease thinking about God's admonition to seek the Lord. Had she sought the Lord before deciding to start poaching? If the same held true for her as for Jehoshaphat, then she might very well meet with disaster.

⁓

When Jorgen arrived the next day at the clearing near the south wall of the town, Odette was already there talking with the children, who were gathered around her and staring up at her with adoring faces.

Did she know how beautiful she was? Her hair shone in the afternoon sun, and her voice was soft and kind. What a wonderful mother she would be. But he should not be thinking about that.

Some of the children caught sight of him standing there watching her and exclaimed, "It's the forester! Jorgen!"

Odette turned, a smile on her lips. "I'm just finishing up my lesson. Come, children. Show Herr Hartman how you write the words you learned today."

They all began to write *Wald, Frau,* and *Mann* with their sticks.

Jorgen looked at their work and praised each one. When they would grin up at him, he would wink or give their shoulders a quick squeeze.

"What is in your sack?" they asked as he dropped his burden, which he had carried slung across his back.

"I shall tell you later, when the gamekeeper comes with another just like it."

The children exclaimed their excitement, trying to guess what was inside. "Toys!" "Sweets!" And one little boy guessed, "Rats!"

"Ew!" several of the girls cried.

"You will just have to wait and see."

"Will you tell the children a story?" Odette asked him.

He had the children all sit on the grass, and he told them a new story he had thought up since the last time he had been with them. They kept their eyes on him—including Odette, who sat with the children.

Just as he was finishing, Herman, his newest gamekeeper, emerged from the trees carrying a sack identical to his own across one shoulder.

Jorgen stood. "The margrave has kindly allowed us to bring thirty skinned hares for you all to take home to cook and eat."

Before he could continue, the children, especially the older ones, let out a loud whoop, cheering and jumping up and down. Why, then, did he feel this overwhelming sadness and shame, like a memory from the past?

Images began to assault his mind. A vendor's face rose before him, a man who had yelled at him for trying to steal some fruit from his stand. A baker who had ordered him from his shop and called him "a filthy beggar." A woman who had wrinkled her nose at his little sister and told her to move out of her way. The face of his sister, Helena, her big eyes staring up at him in horror and pain as she lay dying.

He could not allow those memories to overwhelm him now. Those things had happened long ago. He was no longer the despised orphan child he had been then. But as he gazed upon the children who looked much like he and his little sister must have looked, a fist seemed to grab his insides and twist.

*Focus on the task.* He had already counted the children and knew there were fourteen of them. He cleared his throat. "Each of you may take home two hares to your family."

The gamekeeper opened his sack, and Jorgen did the same. They began to distribute the game to the children, who grabbed them eagerly by a hind leg, talking excitedly about having hare stew or roasted hare on a spit for supper.

Jorgen stepped closer to Odette. "There will be two left over. Who should I give them to?"

Tears were shining in Odette's eyes as she watched the children. She turned to him and blinked rapidly. "Oh. Let me think." She studied the children for a moment. "Pinnosa here and Fritz there." She called to them and motioned them to come toward her. Jorgen gave them each a third hare, trying not to think how much the little girl looked like his sister. Her eyes were shining, but she was pale and she didn't smile. When was the last time she had smiled? No child should ever have that haggard expression.

"How can I ever thank you?" Odette was gazing up at him. The sheen of tears was back in her eyes.

"I shall tell the margrave how thankful the children are."

"But I am sure it was you who asked him to donate this food for the children. Lord Thornbeck would not have thought of this on his own."

"Why do you say that?"

"He never has before."

"It was I who suggested he give some of the hares we were trapping to the poor, but the margrave was kind enough to agree to it."

"Of course. Please give him our thanks."

The children were dispersing, hastening home with their bounty, and the gamekeeper gathered the sacks and turned to leave. He and Odette said farewell and parted.

Even though it had brought back painful thoughts and made him remember things he wished he could forget, he was not sorry he had been able to give away the food to the children. Odette had inspired him to do it. If only she could be his inspiration for a long time to come.

# 11

Two days later, Odette was teaching her lesson to the children when Jorgen appeared at the edge of the forest. He stood leaning against a tree while she finished up.

Odette had been unable to refrain from thinking about the margrave, about the rumors that he had killed his own brother so he could claim the title of Margrave of Thornbeck. Anyone who would do such a thing must be evil and capable of any deception and cruelty. It was yet another reason why it was unfortunate that Jorgen was the margrave's forester.

When the children had all gone home and she and Jorgen were alone, she couldn't seem to stop herself from asking, "Have you seen any more evidence of poaching?"

Jorgen sighed, staring down at the ground with a morose look. "Sadly, yes." He glanced up at her as he shifted his feet. "I found an injured deer with the same type arrow as the one I found before."

"Injured deer?" Her stomach sank, and her heart thudded sickeningly.

"He was dying so I had to finish him." He stared at the trees several feet away. "I do not like doing that—shooting an animal that is helpless and cannot even flee—but I didn't want him to suffer anymore."

"Of course," Odette whispered. "You did the right thing. I am sure he would have died, and you kept him from further misery." Even as she said the words, her breath shallowed.

"But you do not want to hear about suffering animals and poachers. We should talk about something more pleasant." He turned a smile on her that was like the sun breaking out from behind a cloud. But remembering that deer, she wasn't sure she deserved to see the sun or feel its warmth.

"I am interested in anything that interests you," she said honestly. Thanks be to God, he did not know she had injured that stag. Her knees trembled at the thought of him finding out.

"Something that interests me is that the margrave is giving a ball at Thornbeck Castle."

"A ball? He's been the margrave for almost a year now and he has never given a ball."

"He's giving one now. The chancellor advised him to do it, even though the margrave doesn't dance because of his bad ankle. Nevertheless, he thinks it will be a good opportunity for him to meet all the more prominent people of Thornbeck."

"Ah." Who would that include?

"I was surprised I was invited, and of course, you and your uncle. The Burgomeister and his son will be there too."

"Oh. It sounds like it could be . . . pleasant."

"I hear it is to be a masquerade ball. That was also the chancellor's idea."

"A masquerade." What would she go as? She had never been to a masquerade. "What will you be dressed as?"

"I suppose I cannot go as a forester." He said it like a question.

Odette laughed. "You will find something, I am sure. When is the ball?"

"Not for a few weeks. The margrave is inviting some nobles

from other regions and wants to give them enough time to travel here."

"I shall look forward to dancing with you then." Memories flooded her, of how much she had enjoyed dancing with him at the Midsummer festival, his hand around hers. A tiny shiver raced across her shoulders. "In the meantime, I will work on my costume."

"What shall you be?"

Odette thought for a moment. "A swan." She could start searching for feathers for her mask now. "A white swan. And now you shall know how to find me at the ball."

He smiled at her. But there was sadness in his eyes. "My father liked swans. There used to be a pair of them that lived in the lake near Thornbeck Castle. He would take me to feed them bread crumbs."

It was wrenching to see the smile change to anger. He stared down at the ground, his mouth twisting. She had never seen him angry before.

"I am very sorry."

"I believe this new poacher is the same one who killed my father, and I will not let him get away unpunished."

Her stomach twisted. What could she say without arousing suspicion? "It could not be the same person. That was years ago."

"Only four years ago. That poacher shot at my father, then chased him and shot him through the heart. He showed no mercy. And then he disappeared—until now."

Odette forced herself to breathe, forced her voice to stay steady. "Why do you think it is the same man?"

"The feathers on the arrows were the same."

She thought for a moment. She had to be careful what she said. "But . . . were the feathers so unusual? Couldn't more than one person have the same kind of feathers on their arrows?"

He opened his mouth, then closed it, as if considering how to answer her. "I suppose it might not be the same person. White feathers are common."

"Of course! White feathers are very common, probably the most common." Her voice was too loud. She had to calm herself. "Very common," she said quietly.

"My father was a good man. If it is within my power, I will avenge him." He said the words without looking at her. "He did not deserve to die that way."

"Of course not." If only she could comfort him, put her arms around him or touch his hand. Her heart thumped against her chest, both at the longing inside her, and at the guilty feeling of knowing his painful thoughts at the moment were caused, at least in part, by her. "I wish it had not happened. I am so sorry."

After a few moments, he nodded, then cleared his throat.

"I want to thank you for giving me the idea of bringing the animals we snared to the children. It is a joy to know they will eat well tonight." He was looking intently into her eyes. "The world needs more people like you, Odette."

She smiled to lighten the mood. "And you, Jorgen Hartman."

"I should get back to my job now." He took another step toward the forest.

"Will you come next week?"

"I have to meet with the margrave on Wednesday, but I shall see you on Friday, perhaps."

Odette only hoped he would not have found more evidence of her poaching by then.

~⊃

Rutger and Odette sat alone at the table, eating the main dish of roasted pheasant and stewed fruit.

"How was your lesson today with the children?" he asked, just after she had put a bite of meat in her mouth. "Did you see the forester?"

She took a few moments to chew her food. She stared down at her plate and finally swallowed. "*Ja*, he was there."

"Did you ask him what he knows about the poacher?"

"He knows there is a poacher." She forced herself not to squirm in her seat. Not wanting to confess her failure, she avoided looking him in the eye.

"What is it, my dear?"

"He found another arrow."

"Another arrow?"

"I . . . I injured a stag and he got away with the arrow."

"I see."

Although her uncle normally was the picture of contentment and nothing ever seemed to bother him, now she saw concern, even worry, flicker across his face.

"Jorgen was angry about the poaching. He thinks this new poacher is the same one who killed his father four years ago."

Rutger frowned. "That is not good."

"I know." Just hearing Rutger's concern made her heart beat faster and a heaviness fill her chest. "We need to change the color of the feathers on my arrows. Perhaps we could dye them different colors. Then maybe he would think there was more than one poacher."

"My dear, you must not become so upset. Breathe." He demonstrated by taking in a big breath, then letting it out slowly. "Do it with me."

She took in a deep breath . . . Then she saw by the glint in his eye and the upturn of his mouth that he was already seeing the humor in the situation. "This is not a matter to laugh about."

"I will take care of it." His half-amused expression softened. "I will make sure the boys make some new arrows with colorful feathers—perhaps green and brown ones that will not be so easily seen—and change the fletching on your old ones."

"Thank you, but I have already asked them to do that."

"Very well. The problem is solved."

"I would not say it is solved." Jorgen was very upset. But perhaps she had persuaded him to think it was not necessarily the same poacher who killed his father. "He brought two sacks full of hares that he and the gamekeepers had snared, and he gave them all to the children."

"Does the margrave know?"

"He gave him permission."

"So Jorgen is trying to impress you by showing charity to the children. Did he impress you?" He took a sip of wine from his goblet as he studied her over the rim.

She let her lips twist into a frown. "Jorgen is a good sort of man, even if he is the forester. I would not say he did it to impress me."

"Oh, I think he must have. But why does he want you to think well of him? I very much fear he is in love with you, Odette."

"Oh no. He is not the sort of man to fall in love with a woman he hardly knows." She shook her head, blushing and raising her goblet to her lips. After she had taken a sip and swallowed, she said, "We are only friends."

"Are you certain of that? Perhaps you do not know the forester's heart . . . or your own."

She frowned, wrinkling her forehead. "Why are you saying this?"

Heinke came in to refill his goblet, and he waited until she left. "My dear, I do not think you realize the effect you have on men. The fact that you are one and twenty and yet unmarried is a testament to my deference to your wishes and my ability to protect you. You are very beautiful, so beautiful that I have heard rumors around town that I have not found you a husband yet because I want you for myself."

"That is vile and disgusting!" Odette set down her goblet and tried to control her breathing. "That is not true. Surely no one believes that."

"My point is that Jorgen would have to be blind and insensible not to feel some attraction to you. And you should be careful not to fall in love with him. You could have any unmarried man in Thornbeck, and marriage is made more difficult when you are poor. I am simply trying to look out for what is best for you."

Odette nodded and stared down at the table. She wanted love, but if she kept poaching, sooner or later Jorgen would find out. Could he love her then?

Perhaps she should do what Rutger wished and marry someone wealthy, like Mathis. It would certainly make her life easier.

# 12

ODETTE AWOKE WITH a start. A pale light was streaming in her window. Was that twilight—or dawn?

She sat up, blinking. That light was definitely morning, not night. What had happened? She did not remember hunting the night before. She had gone to take a nap but must have slept all night.

She had missed the hunt.

Jumping out of bed, she grabbed her clothes and began to get dressed. But she had nowhere to go.

Odette fell back onto the bed, then curled onto her side. Would the children go hungry today because she had not gone hunting last night? They would have the hares that Jorgen had brought to them. "Thank You, God, for providing the hares," she whispered.

Her mind went to Jorgen, then to the conversation she'd had with Rutger the night before. He believed Jorgen was attracted to her, and she didn't really doubt it was so. But if she was also falling in love with him . . . That was very unwise.

If she could go back to sleep, she wouldn't have to think about it anymore.

A knock at the door made her sit up and listen. Muted voices, then soft footsteps she recognized as Heinke's came from the corridor, then drew closer.

Heinke stuck her head in. "Mathis Papendorp is here to see you."

Her heart lifted, then sank. "I will be downstairs in a few minutes." At least he would be someone to talk to and take her mind off . . . other things.

"Good morning, Odette." Mathis stood at the bottom of the stairs holding a large bunch of fresh pink roses. "These are for you."

"Oh. They are exquisite." She hurried down the steps and took the flowers from his hands.

"Careful. They have thorns."

Odette breathed in the heady fragrance, letting the petals touch her face. "Thank you. They are lovely." She called for Heinke to put them in a vase of water. "There was a vase here on this shelf, but I don't see it now." The beautiful vase Rutger had been looking at a few days ago when they were talking . . . It was gone. But Heinke took the flowers and soon brought them back in a ceramic vase that held them quite well.

"They are the same color as my mother's roses, but I bought these from a seller in the marketplace."

She sniffed them again, unable to stop looking at them.

"You look radiant this morning. Mornings must be your favorite time of day."

She laughed. "Do not flatter me. I am not even usually out of bed at this time of day."

"Oh?" He looked a bit disappointed. Perhaps she could further disappoint him.

"*Nein*, I sleep my mornings away and do very little in the afternoons besides visit my friend Anna, and sometimes I study theology." No one wanted a lazy wife who would embarrass him in front of other men by boasting about how much she knew about the Bible and other holy writings.

"My dear, you can study all you want if you marry me. I can afford to buy you all the books of the Bible, Psalters, whatever pleases you. Odette, I want to marry you, if you will only say yes."

Uh-oh. That didn't go as planned. She forced herself to smile. Wasn't that what she wanted—a husband who was as good to her as Rutger was, who would indulge her with books and tutors and leisure time? If he would indulge her with books, would he not also indulge her by letting her feed the children?

She looked into his pleading eyes. If he would be kind and generous . . . Perhaps she was being foolish by not wanting to marry him simply because she did not feel an attraction to him. Certainly no other maiden in Thornbeck would refuse him. Still, she wasn't ready to pledge herself to this man.

"Thank you for not forcing me to make a decision yet."

"Of course." He took a step back and nodded. "I must go now. My father has appointed me to be in charge of a census of Thornbeck. Everyone must be counted. It is a lot of work, and I have many men I must oversee."

She tried to look impressed. "I am sure you will do a very good job." She reached out her hand, and he took it and brought it to his lips for a kiss.

"Fare well, Odette."

"Fare well."

Jorgen brought two more sacks of hares to the children, watching Odette's face when she saw them. Her blue eyes grew round, a smile spreading over her face as the children cheered and ran toward him. It was to be the last of the hares, for their snaring was at an end, but he enjoyed seeing their enthusiasm—and Odette's pleasure.

He had waited until time for Odette's class to end, and now he handed out the fresh meat and watched the children run home with them.

Odette stood looking at him. "Thank you again. Do you know how unusual you are, caring about children most people would scorn?"

"Maybe because I was one of them after the pestilence killed my parents."

Her expression sobered. "The last time you brought the hares, you looked sad, as though you were thinking of something else."

He rubbed his chin. "I was remembering . . . something." Should he tell her?

"What were you remembering?"

He stared down at the ground, not meeting her eye. "I was remembering when my sister and I were their age. I try not to think about those days anymore."

"Was it very painful?"

He bit the inside of his bottom lip. "After our mother and father died, we were alone. I tried to take care of her . . . of my little sister." He shook his head.

"What happened to your sister?" Her voice was warm and soft.

"A horse trampled her in the street. I ran out to get her, but I was too late. It was a long time ago."

"That must have been horrible." She placed a hand on his shoulder.

A heavy weight settled in his chest as the sights, the smells, the pain in his heart came back to him. "I was in the street, holding her in my arms." His forehead creased, his jaw flexing. "I can still see the people's faces as they stared at me. The women were looking at me with disgust, and the men were yelling at me to get out of the way."

"How old were you?"

Her voice cracked and he glanced up at her. Tears pooled in her eyes.

"I must have been eight or nine." He shook his head, trying to dispel the memory. "I have made you sad. I should not have told you."

"I can see you don't like to talk about it, but I am glad you trusted me enough to tell me." Her hand was warm on his shoulder, but she abruptly took it away.

"It was not long after that that the gamekeeper found me and adopted me. I have lived a good life. God has blessed me . . . more than some."

"I understand." She nodded.

"You have your own painful memories, no doubt."

"*Ja.*" She gave him a sad half smile. "But I was very blessed by my uncle coming and taking me to live with him. He has been better to me than most fathers would have been."

Was she thinking about the fact that Rutger had allowed her to remain unmarried?

"We are agreed, then," she said. "We have both been very blessed." Her happy smile returned. "Thank you again for the hares for the children. I will have the pleasure of knowing they are eating well tonight—thanks to you."

"And the margrave," he reminded her.

"And the margrave."

As Jorgen made his way up the hill to Thornbeck Castle, he thought about the second batch of hares he had brought the day before for the poor children. Odette had looked as beautiful as ever, but he should not have told her about how his little sister died. He did not wish her to pity him. He wanted her to see him as strong and competent.

He had known all along that she lived beyond his social status. Dreaming of her was like hoping to one day become the margrave's chancellor. He had always believed himself capable of the duties of the position. But Ulrich had always been destined for it, since his father was the chancellor for the previous margraves.

How would the margrave even know Jorgen was skilled at organization and diplomacy?

"You have to look for an opportunity to show him," his mother had said.

One way he could get the margrave's attention was by figuring out who was running the poaching ring and black market. There must be more than one person involved to produce as much meat as he had seen at The Red House. One person could perhaps shoot that many deer, but he would need others to dress it for the market and carry it out of the forest. And those selling it probably had no hand in shooting and preparing it, but they must have been employed by someone. So who was behind it all?

When Jorgen was shown into the library, the margrave and Ulrich were huddled over some papers on his desk.

Lord Thornbeck motioned for him to come forward, while the chancellor eyed him coldly.

"Lord Thornbeck, you wished to see me?"

He looked Jorgen in the eye. "The steward has been trying to find out who at The Red House is giving permission to these black-market dealers to sell their illegal goods to the people of

Thornbeck, and also who these black-market sellers are. We are having a more difficult time discovering this information than you might think. It seems my steward is known to be an officer of this castle, and therefore none of the women at The Red House trust him." The margrave frowned absently. "I need someone to go to this brothel and try to gain this information in a stealthy way. I was wondering if you might be willing to . . . make the sacrifice?"

Heat rose into Jorgen's cheeks. "My lord, it is not the sort of place I would ever go."

"I understand, Jorgen. You do not have to do this, but—"

"I will do it, my lord," Jorgen said quickly. "The people there will be unlikely to know me or that I work for you. I can bribe one of the brothel . . . inhabitants to give me the information we need."

"I appreciate that, Jorgen. If you can help me capture whoever is responsible for this poaching ring, I will reward you well, I assure you." The margrave held out a small drawstring purse of plain brown leather. "This should be enough for the bribes."

"Knowing that the poachers have been caught will be a great reward, my lord. I have reason enough to want to capture them."

"I believe your father, the gamekeeper, was killed by a poacher when my brother was margrave. Is that true?"

"Yes, my lord. His killer was never caught, and I believe this new poacher could be the same person who murdered my father."

The margrave gave him a direct look. "I want this poacher caught, whether dead or alive. If you encounter a poacher, you have my permission to shoot him in order to capture him, and if you kill him accidentally, you will not be held at fault. You do carry a bow and arrows when you are in the forest, do you not?"

"Yes, my lord."

"Good. Poaching is a serious offense against the king's property, and I am the king's steward. It must not be tolerated."

"I shall do all in my power to stop them." He would have few qualms about shooting any poacher, especially the one who had killed his father.

"Thank you, Jorgen. And remember." He paused, staring intently into his eyes. "I am not asking you to violate your conscience. Just see if you can find out something."

"I understand, my lord."

⌒

Jorgen made his way to the street behind the marketplace. The Red House was just ahead. Even though the evening was rather warm, he wore the same cloak and hood he had worn when he found the illegal meat market.

The wooden beams that striped the front of The Red House were carved with the faces and names of the former owner and builders of the house, as it had begun as a wealthy merchant's home. The beams were also carved with flowers and birds and animals and painted red, an unusual color for house timbers.

The front door, also red, was open, but a large man stood, his feet planted between the planks framing the door, guarding the entrance. Jorgen whispered a plea to God for help as he strode forward.

The doorkeeper crossed his massive arms and fixed Jorgen with a blank stare. "What do you want?"

"What does anyone want when he comes to The Red House?"

He gave a low grunt, then stepped to one side, allowing Jorgen to cross the threshold.

Heat rose from Jorgen's neck into his face. A few women stood around a counter. A man sat at a table holding a young woman on his lap. She laughed.

One of the women at the counter looked nearly old enough to be his mother, but she also looked like she might be the person in charge. Jorgen flipped his hood down off his head and stepped toward her. She stared at him from beneath lowered eyelids.

Jorgen put down some money. "Two goblets of wine."

The woman never took her eyes off him as she lifted her wine to her lips. He did the same, taking a sip as he continued to take in his surroundings. The walls were covered in hangings that were the same color as the red wine in his goblet. The windows were shuttered, and candles glowed from sconces on the walls and on each table.

"A man who is accustomed to getting what he wants." She squeezed his arm. "You are too young for me, but I have just the one for you." She turned and snapped her fingers at one of the girls.

The girl lurched forward, then walked toward them. She was so very young, and she wobbled as if her legs could hardly hold her up.

"This is Kathryn. She will keep you company. Two marks for me, and five marks for Kathryn, unless you stay longer than an hour." She held out her hand.

Outrage turned to heat, which rose to the top of his head. He ignored it and pulled out the coins, then placed them on her open palm. She grabbed his hand and one of Kathryn's hands and put them together. Without looking at him, Kathryn led him toward the stairs at the back of the room.

Sweat trickled down Jorgen's hairline and between his shoulder blades as he followed her up. She walked slowly, her shoulders hunched forward. She came to a door and reached out to open it. Her hand was trembling, and the one he was holding was cold and clammy. She entered the room and he followed, then shut the door behind him.

She let go of his hand and backed away from him.

Jorgen held up his hands. "I will not touch you. Do not be afraid."

She backed farther away, toward a bed that was almost the only thing in the room. Her face was pale.

"I only want to talk. I will not hurt you." He stared at her face. "You couldn't be more than fifteen. How old are you?"

She sat on the bed, hugging herself. "I am fourteen."

"How? How did you end up here? Who is forcing you to do this?" He wanted to personally, physically throw them in the margrave's dungeon.

A look of confusion creased her face. A tear slid down her cheek. "I had nowhere else to go. The woman you saw . . . Agnes . . . She helped me. She took care of my two little brothers and found them a home after my mother died. She said I could pay her back by coming here and working for her." Two more tears fell, but she made no move to wipe them away.

Who could do such a thing to a maiden so young? And how could he leave her to her fate?

"I don't care what Agnes said. You do not have to stay here. You do not owe her *that.*" How many men would mistreat her if he did not do something? "I will get you out of here. Will you leave here with me?"

She stared at him. "What?"

"If you come with me, I will take you somewhere safe." His mother would take care of her. "A place where you will be fed and no one will bother you."

She frowned. "What place is that? Why would you do this?"

"I want to help you. Is that so difficult to believe?" But of course it was. He suddenly wanted to punish every man who had ever come to this place.

She continued to stare at him as though she was afraid he

would attack her if she looked away. "I cannot leave without someone seeing me. The door is guarded."

"There must be a way." He walked to the one window that overlooked a dirty alleyway. The light outside was fading, and there was only one candle in the room. "I have less than an hour to think of something," he mumbled to himself.

"Why would you want to help me? What do you want?"

"I am a God-fearing man, and any God-fearing man would want to help a young maiden get out of a place like this. Besides that, I work for the margrave." He studied the window, then tried to open it. It swung open, but it was a long way down. He closed it again. "Do you know who owns this house?"

"Agnes . . . I suppose."

"Do you know anything about her selling meat at the back of the house?"

Kathryn shook her head.

"Have you seen anyone coming in who didn't belong? Someone talking with Agnes who seemed out of place here?" He kept his voice as quiet as possible.

She shook her head again. "I've only been here for"—her chin trembled—"two days."

"I am going to get you out of here."

"What will you do with me?"

He detected a tiny note of hope in her voice. And she was no longer crying.

"I will take you to my mother. She lives in the old gamekeeper's cottage in Thornbeck Forest, and she will take care of you. You do not have to stay in a place like this."

"But Agnes . . . She will beat me when she finds me."

"She won't find you. I will not let her. Do you need to take anything with you, Kathryn?"

She stood and reached under the bed, then clutched a cloth bundle to her chest.

Jorgen took off his cloak. He could put it around her. But how would he get her past the guard? "Is there a back staircase?"

"*Ja*, the one that leads to the kitchen."

"Perfect. We can escape out the back."

"There are always people in the kitchen. They will see me." Her lip started to tremble again.

"Put this on." He handed her the cloak. "Pull the hood over your head. I will create a distraction downstairs, and you can rush out in the chaos."

She did as he instructed.

*I am* not *leaving this girl in this place. But I need a miracle.* He tried to think of the saint who was in charge of helping people escape from buildings. He couldn't think of one. *Jesus, help me get her out.*

He went to the door and opened it a crack. No one was there, so he opened it wide enough to stick out his head. No one in the corridor. He motioned with his hand and she came toward him.

"When you get out the back door, run through the alley to the *Rathous*—do you know where it is?"

She nodded.

"Wait just inside the door of the town hall and I will come for you."

They slipped into the corridor, and he closed the door silently behind them.

# 13

JORGEN HASTENED TO the other end of the corridor and found the servants' stairs, which were wooden spiral steps leading down into darkness with no windows to provide any light.

He started down first. "Hold on to me," he whispered, and Kathryn's small hand clutched his right shoulder.

Voices drifted up from below. He crept down the stairs as quietly as possible, but the wooden boards were creaky. When he could see the light on the steps below him, he stopped to listen.

A man was arguing with two women about the best way to roast a pig. "Roasted on a spit makes it crispy on the outside."

"But if you cook it in the pot, it does not dry out."

"I like it boiled in pork fat."

A girl's life was dependent on what happened in the next few seconds. *God, give us favor.* With that quick prayer, Jorgen stumbled down the stairs and into the light of the cooking fire.

"What is that wonderful smell?" Jorgen yelled the words. He stumbled and kicked a copper pot that sat on the floor. The sound reverberated off the stone walls of the kitchen.

"Who are you? What are you doing here?" one of the women asked, her features scrunching.

"What do you want, fellow?" The man was even larger than the guard at the front door. He stepped toward Jorgen.

"I was looking for the privy." He slurred his words and wobbled when he walked.

"There's no privy here. Go in the alley." The man jerked his meaty hand in the direction of the back door.

He had hoped to avoid fighting this man who was as big as a bear, but he had to do something distracting so Kathryn could get away.

Jorgen fell forward into a table. He knocked several copper pots and pans and utensils off the table, and they fell onto the floor with a deafening crash.

Screaming and yelling ensued, and the bear of a man grabbed Jorgen by the shoulder and pushed him up, then drew back his fist and aimed it at his nose.

Instinctively, Jorgen ducked and partially blocked the blow with his arm, and the bear's fist landed a glancing blow to Jorgen's forehead.

Over the man's shoulder, Jorgen saw a dark form race toward the back of the kitchen and out the back door.

Jorgen ducked again as the burly guard threw another punch toward his face. Jorgen was not as quick this time, and the blow hit him below his left eye, knocking him back a step. Before the man could hit him again, Jorgen landed a blow to the man's gut. He bent forward, then brought his fist up to slam into Jorgen's chin.

Jorgen's teeth rattled, but he ignored the pain and slammed his own fist into the burly man's nose.

The man grabbed Jorgen's tunic at his neck, cutting off his air, and pulled him up onto his toes. Blood poured out of the man's nose. "I'm going to kill you!"

Jorgen clawed at his hand, trying to get loose.

When the man took one hand away to wipe at his nose, Jorgen held on to the table beside him, raised his feet, and kicked as hard as he could. The man let go and fell backward into a counter filled with more pots and pans, sending them crashing to the floor. The women in the room screamed.

Jorgen fled, jumping over the scattered pots and pans. He leapt out the door and into the alley, running toward the open market square. His whole head throbbed, especially his cheekbone, but he kept going. He ran to the gray stone town hall, jerked the door open, and stepped inside.

Several people were milling around, talking to each other in the large open room. But he did not see Kathryn. Then something dark caught his eye. He went toward the corner of the room and reached down to pick up his cloak, which lay crumpled on the floor.

His heart sank. Where was she? Did she have somewhere safe to go? Why had she not waited for him?

She had not trusted him. No doubt she felt little inclination to trust anyone after what she had been through. He sighed and tucked the cloak under his arm.

He looked around one more time and a man approached him. "If you're looking for the girl who dropped that cloak, I saw her go inside the shop across the street." He pointed to the candle shop.

"I thank you." Jorgen hurried out and across the street. As he reached toward the handle of the chandler's shop door, it opened and Kathryn stepped out.

"Listen. I know you have no reason to trust me, but I assure you, I only want you to be safe."

She was staring at him with teary eyes. "I am bad. You should not try to help me. Agnes will hate me." She burst into soft sobs, covering her face with her hands.

He started to put an arm around her but stopped himself. He let out a pent-up breath, then bent down and spoke softly. "Agnes is not a good person. You must get away from her. If she sends her guards after us, I am not sure I can fight them off." It was a miracle he had not been beaten into the ground by the one guard. "We must go now." He hoped she could hear the urgency in his voice.

She wiped her face with her hands and nodded.

He held out his arm to her, and she clasped it with both hands. She kept her head down as they walked. Neither of them spoke until they were outside the town gate.

*We did it.* It must have been a miracle.

It wasn't until later that he realized he had not found out anything about the band of poachers or their black-market activities.

"The forester is here to see you." Heinke stood beside Odette's bed looking down at her.

Her brain was so hazy. Hadn't she only just gone to sleep? The hunt had been long and difficult last night. She had not been able to shoot anything and had gotten home just as dawn was lightening the sky.

"Odette! Please wake up. What shall I tell the forester?"

"The forester?" She sat up. "Jorgen?" Her eyes flitted to the trunk against the wall. Had she remembered to put away her bow and arrows? She did not see them anywhere. Had Jorgen seen her walking home with them, wearing her hunting clothes and looking like a boy?

"What does he want?" She threw off the linen bedclothes.

"He said he wanted to talk with you. Shall I tell him you are sick?"

"No. Tell him I will be there in a moment." She jumped out of bed and glanced out the window. It must be midmorning. She'd probably slept about four hours. She rinsed her mouth out with water, then drank a gulp. She popped a mint leaf in her mouth and chewed it.

Heinke came back and helped her on with a pale-green gown. A contrasting emerald-green band with gold stitching decorated the neckline and hemline. The belt was also made of the same emerald-green material and gold stitching as the band. Heinke covered her single blond braid with a silk wimple, secured with a circlet.

Her heart fluttered as she went down the stairs to meet Jorgen.

He stood waiting for her in the large room that served as a sitting room as well as a dining room. As he turned to face her, she couldn't help thinking how good he looked with his hair brushed to one side and wearing his work clothes—a soft leather cotehardie in a shade of green that matched his eyes and a white shirt that peeked from underneath it, encircling the base of his neck. He was hoodless, since it was such a warm day already. Something about the way his dark-blond hair curled around his ears made her want to touch it.

Foolish thought. She should remember that the reason he was here might be because he suspected she was the poacher.

One side of his face was in shadow, and he did not step out into the light coming through the window, even when she approached.

"Odette." The way he smiled—sort of sheepishly—put her at ease. "I hope you do not mind that I came to your home to speak to you."

"I don't mind at all, if you do not mind if I break my fast while you talk." She led him into the kitchen and motioned for him to sit with her at the rough wooden table near where Cook was working.

Cook set bread and sweet cream and pasties filled with stewed fruit in front of them.

Odette bit into an apricot pasty. She had not eaten anything before going to sleep after her long hunt the night before, and it tasted wonderful.

When she looked across the table at him, she quickly swallowed her bite of food, nearly choking. "What happened to your face?"

His left cheekbone was bruised dark purple, and the left side of his lip was puffy with a dark line, like a cut.

"Does it look that bad?" He grimaced and rubbed his jaw.

"Did you get in a fight?"

"It will take me a little while to tell you all of it, and I was hoping . . ."

Odette gestured at the food in front of him, but Jorgen shook his head.

"I was wondering if you would come with me. I need you to speak to a young maiden."

"A young maiden?" She took another bite of food.

"I rescued her from The Red House."

The bite of apricot pasty got sucked down Odette's throat, and she coughed violently. Jorgen stood and pounded her on the back.

Finally Odette ceased coughing. "Did you say you rescued her from The Red House?"

"She has been crying and my mother thinks she will leave, but she is an orphan and has nowhere else to go." He spoke quickly, as though afraid she would stop him. "I thought perhaps you could convince her to stay, or if she refuses to stay, you could find her somewhere else to go."

Odette tried to hide her shock. What was Jorgen doing at The Red House? And what did he mean, he rescued a maiden from there? "Who is crying? Can you begin again? Maybe I am still half asleep, because I thought you said you rescued a maiden from The Red House."

Jorgen sighed. "Forgive me. I know it sounds strange. I was actually . . ." His face turned a little red. He cleared his throat. "I do not normally go to The Red House. It isn't somewhere I would *ever*"—he made a horizontal slicing motion with his hand—"ever go. I only went there to investigate something for the margrave."

Odette raised her brows. What could the margrave want him to investigate at The Red House? "I thought your job was to take care of Thornbeck Forest and catch poachers. The margrave does know what The Red House is, does he not?"

"Of course." Jorgen took a deep breath and let it out. "You see, as strange as it sounds, I *was* investigating the poachers."

Should she believe him? After all, *she* had never been to The Red House, and *she* was the poacher he was looking for. Wasn't she?

He cleared his throat again and spoke quietly. "There is a black market of poached deer meat being sold at the back of The Red House. I am trying to discover who is involved."

But that could not be. Odette forced herself not to speak as she thought this through. Was someone else poaching the margrave's deer? She had never encountered anyone else while she was hunting in the forest. How could someone be selling the poacher's meat? It was impossible since she was the poacher.

She must concentrate on what Jorgen was saying. "Go on. So you went to The Red House to find out about the black market. What happened then?"

He looked down at his hands clasped in front of him on the table. "While I was there, I encountered a young maiden." He held up one hand, still not looking Odette in the eye. "I did nothing to her, I vow to you. I was only there to get information."

"I believe you." He had such a look of embarrassment, she could not help but believe him.

"Thank you. So, this girl was much too young to be in a place like that, doing what . . . what she was supposed to be doing there. I told her I would take her to a safe place, that she did not have to stay there, and she came with me."

"They just let you leave with her?"

"No." He ran his hand through his hair, ruffling the curls at his temple. "I helped her sneak out."

"Is that how you got that bruise on your cheek?"

He nodded.

"And that cut on your lip?"

"But you should have seen what I did to him." The look on his face was something between pride and humor.

"He looked worse than you?"

He shrugged. "You could say that."

She laughed, but her heart tripped over itself at the thought of Jorgen rescuing this girl. "How old is she?"

"Fourteen."

"Dear heavenly saints!" Odette pressed a hand to her stomach. She had forgotten to eat while he was talking, and now the two bites of pasty in her stomach roiled as if they might come back up.

"I took her home. She spent the night there last night, but now she is crying and says she should leave. She says she will taint our house, and she is afraid that now that she has not paid her debt to Agnes, she will do something bad to her little brothers."

"Agnes? Her little brothers?"

"Agnes is the woman at The Red House who helped find her little brothers a home when their mother died. She said if Kathryn—that's the fourteen-year-old maiden—would work for her, she would find them a home."

"No." Odette pounded her fist on the table. "We must not let her think she has to give in to this terrible woman."

"I will have to find her brothers, or she will go look for them herself."

"Do you know where they are? I will go get them!" Odette rose from her seat. "How dare that woman do such a thing to helpless children? We should have her thrown in the pillory or locked in the dungeon."

"We must have evidence first, Odette. If we want her to be stopped, we must keep our heads and find evidence that she has broken the law. I am not sure that we have proof she has violated any laws yet, and we do not know where Kathryn's little brothers are."

"Of course. Still, how could anyone do such a thing to a fourteen-year-old?"

"Why don't you sit down and eat your breakfast. Then you can come with me to talk to her." The half grin on his face made her wish he was as rich as Mathis Papendorp.

Three young orphans were in need, and Jorgen wanted her assistance in helping them. She didn't want to think about the mayor's son.

# 14

ODETTE DID AS Jorgen suggested and ate her food. Soon after, they were walking toward the gate closest to Thornbeck Forest and to the gamekeeper's cottage. Jorgen led her through a well-worn path—a path she avoided at night so as not to leave footprints.

"I am sorry for intruding on your day." Jorgen held a tree limb out of the way so she could pass. "I did not know who else to ask, and I know you care about people, especially orphans."

"I had nothing to do today anyway." *Except sleep.*

"I do thank you. I hope she didn't leave while I was gone."

She wasn't the only one who cared. Jorgen obviously cared, too, so much that his forehead was creased just thinking about her leaving.

A sudden thought sent a strange pain through her. Did Jorgen feel something for this girl, some attachment or attraction?

She should not even have such a thought. The girl was only four-teen. Of course, fourteen-year-olds often married, and they married much older men. Usually it was for the gain of their fathers, but it was not unheard of for a man of Jorgen's age to marry a four-teen-year-old girl. But this girl was in a bad predicament and her situation was pitiable indeed. Odette should be thinking only of helping her.

They reached the old gamekeeper's cottage, and she thought it looked pleasant, with flowers growing all around it and a roof so neatly thatched it was like a hat made of one piece of cloth.

Jorgen opened the front door, calling, "Mother? Kathryn? I have brought my friend Odette to see you."

Odette followed him inside. The front part of the house was one long room, complete with a hearth and a table and stools. A few comfortable-looking chairs stood at the other end of the room. Some colorful tapestries decorated the walls, and the windows were thrown open to let in the light. It was a homey kind of place that smelled of freshly baked bread.

"Mother?"

"Coming!" a voice called from down the open corridor at the back of the room. A moment later, an older woman with sagging cheeks and a pleasant smile appeared in the corridor connecting the front room to the rest of the house. She turned and motioned to someone behind her. "Come, come."

A young maiden stepped forward to stand beside the elderly woman. She met Odette's eye for a moment, then looked down.

"Odette, this is my mother and Kathryn. And this is Odette."

Kathryn did not look up at her, but Odette could see enough of her face to know that she had been crying.

Jorgen's mother grasped Odette's hand in both of hers and squeezed it. She was only as tall as Odette's shoulder and rather plump. "I thank you for coming, my dear. Was it a very long walk?"

"Not so long."

"Shall I fetch you some milk? We have our own cow, so it is fresh, and we have a little underground storage house by the stream that keeps it cool."

"That sounds good. Perhaps Jorgen and Kathryn would like some too?"

"I will help you, Mother." Jorgen gave Odette a look, then went with his mother.

Kathryn stood unmoving, her head still bowed.

"Will you come and sit with me over here?"

Kathryn gave an almost imperceptible nod and followed Odette to the other end of the room. They sat, each sinking into the feather cushions of the wooden chairs, decoratively built from crooked tree branches. It may have looked rustic, but it was the most comfortable chair she had ever sat in. Kathryn sat with her legs folded underneath her.

"Jorgen tells me his mother is pleased to have you staying here with her. I am sure she gets lonesome, with Jorgen gone most of the time and no other family."

Kathryn seemed to consider Odette's words. Perhaps the girl had not thought that she might be serving a purpose by being with Jorgen's aging mother.

When Kathryn said nothing, Odette went on. "I hope you will stay with her. I have never met her before, but she seems like a kind person."

After a moment of silence, Kathryn said softly, "She is a kind person. But I do not think I should stay. Jorgen had to give up his bed for me. Besides, I have a debt I need to pay."

"What sort of debt?"

Kathryn finally looked at her. If she wasn't mistaken, Odette read resentment in their deep-blue depths. "You would not understand. Sometimes orphans must do . . . bad things to stay alive and get food for their younger siblings."

"How surprised you would be to know that I do understand. I foraged through other people's garbage to get food for myself. I had no siblings, but when my mother and father died, I went to live with a neighbor's family. They did not want me and treated me like a servant. I was five years old. It was not until years later that my uncle came and took me to live with him. I do understand, and you do not owe anyone anything, especially if they want you to do something that makes you feel bad."

"Jorgen told you, didn't he? Do you know what will happen to my little brothers?"

"No."

"I cannot let them be mistreated or turned into the streets to starve. Besides, Agnes was kind to us. She fed us and gave us clothes. I have to do what she says, for my brothers' sakes." She was near tears again.

"What if Jorgen and I can help your brothers? Perhaps we can find another place for them to stay."

"Do you think so?"

"I do. But, Kathryn, no matter what happens, you should not ever go back to The Red House or to that woman, Agnes. Anyone who asks you to do what she did is not a good person. Please. You must stay away from her and not feel any loyalty to her."

"But . . . I do feel loyalty to her." Kathryn's chin quivered and tears flooded her eyes again. "Maybe I should not, but I do. She took us in off the street and even took care of my littlest brother when he was sick, when no one else offered to help us."

"Those were all good things, but if she did them only to trap you into working for her, then she does not deserve your loyalty, Kathryn. Truly, you should believe me."

Two tears tracked down the girl's pale cheeks. "It does not matter about me. My brothers are the ones who matter. They are innocent, but I have done bad things, things you cannot imagine. What if I am not worth all this trouble? What if I was born bad and will always be bad? I should just do what Agnes wants me to."

"You must know that is not true." How could anyone think

that way? "You are still practically a child. You should not be made to work—"

"I am not a child." Kathryn turned blazing eyes on Odette.

"No, no, you are very mature. But what I am trying to tell you is that you could have a good life. You do not have to throw yourself away at The Red House. Your life could be better than that. Don't you feel a hope inside you for something better?"

It had been that hope for something better that had kept Odette from sinking into the same despair Kathryn obviously was feeling. Odette had believed that someday she would feel power over her circumstances. She would be able to get away from the people who had taken her in but did not care about her. There would come a time when she could take care of herself and would no longer have to forage for food in people's trash heaps—or depend on people who mistreated her—to survive.

If Odette had felt more grateful to the people who had taken her in, perhaps she would understand how Kathryn was feeling about Agnes. But she had only wanted to get away from them and their mistreatment.

"You want to show your gratitude for what Agnes did for your brothers, but this is not the way to do that. Someday, when you are able to, you can give Agnes money, if you feel you need to repay her."

Kathryn was not looking at her. She was fidgeting with the edge of her sleeve. "Why did Jorgen ask you to come and talk to me?"

"He was afraid you would leave, and . . . I suppose because I know a lot of orphans. I teach lessons two days every week outside the city gate to any child who wants to come."

She glanced up at Odette. "Do you teach them to read?"

"I do."

"I have always wanted to learn to read."

"If you stay here with Jorgen's mother, you can learn. It would be my pleasure to teach you."

"I will still need to make sure my brothers are well." She sank back into the chair and sighed. "But I think I might stay."

Jorgen and his mother came in carrying a pitcher and some pottery cups. The way Kathryn looked at him, with adoration and attentiveness, made Odette feel uneasy again. Was she afraid Jorgen might take advantage of the girl? No, that wasn't it. Was she afraid he might fall in love with her and marry her? Perhaps, a little. Or did she suspect the girl would try to put to use what she had learned in her two days at The Red House in order to seduce Jorgen?

The heat in her cheeks and the roiling of her stomach told her—that was it.

⁓

Jorgen glanced at Odette, at the expression on her face as she sat with Kathryn, and he knew what he had to do.

As his mother poured the milk for them, Jorgen motioned to Odette. "Can I speak with you?"

Odette stood and allowed him to open the door for her as they walked outside.

Jorgen rubbed the back of his neck before facing Odette. "Do you know somewhere Kathryn could stay?" How could he explain his reasoning? "I could not allow her to stay in that terrible place, but our house is small, and I think it is uncomfortable for her . . . and for me."

"Uncomfortable?"

Jorgen looked her in the eye. "I have no wish to be betrothed to a fourteen-year-old girl, and therefore I do not think it's a good idea to have her in my house. One of us needs to go." Desperation resonated in his voice. "It is not that I am afraid of what might happen. It's more that I am afraid of what people will think, and what Kathryn might begin to think."

Odette smiled slowly. "Jorgen, you are almost too good to be true." She covered her mouth, as if stifling a laugh.

"I do not know what you mean. This is not a humorous situation."

She shook her head. "I mean that you are very sweet." She cocked her head to the side in a most fetching way. "I think."

"Now what does that mean?"

"I wonder whose reputation you are trying to protect." Now there was a shrewd glint in her eye.

"Hers and mine!" He lowered his voice. "Both."

She stared into his eyes, shaking her head. He wanted to ask her what she was thinking, but he decided to just enjoy the soft, sweet look on her face. She probably wouldn't tell him anyway—or if she did tell him, he would not understand.

"So," he prompted, "do you know of somewhere? Perhaps she could stay with you."

Her brows went up, but they came back down and she bit her lip. "No, I do not think that would work."

He didn't see why not. Rutger's house was three times bigger than the cottage he shared with his mother.

"I don't think Rutger . . . That is, I would have to ask him first. He is unmarried, too, you know."

He sighed. "I had not thought of that."

"But he might know of some place. He knows nearly everyone in Thornbeck."

"Could you ask him today?"

"Yes, and she can come home with me now. I can take her to meet Anna—perhaps she could stay with Anna and help with the children! I will ask her, and we can talk until it is time for me to teach my lesson to the children this afternoon."

"Thank you, Odette." He clasped her hand in his but then realized he probably shouldn't have, as his heart did the strange stuttering it did every time he touched her or got too close.

She squeezed back. "Thank you for saving her. I hate to think what would have happened to her if you had not."

Yes, and he hated to think what would happen if he ever asked to marry Odette. He was growing fonder of her by the day.

Later that day, Odette left Kathryn at Anna's house, where she was playing with Anna's two-year-old, Cristen. It was around the time Rutger usually came home, and Odette caught up with him on the steps between the first and second floor.

"May I ask you something?"

"Of course, my dear." Rutger stood halfway up, looking down at her.

"It is a bit of a long tale." She laughed nervously. "Jorgen rescued a girl from The Red House and took her to his home where she would be safe."

Rutger's mouth went slack and his eyes opened wider. "What do you mean he rescued a girl from The Red House?"

She nearly laughed at his reaction, as it was so similar to her own. "She was working there—a fourteen-year-old orphan girl. But Jorgen asked her if she wanted to leave. He helped her escape."

Rutger's face tensed. "What was Jorgen doing at The Red House?" His voice was raspy.

"It is not what you would think. He was trying to find out about a black market of poached meat."

Rutger rubbed his chin with his hand.

"But that is not what I wanted to tell you. Do you know of any place where this girl—her name is Kathryn—might be able to stay? It is rather uncomfortable for Jorgen to have her staying at his home, and I thought perhaps she might stay with us."

Again Rutger's mouth went slack. "You know why she cannot. Surely you do not want her finding out your secret. She could turn you in to that forester, who would give you over to the margrave. They would think *you* were supplying meat to this black market."

Odette wondered again who, besides her, could be poaching the deer in Thornbeck Forest. And Rutger was right. If Jorgen ever caught her poaching, he would think she was the one supplying the black market. "You have a lot of influence. Perhaps you could find out who is behind this black market."

He didn't look at her. "Perhaps I could. Perhaps I could."

"As for Kathryn, I will ask Anna if she could stay with her. Of course, she will have to ask Peter, but Kathryn could help them with the children in exchange for food and a place to sleep."

"If that doesn't work out, I shall help you find a place for this girl."

"She is also worried about her two little brothers. Agnes, the woman at The Red House, knows where they are."

Rutger brushed past her on the narrow steps. "You may leave it to me, Odette. I shall find them and make sure they are being cared for."

"You will? Oh, thank you! You are the best uncle in all the world."

Just before she threw her arms around him, she thought she saw him cringe, a tiny flash of pain crossing his face.

When she stepped back, she studied him. "Is something wrong, Uncle Rutger? Are you getting sick?"

"Of course not. I am very well. And I shall find Kathryn's little brothers. Do not worry."

Rutger would take care of it. He always took care of everything. He was such a good man.

# 15

JORGEN BOWED TO the margrave. "Lord Thornbeck."

"What have you discovered about our poachers and black-market brigands?" The margrave limped his way to his desk as he leaned on his cane. He was a large man, and limping and being forced to use a cane did not rest on him lightly, even after a year. He scowled most of the time, his forehead creased in a way that had made Jorgen sense the margrave was either in constant pain or thinking unpleasant thoughts.

"My lord, I did go to The Red House yesterday to try to find out what I could about the black market, but I am afraid I discovered very little."

"Do you know who owns it?"

"Possibly a woman named Agnes. She had put a girl to work there, an orphan girl who was only fourteen, and I . . . I helped her escape."

The margrave stared at him. "Was she able to tell you anything about the black market?"

"No, my lord."

"And the poacher has not been captured either?"

"I plan to start watching the forest at night."

"That could be dangerous."

"Nevertheless, I am determined to capture him. And the black-market sellers as well."

"I will have my steward look further into The Red House and its owner. He has also been unable to find out much about it. I will have him inquire more about Agnes." He frowned. "My problem there is that I think my steward is a bit too fond of The Red House. He is well known there and perhaps is not the best person to send. But that is not your worry." The margrave grimaced and rubbed the back of his neck. "There is one more thing I wanted to ask. You will come to the big masquerade ball we are having here at the castle?"

"Yes, my lord."

"You must dress elaborately or wear a costume. It is the new fashion, I am told." His scowl deepened. "I doubt you are any more excited about it than I am. But perhaps you have a girl you wish to come. Tell me her name and I shall be sure she is invited."

"I think she is already on the invitation list." As soon as the words were out of his mouth, he wished he could take them back in. "That is . . ." His face burned.

"Very well." The margrave nodded, almost smiling. "Thank you for this report, Jorgen. I hope you will catch that poacher soon. If the king comes and finds all his deer gone from Thornbeck Forest and he cannot hunt them on his visit, he will be sorely displeased. I cannot allow that."

"I understand, my lord. I will not fail you."

Jorgen made his way toward the clearing where Odette gave lessons to the children. As he walked, he planned how he would capture the poacher. He would scour the forest every night, searching the clearings where a deer would most easily be seen. He had let the poaching go on too long. He wouldn't be surprised if the margrave grew tired of his incompetence and replaced him.

And even though a lot of deer were missing, he still believed it was possibly only one poacher, although with helpers. One person shooting one or two deer every night could produce a lot of meat, enough for a small black-market business.

He emerged into the clearing where the children were already gathered. Odette was walking toward them on the path from the town gate, along with her friend Anna, with Kathryn trailing just behind them.

Jorgen was pleased to see Kathryn with Anna and Odette.

Odette gave her attention to the children, as she always did, and Anna and Kathryn came and sat with him. Anna chatted about many things, but Kathryn hardly said a word. However, she seemed to stare at him nearly every moment.

Someone was riding toward them. A man appeared on a white mule, coming not from town but from the other direction.

As he drew nearer, Jorgen recognized Rutger. Odette waved at him but continued her lesson. Rutger steered his mule toward them and dismounted.

"You must be Kathryn." He fixed his gaze on the girl, who kept her head down and looked up at him through the hair hanging over her face. "I wanted to tell you that I have found your two brothers and you will be going to live on the farm where they are living."

Kathryn lifted her face and stared at him.

"I have arranged everything. You will live in the house with the Schindler family and will do some light work for them in exchange for your food and other provisions."

"My brothers? You found my brothers there?"

"Yes, and you will join them."

"Thank you." Her voice was hoarse.

"I can take you there now, if you wish. Then I will send one of my servants to bring your belongings to you."

She nodded eagerly. Rutger helped her mount his mule, and he took the reins, walking beside her.

As they started off, Odette clasped her hands, smiling. "This is so wonderful. I could not have planned anything more perfect."

Jorgen watched them ride away, and he sighed in relief. As Odette said, it had worked out perfectly. Kathryn would be able to stay with her brothers.

But he didn't like how tired Odette seemed. She looked beautiful, as always, but her shoulders and eyelids drooped, and she didn't speak as energetically with the children as she normally did.

When the children began to leave, Odette was smiling, but the dark smudges under her eyes made him wonder if she was sick.

"Odette, you seem tired. Are you well?"

She opened her mouth as if to speak, then closed it.

"You do look tired, Odette," Anna said. "Have you not been sleeping?"

"Oh, I am not very tired. I am well. I . . ." Odette seemed to be considering what to say. "I have not been getting enough sleep. But I will try to sleep more tonight."

Anna looked at her curiously. "Why are you not sleeping?"

Odette gazed beyond her friend and shrugged. "Sometimes I do not sleep well. It is naught to worry about. All is well. Shall we go?"

Jorgen could not push away the feeling that all was not well.

"Odette, I want you to sleep here tonight. You apparently aren't sleeping well at home."

They had gone back to Anna's house to talk, and now they had just eaten supper and it was getting dark. Odette wanted to stay, but how could she?

"Jorgen was right. You look exhausted."

Odette couldn't stifle a yawn. She had to go out hunting tonight. Perhaps she could stay until the household fell asleep and then slip out. She could say she went home early because she couldn't sleep when she wasn't in her own bed.

"Of course I can stay the night." Odette plastered on a smile.

Anna sent a servant girl to tell Rutger that she would be staying there for the night. "I just do not want you to go home when you seem so tired. I will give you something the nurse gives the children to help them sleep when they are sick. That will be just what you need."

With Peter playing with Gunther before his bedtime and the nurse having just put baby Cristen to bed, Odette and Anna sat in the first-floor room talking.

"And you seem a little nervous too. Are you sad that Rutger doesn't want you to marry Jorgen?"

Odette did not answer right away. Perhaps it would not hurt to admit the truth to Anna. "You must not tell anyone what I say."

"I will not, of course. We always keep each other's secrets."

"I do like Jorgen." She sighed. A tingle went down her arms as she imagined his face, his smile, his eyes, the way he looked when he spoke, how kind he was with the children and with her. She especially admired the way he had saved Kathryn. It was sweet and heroic. It reminded her a little bit of how Rutger had come and saved her from those people she was living with and toiling for.

Wasn't she even more exhausted now that she was not slaving

away or scrounging, but poaching deer to feed the poor? But that was different. She did that because she wanted to.

"You like Jorgen. *Ja*, go on," Anna prompted her.

"Jorgen is . . ."

"Kind? Handsome? In love with you?"

"In love with me? I would not say that."

"I have seen the way he looks at you sometimes. I believe I am justified in saying he loves you."

"I think Kathryn is in love with him."

"Of course she is. He saved her. She would hardly be human if she was not in love with him."

"Perhaps he will marry her."

Anna wrinkled her forehead. "I don't think that is likely. She is a pretty girl, but Jorgen doesn't seem like the kind of man who would want someone so young and timid."

That was a good point.

"You still did not answer my question. Are you sad because Rutger doesn't want you to marry Jorgen?"

Again, Odette took her time answering. "I don't believe Rutger would stop me from marrying a poor man if I wanted to marry him, but perhaps it would be selfish of me." Jorgen couldn't help her feed the children like Mathis Papendorp could. Marrying Jorgen seemed selfish for many reasons.

"But Jorgen is not exactly poor. He is not the wealthy burgher you would be expected to marry as Rutger's niece, but he does have some status as the margrave's forester." After a moment of silence, Anna asked, "Would you marry him if he asked you?"

Would she marry the man who would hate her if he found out she was poaching? That seemed a bit self-destructive. And yet . . . "I like him very much."

"*Ja, ja.*" Anna's tone urged Odette to go on.

"I enjoy talking to him."

"*Ja, ja.*"

Sometimes she wondered what it would be like to kiss him or be embraced by him, but she wasn't ready to admit that to Anna. "I think he is handsome."

"You would be blind not to."

"But I cannot go around falling in love with and marrying every man I talk to. No, I would not."

"Oh, Odette. Why are you so guarded? What are you so afraid of?"

Was she guarded? Wasn't it wise to be guarded? "I don't want to get my heart broken. I only have one heart, you know." But it wasn't that. She was willing enough to risk her heart. But she wasn't yet willing to sacrifice the children who depended on her for food.

It was increasingly difficult not being able to tell Anna everything. But what choice did she have?

⁓

Odette awoke with a start. She had been dreaming about falling into a deep pit. Where was she? Was she too late to go hunting? Someone was breathing in the same room where she slept. Oh yes. That was Anna. She was sleeping at Anna and Peter's house.

Odette slid off the side of the bed. Quickly and as quietly as she could, she got dressed. It was not far to her own house, and she would change into her hunting clothes and retrieve her longbow and arrows.

Anna made a sound in her sleep. She turned over, her arm flopping down on Odette's pillow. Odette held her breath. Was Anna still asleep? Or was she opening her eyes and realizing that Odette was no longer in bed?

Anna's deep breaths started again, a little raspy and just loud enough and regular enough to assure Odette that she was asleep.

Holding her breath, Odette slipped out.

Once she had gone home and changed, she found the three boys who accompanied her. They were sitting in their usual rendezvous spot, but they were all asleep. One of them awoke as she approached and pushed the shoulders of the other two, waking them. Silently they all moved forward into the dark forest.

Hoping to have better fortune than she had had the night before, Odette moved to one of her favorite spots to watch and wait. She had not frequented this place in a few weeks. Perhaps this was where the deer were feeding now.

Odette squatted, an arrow nocked and ready. She kept her eyes trained on the tiny clearing several feet in front of her since the deer were typically so silent she would never hear them. So she waited, her eyes burning.

How lovely to be asleep in bed just now. No doubt Anna would awake in the morning and either come looking for her or send a servant. Odette would have to rise and assure her she was well, pretending she was not still exhausted from being out all night.

But she did not want anyone to go hungry simply because she would rather be in bed sleeping. She had not been able to kill anything the night before. She could not fail a second night.

She heard a slight rustling sound. A large stag appeared. Odette had anticipated him, so she was already aiming. As soon as he stilled, she let the arrow fly.

It found its mark. The deer took two steps, then fell to the ground.

The three boys leapt into action from behind her. They raced toward the hart and began the hard work of readying him for being transported out of the woods.

"Who is there?" a man's voice called.

The boys all stopped what they were doing and stood perfectly still—as still as Odette's heart. But then it began to beat again, so hard it hurt her chest.

A crack sounded not far away, then another, as someone was walking toward them.

The boys started running. Odette turned and ran as one of the boys flew by her.

"Halt!"

# 16

TREE LIMBS SLAPPED her in the face as she ran through them. She stumbled over roots and bushes, but she kept going. Her heart was slamming against her chest, and the smell of sweat and animal blood filled her nostrils, even though there couldn't have been any blood near her.

Odette was sure that the voice belonged to Jorgen.

A cry rang out above the crashing sounds she and the boys were making as they ran through the forest. Had one of the boys been caught? Would he tell Jorgen the truth about who was doing the poaching and why?

As she continued to run through the trees and undergrowth, her head throbbed with every footfall. She emerged from the trees at full speed. The boys were nowhere to be seen, but they had run in different directions. They would find hiding places somewhere.

Odette found the hole in the town wall, just big enough for her to squeeze through, where she always came and went after dark. She moved the loose stones and squirmed her way through, then put them back in place before hurrying through the back alleys of the town. She climbed over the garden fence and went in the back door.

She leaned against it, trying to calm her breathing. *O Father*

*God, please do not let Jorgen find out what I have been doing.*
Thinking of how her poaching would look through Jorgen's eyes,
a stab of pain went through her stomach. She was stealing. Those
deer belonged to the king and the margrave, not to her, even if she
was doing it for good reason.

But perhaps the boy would not tell Jorgen about her. Perhaps
he even got away, slipping out of the forester's grasp before he could
take him back to the margrave's dungeon.

Odette's skin felt cold and clammy around the collar of her
leather cotehardie. Her sweat had chilled as she ran, and her head
was as light as a cloud, as if it might float away. Her stomach roiled,
and she placed her hand on her midsection. "Do not get sick. Do
not get sick," she told her stomach.

She closed her eyes and tried not to think about Jorgen or the
poor boy he had caught. There was naught she could do about
it now. She would breathe evenly, in and out, and concentrate on
getting to bed without anyone hearing her.

She crept up the steps to her chamber door, which she had
left ajar. The door creaked when she pushed on it. Once inside,
she moved as quietly as she could to the other end of the room.
She opened the trunk and placed her bow and arrows inside, then
started to remove her hunting clothes.

"Where have you been?"

Odette spun around. "Anna." She clutched her hands over her
chest to keep her heart from leaping out. "You frightened the life
from me. What are you doing here?"

"I was worried about you when you left my house in the middle of the night. And what are you wearing? Odette, this is strange.
Where did you go? What did you do?"

"Anna, I . . ." How could she lie to Anna? At the thought of
telling her the truth, her heart started pounding again, thundering

in her head, so hard it made her feel weak. But was that fear making her sick? Or was it the exhaustion of keeping her secret? She had never told a soul, but it would feel good to be able to share it. She could trust Anna, couldn't she? "If I tell you, do you vow not to tell anyone?"

Anna, who was lying in Odette's bed, sat up and threw off the covers. "I won't tell a living soul." She scrambled out of the bed and went to help Odette undo the lacings on her leather stockings and her leather cotehardie, which protected her from thorns and tree limbs.

"I do not quite remember how it started," Odette said.

"How what started?" Anna worked at a knot in the lacings on her left stocking.

How should she word this? "I am . . . I have been poaching deer from Thornbeck Forest. At night. Every night for the past year." She felt weak, so weak her knees nearly buckled.

"Odette!" Anna gasped. "Poaching! This is unaccountably strange. But . . . But . . . Why? Why would you do such a thing?"

Her stomach twisted at Anna's tone. "I am feeding dozens of orphans and poor families." That justified her actions, did it not? "Why should the animals live and die in the forest and be no good to anyone?" But it sounded like a pitiful excuse, now that she was saying it out loud.

Anna covered her open mouth with her hand. The moonlight through the window showed how big her eyes were as she stared at Odette. "You . . . you are so . . . brave." She let out a strangled laugh. "You go out every night and kill deer in the margrave's forest? I have never heard of anything so exciting!" She laughed again.

"Shh. Someone will hear you." Odette allowed herself a tiny smile at Anna's enthusiastic reaction.

"I wish I could see you out there, stalking through the trees, hunting down your prey, and killing the margrave's deer to feed the poor. It is romantic."

Odette sank down on the bed. "It's hardly romantic, but I am relieved you aren't scolding me." She sighed as she lay back on her pillow. "It is exhausting."

"However *did* you begin doing this?" Anna leaned over her, her face obscured in the dark room.

Odette thought for a moment. "I wanted a way to help feed the poor, something I could do all on my own. I had done a little poaching of smaller animals when I was a child. I learned to use a bow and arrow, and I was good at it. There were so many deer in Thornbeck Forest. It seemed like it wouldn't hurt to shoot a few and give them to the hungry people. Rutger and I worked out a plan where he would have some of the young men who worked for him go with me and cut up and carry the meat after I killed it. And Rutger has some other people who distribute it to the poor."

"Oh." Anna sat facing the foot of the bed. "But . . ."

When she didn't continue, Odette asked, "But what?"

"Does it not seem strange to you that Rutger would allow you to take the risk? If you are caught, the margrave might cut off your hand. He will be furious and will throw you in the dungeon. And what about Jorgen? If he discovers that you're poaching . . ."

"I know, I know." Odette's heart twisted inside her. "I don't want to hurt Jorgen, but I also do not want to abandon the poor who are counting on me to feed them."

Anna nodded. "But, Odette, how long do you plan to do this? It must be exhausting, going hunting every night. When do you sleep? If yesterday was an indication, you are not sleeping. You looked so tired."

"I don't know. Perhaps someday I can stop. But to be honest, I don't see how it will ever be possible. Unless . . ."

"Unless what?"

"Unless I marry a rich man who will use his money to feed them."

"Odette, you aren't responsible for every single hungry person."

"But I just cannot bear to think of them going hungry when I can do something about it. Besides, I like hunting, and I believe I am doing something good and that God will reward me for what I'm doing."

"It seems to me . . . But perhaps I should not say that."

"What? Go on and say it. You know I won't be angry with you."

"I just think that Rutger, as your uncle, should be more concerned for you and your well-being. He should not encourage you to break the laws of the land."

"Well, Rutger knows I want to help the poor and that I am a woman who will not be easily dissuaded. He also allows me to study with a tutor and to study any subject I wish, and I am grateful for that." But there was a niggling feeling that Anna was right. Why did Rutger not try to stop her?

"You should not feel as though you must hunt *every* night, Odette. Truly you shouldn't. You will make yourself sick. Besides, it must be hard on you to be always afraid of being caught. I could never handle the strain of such a thing." She reached out and squeezed Odette's arm. "But you have always been stronger than I am."

Stronger? Or more foolish? "Perhaps you are right about not hunting every day."

"So you will only hunt five nights a week?"

"I suppose. But it feels selfish to cease hunting every night. People will go hungry."

"Odette, you are not responsible for every person in Thornbeck!"

"Perhaps not." The sun was coming up, and the room was now

light enough from the gray light coming through the windows that she could see Anna's face. "But if I can feed them and I don't . . ."

"Now you are just torturing yourself. God knows you cannot feed everyone. Even you have limitations. And I think you should consider that perhaps poaching deer in the margrave's game park may not be the right thing to do anyway."

Odette opened her mouth to protest, but Anna interrupted her.

"I am only asking you to consider it. Promise me you will."

"I will." She leaned forward and put her head in her hands. "I may have to stop poaching anyway. I think Jorgen caught one of the boys who help take the meat out of the forest."

"What? When?"

"Tonight."

"Do you think he recognized you?"

Odette shook her head. "But if he caught one of the boys, it is possible he would have told Jorgen that I am the poacher."

"Oh. But you do not know if he caught him or not?"

"I am not certain."

"Then you must assume he did not. You must determine not to worry about it and go to sleep. You must sleep, Odette."

"What about you?"

"I will sleep too. I lay awake most of the night praying for you."

A lump formed in Odette's throat. No one had ever told her before that they were praying for her. "Thank you, Anna."

"Of course, you mad, wonderful, courageous woman who steals the margrave's deer."

Mad. That was a good description of it. Truly, she must be mad.

"Have you received any letters from The Red House girl, Kathryn?" Rutger asked.

Odette shook her head as they ate their midday meal together.

"You have been quieter than usual the last several days."

"I have not heard anything from Kathryn, but I do not believe she is able to read or write. And I am well."

"I saw Anna leaving this morning. I hope she did not keep you from sleeping."

"Oh no." Odette shook her head. What would he say if she told him what had happened last night? And that she had told Anna her—their—secret.

"How is Anna?"

"She is well." She stared down at her food, not feeling very hungry.

"Have you learned anything else from Jorgen? Has he found out anything else about the poachers?"

"I . . . I don't know." She might as well confess. "I think he caught one of the boys last night."

Rutger started coughing, as his fruit-juice compote must have gone down the wrong way. He took another swallow.

When he could speak again, he rasped out, "What did you say?"

"Jorgen heard us last night and yelled at us. I do not think he was able to see me. We ran, and I think he may have caught Wernher."

Rutger's face seemed to turn a light shade of gray. He took out his handkerchief and dabbed at his face. "Why do you think Jorgen caught him?"

"I heard Wernher cry out."

"Will you see Jorgen today?"

"Not today."

"You should have told me. You should have woken me up as soon as you returned home."

"I'm sorry. I knew there was nothing any of us could do."

He heaved a sigh. "All will be well, I am sure. I shall try to find out what happened, if he was captured."

"Oh, thank you, Rutger. I am worried about him. But how will you find out? What will you do?"

"Do not worry, my dear. I have resources."

"Do you have any influence with the margrave?"

He hesitated, then shook his head. "The margrave is a powerful man, but he has lived away from this region his whole life. I do not know anyone who has any influence over him, except his chancellor, Ulrich. And probably Jorgen. But I will find out if Wernher made his way home."

"Do you think the margrave is a fair man, given the rumors?"

"I know little about whether he is fair, but he placed a harsh punishment on a servant who was caught stealing several months ago."

If the margrave was capable of killing his own brother, what would he do to poor Wernher? Would he torture him and force him to tell whom he was working for? She and Rutger would lose everything. They might even have to leave Thornbeck in disgrace. No wonder Rutger had looked a bit ashen when she told him about Wernher.

"Since tomorrow is Sunday, and I am always so tired when I'm at church, I thought I would not go hunting tonight, to take a Sabbath rest. Perhaps I will rest two nights a week." If she wasn't taken to the dungeon today by the margrave's guards.

Rutger looked concerned. "Of course, my dear. I think that is a good idea."

"I will go up to my room now. Will you tell me what you find out about Wernher, as soon as you can?"

"Yes, my dear. Now do not worry. Naught is ever accomplished by worrying." Rutger gave her a small smile, but it seemed rather brittle and forced.

He was as worried as she was.

# 17

Today was Sunday, and she actually felt well rested and might not fall asleep while she prayed, as she had often done in the past.

Rutger had informed her that Wernher had slipped through Jorgen's grasp and escaped. She shuddered inside at how close she and the boys had come to Jorgen catching them. She would be sure to thank God for Wernher's escape.

If she saw Jorgen at church, would she be brave enough to ask him how things were going with his hunt for the poacher?

Odette walked with Rutger to the cathedral, which was not far from their home. Odette pulled her veil over her face as she entered the echoing nave. She dipped her fingers in the holy water and made the sign of the cross. Then, bowing her head, she genuflected before the crucifix depicting Jesus suffering on the cross. After a moment of silent prayer—*God, forgive me of my sins and remember them no more*—she made her way toward the altar, finding a place to stand where she could see the priest.

Odette glanced around but did not see Anna or Jorgen. Rutger joined her, bowing his head and kneeling to pray. Odette did the same, making the sign of the cross over her chest.

Usually Odette felt little or no guilt for her poaching activities. After all, she was feeding the poor. But today she couldn't seem to stop confessing it to God as she prayed.

*I have broken the law of the land. I am sorry I could not have fed the children any other way . . . Forgive me if what I am doing causes Jorgen pain or trouble. I do not want to hurt anyone. Forgive me for breaking the law and stealing from the margrave and king.*

It was at the edge of her mind to say she wished she didn't have to hunt anymore. At first it had been exciting, but now . . . She rather dreaded the killing and the guilt of knowing she was stealing the margrave's—the king's—property.

*I am so confused. Is it not right to feed the poor? Lord God, provide another way, if it be Your will to do so.*

Brother Philip knelt not far away. He then prostrated himself on the stone floor, facedown, as he often did. Odette had once asked him why he did that, and he scowled, grunted, and said, "Because I am overcome by the realization of my sin," as if it should be obvious. What would he say if he knew about Odette's poaching? There probably wasn't enough prostrating in the world to absolve herself of that sin, at least in Brother Philip's eyes. But she didn't have to absolve herself in his eyes, only in God's.

A man with thick dark-blond hair caught her eye. Jorgen walked up the center of the nave and took a place on the other side, parallel to her.

She should be meditating on her sins from the past week instead of letting her heart flutter over the thought of speaking with Jorgen. Odette bowed her head and closed her eyes. But instead of examining herself and meditating on Jesus, an image of Jorgen's face rose before her as he discovered that she was the poacher he was searching for—the image from her recurring dream.

The choir of boys recited some hymns in plainsong, then the priest began the Liturgy of the Word and gave a short homily. When he began the Sacrament of Eucharist, Odette closed her eyes and concentrated on the meaning of it. How sad she felt for those who did not understand Latin, for it always lifted her heart to meditate on the words and to believe she was in the very presence of God.

When she went forward to receive holy Communion, her eye caught Jorgen's as he filed in behind her.

The back of her neck prickled. What was he thinking, walking just behind her? He had caught Wernher two nights ago, even if he had lost him soon after. Had he figured out that she was the poacher? How had he looked at her a moment before? She'd only glanced at him. She didn't think he looked angry, but she couldn't be sure.

She was being foolish. Of course he did not know she was the poacher. Her face burned with the heat of the midday sun nonetheless.

When the priest dismissed the people, Odette hoped she didn't look obvious as she made her way toward Jorgen, trying to keep him in the corner of her vision. People were moving down the middle toward the entrance, blocking her view. Finally she could see him again. Dark circles under his eyes joined the bruise on his cheekbone and made him look worn out. His brows were drawn together, but when he saw her, his face relaxed.

Mathis Papendorp stepped between them. His smiling face loomed before her.

"Odette, you look beautiful."

"Thank you, Mathis. It is a wonderful day to be in church, is it not? Are you feeling absolved?"

He opened his mouth, then faltered. "Absolved? Why, yes, I suppose so."

"I do as well." Odette smiled. "It is good to see you, Mathis. I wish you a good week."

"Thank you. I wish you a good week as well, Odette." He

looked at her for a moment, then whispered, "I am giving you time to think, as you asked me to. Please do . . . think of me fondly."

She opened her mouth but wasn't sure what to say. So she smiled and nodded.

He reached out and squeezed her hand. "Fare well, Odette."

"Fare well, Mathis."

As soon as he turned away, Jorgen said to Rutger, who stood just behind her, "May I escort your niece home?"

"You may." Rutger nodded to him and joined the crowd heading for the door.

Jorgen held out his arm to her. He did not look at all angry, and her shoulders grew lighter.

"You look well rested," he said.

"Thank you, but I was thinking you look the opposite."

Out of the corner of her eye, she caught a glimpse of Mathis staring at them with narrowed eyes. He had stopped not far from the door of the cathedral, but now he scowled and stalked out.

Odette hoped she had not hurt his feelings. But standing so close to Jorgen, touching his arm, she couldn't help but focus her attention on him. "Have you had some difficult nights?"

He sighed. "You do not want to hear about my troubles."

They walked out into the sunlight, and Odette found herself pressed close to his arm as the people jostled them. They waited for two arguing women to pass before continuing on their way. Rutger was ahead of them, too far away to hear their conversation.

"I do not mind listening to whatever is troubling you." She spoke the truth, even if her greater curiosity was for what he had found out.

He shook his head, pressing his lips between his teeth. "I caught a boy in the woods a few nights ago."

"Was he the poacher?"

Jorgen shook his head again. "But the poacher was there and had just killed a deer. I think the boy and at least one other person were about to carry it away." He was quiet for a moment, staring straight ahead.

"So you caught him? Did he tell you who the poacher was?"

"No." He looked down at his feet as they walked slowly, letting Rutger move farther away. "I lost him. He wriggled out of my grasp. I chased him a long way, but I lost him." He sighed again.

It felt wrong, but her heart swelled with a surge of relief that the boy had gotten away, while Jorgen's face was a picture of burdened disappointment. A stab of guilt pierced her chest.

"I am sorry. I know how badly you wanted to catch him."

"I *need* to catch him. What kind of forester would I be if I cannot catch a poacher, one who seems to be poaching so much and so often? The margrave will lose confidence in me and replace me with someone else."

"Surely he would not do that. He must know you are doing your best."

"And the chancellor dislikes me and is probably leaping at every opportunity to malign me to the margrave."

"How could anyone dislike you?"

"Ulrich seemed to dislike me from the first time I saw him when we were children. Then he seemed to become jealous when Lord Thornbeck appointed me forester. I think he has been afraid of losing his position ever since the former margrave died in the fire."

"Some people are jealous. The margrave probably sees his true nature."

He shrugged. "Possibly."

"And perhaps he sees that your strong character is the exact opposite of that petty chancellor's."

He smiled a little and gazed down at her. "You are very loyal, are you not?"

She thought a moment. "I am loyal, but I hope I am only loyal to people and causes that are worthy." She smiled up at him. "You are a loyal person, too, are you not?"

"I suppose."

Thinking of his loyalty to the margrave, she asked, "Do you think it is ever possible to be too loyal?"

His brows came together. "Perhaps." Then he nodded. "It is possible, if one is loyal to the wrong thing . . . or the wrong person."

"Very true." If the margrave had killed his brother so he could take his place, then Jorgen's loyalty to the man could get him in a lot of trouble and cause him to do things that were wrong. She hoped he would see that, sooner rather than later.

But could she also be loyal to the wrong person or thing? She was only loyal to God, her uncle Rutger, her friend Anna, and the poor. No, her loyalties were certainly righteous.

⁓

Odette walked beside Anna as they made their way home the next day with baskets full of fruits and vegetables from the market. Odette had a servant for that chore, but she had enjoyed choosing them in the bustling Thornbeck *Marktplatz* and talking with the various sellers.

"These melons look so sweet." Odette thumped the round fruit with her finger.

"You paid too much for them," Anna scolded. "The woman would have taken less."

"I did not mind. Besides, she looked as if she needed it more than I did." Her dress had been patched multiple times, and she wore no shoes at all.

A woman stood beside a cart with bunches of flowers and others planted in earthen pots. The seller held out a pot of bright-red geraniums and called, "Flowers make the heart merry!"

Odette was drawn like a honeybee to the red geraniums. She and Anna exclaimed over their favorite ones. While Anna bartered with the seller, offering her some carrots and leeks for a bunch of flowers, Odette wanted the geraniums.

A man's voice near her caught her attention as he said, "That new girl is back at The Red House. Remember the young one with the pretty face?"

Odette glanced to the right. Two men were standing in front of a baker's shop only a few feet away. One held a long loaf of bread under his arm. The other bent toward him, as if imparting a secret, with a leering grin on his whiskery face. She itched to slap that grin right off him.

The other man grunted and nodded.

"We should go over and give her a greeting, eh?" He laughed, an ugly sound.

"Agnes is protective of that one. She might not let you—"

"Aw, Agnes likes me. She lets me have any girl I want."

Odette's stomach turned as the blood drained from her face. She glared at the two men, but they did not even see her as they moved away from the front of the bakery and down the street.

Odette grabbed Anna's arm. "Did you hear that?"

"Hear what?" Anna was just turning away from the flower seller with her bunch of flowers.

Odette stepped aside, out of the street, pulling Anna with her. "There were two men over by the bakery, and one of them said something that makes me think Kathryn went back to The Red House."

"Oh no, I cannot believe that. It might not be Kathryn. It couldn't be. She is with her brothers at the farm."

"I have a strange feeling it is her. I have to find out."

"How will you do that? You cannot!" Anna put her flowers in her basket and grasped Odette's arm. "What are you thinking?"

Odette knew she probably shouldn't tell Anna, since she might try to stop her. "I cannot let Kathryn be molested by that disgusting man. I will simply go to The Red House and see if she is there."

"They will not let you in that place."

They would if she wanted to work there.

Odette stood in front of The Red House with Anna still holding on to her arm.

"Odette, what are you going to do?"

She turned to her friend and looked her in the eye. "Nothing bad will happen. I only want to find out if Kathryn is here." She thrust her basket into Anna's hand. "I will be back in a few minutes."

She turned away from Anna's distraught expression and strode toward the front door of The Red House.

The guard at the door trained his eyes on her as she approached. He uncrossed his arms and turned his body to face her. "What do you want?"

"I want to talk to Agnes."

"Why? What about?" He narrowed his eyes. Otherwise he didn't even move, as though she were no threat at all.

"She will want to talk to me."

"Go away. This is not the kind of place for a maiden like you."

"How do you know what kind of maiden I am?" She felt a bit

queasy in her stomach at what she was implying. She clenched her jaw and said firmly, "I want to talk to Agnes."

He leaned toward her menacingly. "Why?"

"I want to work for her."

He leaned back with a lift of his brows. "You do?"

"Yes."

"Very well." He opened the door and preceded her into the house.

When they walked in, everyone in the room turned to look at her. One woman, wearing clothing that covered more of her skin than the rest of them, turned and put her hands on her hips. "Who is this you have, Conrad?"

"She wants to talk to you, Agnes."

The woman looked at Odette from head to toe. "What do you want?"

Odette walked toward her. "I was thinking of working for you. I had heard that my friend Kathryn was working here, and if she is here, then I want to work here too."

Agnes crossed her arms over her chest, continuing to eye Odette.

"Is she here?"

"Why would that matter to you?"

"Because I want to be where my friend is."

"So you want to work for me." Agnes gave a smirk. "Have you ever done this kind of *work* before?"

One of the women staring at her from several feet away snickered. The bodice of her dress was indecently low, and Odette averted her eyes. The young woman beside her laughed even louder. Two men sitting at a table grinned at her as they looked up from their game.

Odette lifted her chin, hoping they couldn't see her blush in the dimly lit room. "There is a first time for everything. I am desperate for work, and this is what I want to do, if Kathryn is here. She said I could make a lot of money in a short time."

Agnes stared at her as a slow smile spread across her face. "Then go get ready for work. Conrad will show you to your room."

"I want to talk to Kathryn first."

Agnes leaned in, as though to whisper to her. "I am not playing games here. This is a place of business. I know you want to save your girl, but she is my girl now."

Odette leaned away from her, noting the coldness in her hard blue eyes. Part of her wanted to turn and run back out the door. But Kathryn was here, and Odette was not leaving without at least talking to her.

She faced the stairs at the back of the room and marched straight toward them, not looking back. She heard Agnes whispering, then a grunt from the guard as Odette started up the steps. As she reached the shadows, she began to hurry, then to run up the steps.

Heavy footsteps pounded the stairs behind her. She ran down the long corridor calling out, "Kathryn! Kathryn, where are you?"

Her heart beat so hard she could hardly breathe. The guard was still behind her, his steps drawing closer.

A door at the end of the corridor opened and Kathryn's face appeared. Her eyes grew wide. "Odette."

Odette ran to her. Kathryn moved back as Odette rushed into the room, then shut the door behind her.

As soon as she was inside, she heard a loud noise against the door. She stared at it, but it stayed shut. "What was that? What is he doing?"

"He barred the door from the outside." Kathryn's voice was quiet, and when she looked at Odette, her mouth hung open. "What are you doing here?"

"I came to ask you the same question."

"I can do what I want." Kathryn turned away from her and sat on the bed in the center of the room.

"But, Kathryn, why? I do not understand. What about your brothers?"

Kathryn's frail shoulders went up and then down in a quick shrug. She still did not face Odette.

"Did you not want to stay with them? Were the people at the farm unkind to you?"

She was still and quiet. Finally she said, "They weren't unkind, but I did not feel like I was doing enough to pay for being there. Agnes came and talked me into coming back. She reminded me of the promises I had made to her and how much she had helped my brothers and me." Kathryn's voice quivered. "I know it must seem wrong to you, but . . . what else . . . am I good for?" She sobbed softly.

Odette sat beside her, putting her hand on Kathryn's shoulder. "Kathryn, this woman, Agnes, is using you. You do not owe your loyalty to her. You do not have to do this! You are so young, and your life can be different from this. You are much too good for this kind of life."

She shook her head furiously. "No, I am not. I have done things, bad things. You do not understand. I am not innocent and clean like you. I am damaged . . . ruined." She said the words like they caused a bitter taste in her mouth.

"That is not true. You are a beautiful young maiden who can start fresh and clean right now. People have done bad things to you. I am sure that is true. But you do not have to stay in that awful place where they have tried to imprison you. You can be the woman you were always meant to be, the woman who is deep inside you. Just because people did bad things to you, or you did bad things in the past, does not make you bad. You can choose to be free, free from all that."

Tears flowed down Odette's own cheeks as she spoke, as she realized it was true of her too. People had said ugly things to her when she was young, when she had scavenged for food and even stolen food a few times. But even as she was not those things they said—beggar child, worthless, orphan trash—Kathryn was not either. "You are better than this."

"How do you know God has not cursed me to do these things? He could have kept my parents alive. He could have saved them, could have saved me." She sobbed harder.

"He is saving you now." Odette gripped Kathryn's arm, trying to make her listen. "He saved you when Jorgen came and found you here. He saved you when Rutger took you to the farm where your brothers are living. We can leave here now and you do not have to—"

"We cannot leave! They have locked us in. Oh, what have you done, Odette? They will do these terrible things to you now. And it is all my fault."

"No, no, we shall get away. No one is going to do anything to me." But Odette's insides were twisting, her cheeks burning as she tried to think how they would escape.

# 18

"WE WILL GET out of here." Odette sat on the bed patting Kathryn's shoulder. "They would not dare to hold me against my will." *Even though I told them I wanted to work here.* How would they escape? Especially since Kathryn had already escaped once before. They would never allow Kathryn to leave a second time.

While the girl's shoulders shook with sobs, the thought of what she must have done, here in this very room, sprang up before Odette's eyes, and she shuddered. *God, help her get out of here and never come back. Help her understand she does not have to stay here.*

Odette walked to the window, which looked out over the street. Below, people were walking around, carrying bundles and sacks and baskets full of good things from the market. A man walked by as he took a bite from a bread roll in his hand. They were going about their normal daily chores and shopping, not knowing that just above them a young girl's life was hanging uncertainly. Kathryn was doomed to a sordid, ugly life, depending on what happened in the next day, hour, or minute, and Odette's innocence could be snatched away just as quickly.

"O Lord God," she whispered toward the overcast sky, "please get me out of here. Get us both out of here. We are but dust and ashes in Your great universe, God. But for the sake of our Savior, Jesus, remember us and help us."

"I am so sorry you came here for me," Kathryn said, watching her from the bed. "You never should have come." Her face was tear-stained and blotchy.

"Do not worry. I will think of a plan. Sooner or later they have to unbar the door. We must find something we can use as a weapon and force our way out." Odette looked around the room for something she could use to bash someone over the head. "Or we could always kick them between the legs and punch them in the throat. Rutger taught me that those are the two places to strike if a man ever attacks me."

Kathryn's face seemed to grow even paler, her eyes wider. "But they would punish us, maybe even kill us, if we did something like that."

"The idea is to render them too weak to hurt us, just long enough for us to escape."

Kathryn still looked terrified. "You should go without me."

"Do not be afraid. Just trust me."

Kathryn wiped away another tear, pressing her lips together.

Jorgen walked toward his mother's favorite bakery. It was the anniversary of his father's death, and although she avoided admitting it, he knew she always felt sad around this day. So he had decided to buy her a cake, a luxury she never allowed herself, and take it to her. She would fuss at him for walking all that way, and especially since he had been going out every night to search for the poacher and getting less sleep. But it was worth it to give her something else to think about besides Father's death.

Was someone calling his name? Jorgen turned his head but did not see anyone he knew on the crowded street. He kept moving forward.

"Jorgen!"

Anna was running toward him. When she reached him, she was so out of breath she could only pant.

"What is it?" By the look in her eyes, it was something bad. "Has something happened to Odette?"

She closed her mouth to swallow, then said, "Odette is at The Red House. You must come and get her."

"The Red House?"

"She heard that Kathryn was there. She went inside to find her."

Jorgen was already walking fast toward *Waschefrau Strasse.* "How long has Odette been in there?"

"Longer than I thought she would be. I told her not to do it, but she said she just wanted to see if Kathryn was there and to talk to her."

What would they do to her? Jorgen broke into a run, leaving Anna behind, weaving in and out between the people.

When he turned down the street where The Red House stood, he slowed his pace. The guard at the door was already glaring at him. "Get out of here," the guard said in a deep voice.

This was no time for playacting. Jorgen was no good at it anyway. He stood tall and looked the taller guard in the eye. "I am Jorgen Hartman, and I am the Margrave of Thornbeck's forester. He will not suffer you to thwart my official business here. He will shut down this brothel, and Agnes and the rest of you will be on the street."

The guard's glare grew even blacker. "You are that man who took Kathryn away from here."

"I am. The margrave knows all about that as well. He will also hear that you are keeping a young maiden here against her will, a young maiden who is the niece of a wealthy burgher named Rutger Menkels."

When he said the name "Rutger Menkels," the guard moved back a half inch, the expression in his eyes changing. Rutger was one of the wealthiest people in Thornbeck, but did that warrant a reaction from this stoic oaf of a guard?

"Come. I will take you to Agnes."

Jorgen almost stepped on the guard's heels as he followed him inside the dingy, half-lit room. Agnes's shrewd eyes caught sight of them and she came forward. The guard met her halfway and whispered in her ear. A change came over Agnes's face, much like what had happened with the guard. Then she waved the burly man away and proceeded toward Jorgen.

"Where is she?" Jorgen demanded.

"Where is whom, dear boy?"

"You know who. I will not stand here arguing with you. I will find her myself."

He started toward the stairs, but the guard stepped in front of him and blocked his way. Jorgen tried to walk around him, but the man grabbed Jorgen's arm. Jorgen slipped out of his grasp and turned to face the room. The guard caught hold of his arm again, his fingers biting into Jorgen's flesh.

"I am the margrave's forester! You are holding two young maidens here against their will, and the margrave will not allow this to go unpunished."

"Two maidens?" Agnes feigned surprise as she placed her hand over her heart. "I was not aware of that. I assure you I would never do such a thing. Can you tell me the names of these two captive maidens?"

"Kathryn and Odette."

"Are you certain they are here against their will? Perhaps they choose to be here."

A couple of chuckles followed her words. Every person in the room was staring at him.

"If you can prove that they did not come here of their own freedom and choice, then I am sure the margrave will have reason to throw me in the dungeon. But as they both came here freely . . ." She clicked her tongue against her teeth. "I believe the margrave might ask you what you are doing here."

Jorgen growled deep in his throat as he struggled to loose himself from the grip of the guard. "If they came here freely, then allow them to leave freely."

Agnes stepped closer to him and smiled. She touched a finger to his temple, then drew a line down his face to his chin. "You are too handsome to incite my ire . . . far too handsome. And far too passionate in your determination for me not to believe that you are in love with one of those young maidens you speak of freeing." Her smile widened, showing two missing front teeth on the top. "Which one is it? Kathryn? Or Odette?"

"Let me go. I am the margrave's forester."

"You are the margrave's forester. So why are you here? No, do not answer that again. I would never mistreat a man who is so close to the margrave." Her words dripped with insincerity. "I shall allow you to go upstairs and free the maidens you speak of. I am tired of this game. Kathryn is no longer welcome to come back, and you may tell her I said so." She snapped her fingers. The massive oaf holding on to his arms released him.

Jorgen ran up the stairs. When he reached the top, he called, "Odette!"

From somewhere on the other side of the door, someone was calling her name. "Odette!"

"It's Jorgen!" How had he found them? How did he know she was there? "Here!" she yelled at the door. "We are here!"

"Where? Where are you?" His voice sounded strong and calm, but urgent.

Odette kept calling to him so he could follow her voice. Her heart beat fast and hard. Were they allowing him to release her and Kathryn? Or would the guards try to stop him?

His footsteps grew close. "Here! We are in here!" She heard the bar scraping, wood on wood, and then the door swung open. Jorgen's face was tense, his brows drawn together and his fists raised, as if ready to punch someone.

He stepped one foot over the threshold and she threw her arms around him. She buried her face in his shoulder, but only for a moment. He held on to her arms as he stared down at her face. "Are you unhurt?"

"*Ja, ja*, we are well. But we should go." She turned to fetch Kathryn, who stood behind her.

"Go on and leave me here." Her face crumpled. "Go on."

"We are not leaving without you." Odette grabbed Kathryn's arm.

"My things." Kathryn pulled away and sank to her knees beside the bed. She pulled out a bundle, which she tucked under her arm.

"Come." Jorgen motioned for them to follow him out the door.

Odette held her breath, waiting to see if Kathryn would go with them. She stepped forward, and Odette let her go out the door behind Jorgen.

Jorgen turned to the right, heading toward the front stairs.

"Are we not going out the back way through the kitchen?" Kathryn asked.

"No. They are going to let us go through the front door." Jorgen's voice was resolute.

Odette's stomach sank. Would they have to fight their way out?

"They will never let me leave." Kathryn's shrill voice threatened tears. "Leave me here."

"No. They will allow you to leave."

Kathryn held on to his sleeve and Odette held on to Kathryn's arm as they made their way to the other end of the corridor and the top of the stairs. Without hesitating, Jorgen started down.

Everyone in the large open room at the bottom of the stairs watched them. Kathryn kept her head down, but Odette glared at them all, meeting each person's eye, including Agnes's.

Agnes glared back. "None of the three of you are to ever set a foot in The Red House again. Do you understand?"

No one said anything for a moment. Then Jorgen said, "None of us will want to."

"What about you, Kathryn?" Agnes's voice was taunting. "Will you be back?"

Kathryn's hands were shaking and she cringed, her shoulders bowed forward.

"She will not be back either," Odette said stoutly.

Agnes merely smirked.

They walked out into the daylight, and Odette was never so thankful to leave a place in her life.

Jorgen said nothing as he set a rather fast pace down the street. But as Kathryn still held on to his sleeve, he reached toward Odette and clasped her hand in his. She moved closer.

He gazed down at her. "Thank God you were not hurt."

Had she never noticed how inviting his lips looked? What would it feel like to kiss them?

*Foolish, foolish girl to think of* that *at a time such as this.* "Thank you for saving us from that terrible place, Jorgen." She felt breathless, and it had nothing to do with the way they were hurrying along.

He was no longer looking at her but was guiding her and Kathryn through the street, dodging horses as well as people. He glanced at her for a moment. "It was incredible good fortune that Anna happened to see me and that I happened to be walking that way."

His voice seemed tight, controlled.

Anna was running toward them. "Oh, you are well, you are well!" She threw her arms around Odette. "Did they hurt you?"

"I am not hurt, thanks to you and Jorgen."

Anna hurried over to Kathryn and embraced her too. "I thank God you are both safe."

Jorgen was staring down at Odette. He seemed about to say something.

"I have your things from the market," Anna said. She ran over to a chandler's shop and came back out carrying Odette's basket.

"I had forgotten all about it." Odette took it from her. "I don't even remember where I left it. Thank you, Anna. You are a godsend." She hugged her friend again.

"Peter will be worried about me," Anna said. "I should go now. Fare well."

They started walking again. But Kathryn was looking uncomfortable and near tears again. Odette went to walk beside her, put her arm around her, and said to her quietly, "That part of your life is finished. You are free from Agnes and The Red House. She set you free when she said you were never to come back there again. I know you felt you owed her something, and there was some part of you that told you that you belonged there, but that is a part of you that has no place in your future. Kathryn? Do you understand?"

She nodded and wiped at a tear on her cheek.

She only hoped Kathryn would take to heart the words she was speaking to her. If only she would cast away the broken part of her, the part that thought she didn't deserve to live free and without someone using and abusing her. It had taken Odette a long time to stop feeling guilty that she had an uncle who was wealthy and who gave her everything she needed and wanted. For so long, part of her still thought she deserved to be despised as a lowly beggar child, forced to work like a slave and not allowed to have three meals a day. But that part of her was not welcome in her thoughts and her heart now. She simply had to convince Kathryn of that same thing—that her brokenness was a part of her past, not her present nor her future. It was possible to start anew . . . and to be joyful about starting anew.

Jorgen stopped, and Odette looked up to see that they had arrived in front of her house. Holding on to Kathryn's arm, she turned to Jorgen. "Please come inside."

Inside the first-floor room, Odette asked Jorgen to wait for a moment, then she took Kathryn to the kitchen.

"Heinke, I need you to prepare a bath for Kathryn. And, Else," she called to the older woman who helped Cook in the kitchen, "will you take care of her and help her wash her hair?"

"Of course." Else put her arm around Kathryn's shoulders. She was a motherly type, exactly what Kathryn needed. "Come, love, and you can get a good scrub. Nothing like a warm bath."

Odette hurried back to where Jorgen was standing just inside the front door. He didn't see her come in. He still looked a bit angry, as if he was thinking of something unjust. He was so tall and strong, and his hair looked soft, the way it curled around his ears. If only she could gaze at him forever. Tears stung her eyes.

Jorgen turned and reached out to her. Tears spilled from her eyes and she stepped into his open arms, pressing her cheek against his chest.

"My brave girl," he whispered against her hair as he swept it away from her face. "Do not cry."

How could she cry now? She made an effort to stop, taking deep breaths, but oh, how good it felt to be held in his warm, strong arms, to press her face against his broad chest. Concentrating on the warmth of his body made the tears dry up.

She had no right to let him hold her like this. She didn't want to hurt him, and she could not marry him, so she should step away from him right now.

But she didn't have the strength to push him away. She would stay like this for a bit longer. "Thank you." She closed her eyes, memorizing how warm, how safe, how exhilarating it felt to be embraced by him. She breathed him in as guilt assailed her. "Thank you for saving us today. I do not know how we would have escaped had you not helped us."

"I am pleased I was there, where Anna could find me. And grateful you were not hurt. You weren't hurt, were you?"

"Not at all." It was time to break away. She must. She took a deep breath, trying to make sure she remembered his smell—like evergreen trees, fresh air, and something else, something enticing—and let it out slowly.

With reluctance, she loosened her arms from around his waist and took a step back. But Jorgen did not let go. His hand stayed on her back, while the other came up and pressed against her cheek as he looked into her eyes.

The moment seemed frozen as they gazed at each other.

When his eyes focused on her mouth, her heart started to pound and her breath left her chest. Would he kiss her? Did she dare kiss him? It would be easy to rise on her tiptoes and pull his head down to hers. She did not think he would resist.

A door slammed, causing Odette to jump. Cook's voice came from the back of the house and called for Heinke to come and help her. "Make haste! The milk will sour before you get here."

Odette let out a nervous half giggle, and Jorgen mumbled, "I should not," as if to himself. He was still staring down at her, but his expression had lost its intensity.

He pulled away, stroking her cheek so quickly she wondered if it was accidental. "I must go. Take care of Kathryn."

"I will."

Did he want to kiss her? Was he thinking about it? Or had she imagined it?

# 19

THE NIGHT OF the margrave's masquerade ball had arrived.

Two weeks had gone by in which Odette saw Jorgen only a few times when she gave her lessons to the children. And Mathis had visited her twice, to bring her flowers and to tell her about his costume for the masquerade ball.

"What are you wearing to the ball?" Mathis had asked her.

"I cannot tell you, or else, what is the fun of having a masquerade ball? You shall have to guess which maiden is me." Perhaps it was not a good idea to tease Mathis, but she hoped he would not recognize her for a while and she could dance with Jorgen for the first few dances.

Rutger told her that many titled ladies and men would be attending the ball, as well as the most distinguished residents of Thornbeck. Odette and her uncle were invited, but she was sad that Anna and Peter were not. At least Jorgen would be there. Although she should not indulge her attraction to him so much, being able to talk with him would soothe the nervous flutterings in her stomach at being around so many highborn people.

Meanwhile, she couldn't help being excited about her swan costume. Rutger had spared no expense with Odette's mask. It was made of white swan feathers, and the eyeholes were outlined in black, but the rest of the mask was snow white. Her matching headdress framed her hair with white feathers.

Her gown was also white, with silver stitching on the bodice. The belt was decorated entirely with silver thread, and white feathers were attached to the shoulders of the gown. Her blond hair had been arranged high on her head but fell down her back in loose curls, with white and silver ribbons woven throughout.

Rutger was employing his carriage for the occasion, and Odette was grateful not to be walking or even riding a horse, which might have ruined her costume. She hoped the other ladies at the ball were dressed as elaborately as she was.

Sitting on the cushioned carriage seat, she reached up and touched her mask. It felt strange having something on her face. Would anyone guess she was hiding as many secrets as the mask might suggest?

Rutger was not wearing a mask, but he wore a turban in the style of the Saracens, as well as an elaborate matching robe, also in the style of the people who lived in the Holy Land. He said the men would not be expected to wear masks, and some of them might not even wear a costume.

Odette alighted from the carriage feeling like a princess. Rutger escorted her up a few steps to the castle entrance. She might have imagined it, but the servants at the entrance seemed to open their eyes a little wider and let their gaze linger when they saw Odette.

Was her headdress too elaborate? Had her mask become askew? She reached up and put her hand on the mask, but it seemed to be in its proper place.

Once inside, they joined a line of guests waiting to greet the Margrave of Thornbeck.

The other ladies also wore masks. The woman in front of her wore a bright blue-green mask with elaborate designs on the sides to imitate the tail feathers of a peacock. She wore a headdress of real peacock feathers that matched the mask.

The men wore very fine clothing, but only a few others besides Rutger were wearing costumes. One was dressed like an Indian sultan, another like a Roman senator, and another like a Far Eastern Mongol.

Odette caught a glimpse of a man who stood talking with the margrave. The back of his head reminded her of Jorgen. He was dressed in a fine brocaded cotehardie of various shades of blue and gold that came below his hips. The sleeves were slit in several places all the way down his arms, showing white linen underneath. White ermine cuffs accented the wrists, hem, and shoulders of the outer garment. He also wore a felt hat with a peaked brim and a feather.

Just as he finished speaking with the margrave, he turned and smiled at Odette. Her breath caught in her throat at how good he looked.

A moment later, he was hidden from view as a large man wearing an enormous turban moved between them. When the man was finally out of her line of vision, Jorgen was gone.

When Odette and Rutger were face-to-face with the margrave, she was struck by how young and handsome he looked. The margrave was not at all the boorish former knight she had imagined. His hair was dark and slightly wavy, his eyes brown, and his cheekbones high. He was tall and broad shouldered, and he looked them in the eye as Ulrich, the chancellor, read their names from their invitation and introduced them.

Pity squeezed her heart at the way he leaned on his cane, no doubt due to his injury when the west wing of Thornbeck Castle burned. Odette and Rutger made the appropriate greeting, and the margrave said the proper acknowledgments, and they moved on to allow him to greet the guests waiting behind them.

Now they were just outside the ballroom, and there was Jorgen, waiting for them. He smiled with his eyes as he watched her, the corners of his mouth tilting up. But as Rutger stepped ahead of her, Jorgen greeted her uncle first, who paused to converse with him.

Odette could hardly concentrate on what they were saying as she stared at Jorgen—clean-shaven, skin browned by the sun, his blond hair perfectly in place, the bright blue of his waistcoat contrasting with the white of his shirtsleeves. His eyes had never looked brighter as he turned from Rutger and smiled.

Jorgen reached out to her and, moving as if in a dream, she placed her hand in his. He raised it to his lips and kissed her knuckles.

She had been kissed on the hand numerous times before and never felt a thing. So why did his lips on her skin send a tingle through her, across her shoulders and down her back?

"Odette, you are the most beautiful swan I have ever seen." He held out his arm to her.

"Thank you. And you are the most handsome prince I have ever seen."

The humor returned to his eyes as they made their way inside the ballroom. "For one night only. These clothes must be returned tomorrow to their rightful owner."

"It is not the clothing of a man that makes him a prince."

His smile grew wider. "You are very clever tonight, as well as very beautiful."

"How do you know I am beautiful? My face is covered by a mask."

"Only half of your face. I know what the other half looks like." He gazed down at her, his eyes mesmerizing. "And it is beautiful."

"I never took you for a flatterer, Jorgen. You will make me think more of myself than I should."

"I do not think that's likely."

The musicians and singers began a lively tune as Jorgen and Odette entered the ballroom.

"Will you tell me who is here?" Odette spoke near Jorgen's ear. "I am afraid I hardly know anyone except you."

"I will do my best. I believe the woman with the red dress is the Duchess of Peisterberg, and the young woman with her, wearing the blue mask, is her daughter."

How exciting it would be to meet a duchess! Or a duchess's daughter. They both had feathers on their masks, which were even larger and more elaborate than her own. "Their gowns and masks look lovely."

"Not as lovely as yours," Jorgen said without hesitating.

Her heart seemed to fly out of her chest and soar around the arched ceiling of the ballroom of Thornbeck Castle. Jorgen Hartman, rescuer of damsels in peril, might . . . perhaps . . . love her.

But she should be ashamed of feeling joyful about such a thing! Jorgen was too good and kind, and he had seen too many tragic things in his life, for her to hurt him and break his heart. He should not love her. She should shun him, reject him now, before his heart was engaged.

But glancing up at him, she knew that her heart was in just as much danger. *Oh, dear saints in heaven.* It seemed just as likely that *she* was in love with *him*.

"How is Kathryn?" he asked.

Of course, he had no idea what she was thinking. With the mask covering half her face, she could think anything and no one would know. She felt almost as if she were someone else, someone bolder, someone who could be flirtatious and carefree. Tomorrow she could go back to being sensible, to understanding that no matter how strong and noble and kind and good Jorgen was, he was still a forester and not the person her uncle—or she—would ever choose for her to marry. But for tonight, inside this formidable castle and this beautiful, palatial ballroom, she could think outrageous thoughts and imagine the impossible.

"Kathryn is well. She is staying with Peter and Anna, as you know. She insists on sleeping in the servants' room and helping them with their work and also with the children. Allowing her to work as a servant seems to be the only way to keep her from leaving."

She peeked out at Jorgen through the eyeholes in her mask. He had no idea how many secrets she was keeping from him. Was he keeping any secrets from her? Or was he truly what he seemed: a hardworking forester, loyal to the margrave, who wrote stories and rhymes that children loved? Well educated for his station in life, he also danced well and was protective of women.

In her heart, she believed his conscience was as uncovered as his face, as untarnished as his clear blue-green eyes.

He nodded in answer to her information about Kathryn.

"There is the margrave's sister." Jorgen nodded toward a man and woman just entering the ballroom. "And that is her husband, the Earl of Augenhalt."

Odette marveled at her beauty. Even with the mask, her perfect lips and translucent skin shone in the candlelight. Her gown was pink silk, shimmering with metallic embroidery and trimmed in fur. She smiled as she greeted the other beautiful people, moving gracefully about the room.

Her husband did not smile, and he was not as handsome as she was, but he had an air of deference as he walked beside her, as if he was ruled by her wishes as he allowed her to greet whomever she chose and talk as long as she liked.

"So much beauty," Odette breathed, shaking her head.

Jorgen nodded, but he did not seem nearly as awed as she was.

Rutger stood on the other side of the ballroom. He was talking with a man. Odette wasn't sure who he was, but he looked like Mathis Papendorp, wearing a strangely shaped hat and colorful robe.

The dance ended. The swish of the dancers' shoes and hems ceased with the music. Jorgen turned to face her. "Will you do me the honor of dancing the next dance with me?"

"It would be my pleasure, my lord." She bowed formally and placed her hand in his. The touch of his fingers sent her heart to dancing, and her mind flitted to being held in his arms after he had saved her and Kathryn from The Red House. *How pleasant to be touched by Jorgen.* She might have felt a bit of conviction and guilt at such a thought, but behind her mask, she smiled flirtatiously at him, letting the warm sensations spread all through her, from her hand to her cheeks.

The music started, and he led her toward the center of the floor. The dance was slower and more complicated than the folk dances they had danced at the Midsummer festival. Fortunately Rutger had made sure she knew how to dance them by hiring her a dance master when she was younger. Was Jorgen familiar with the more formal dances?

The dance started before she had time to decide whether to ask him. He moved with confidence, and she followed his lead. Even though the dance floor was filled with beauty and color enough to dazzle any eye, Odette had no desire to look away from Jorgen as she stepped toward him, clasped his hands, then let go as they stepped back. They turned around one way, then the other way, and then came back to the center to clasp hands again.

Jorgen, in his blue brocaded cotehardie with its ermine trim, looked every inch as princely as any prince or duke or margrave at the ball. And the look in his eyes made him even more handsome.

The music and the dance stopped, and Jorgen glanced around the room. He leaned toward her and said softly, "Everyone is looking at you, the most beautiful woman here."

"I think they are looking at you, Jorgen. They are asking themselves, 'Who is that handsome prince?'"

He looked as if he didn't believe her, lifting one brow and one corner of his mouth. "Thank you, but I was being truthful."

"As was I."

"Jorgen!" Mathis strode up to Jorgen's side. "I hope you are not going to dance with this lovely swan all night."

"I had hoped I would." Jorgen winked at her.

Odette smiled at him. When she looked back at Mathis, his brows had drawn together in an angry V. Quickly she said, "I am a little tired. Perhaps Jorgen could find a place where I might sit."

Mathis still did not look pleased. "I will find you later, Odette, when you are feeling better." He took her hand and kissed it before walking away, as though he saw someone over her shoulder he wanted to talk to.

Jorgen led her away from the dancers as another song began. "There are some chairs in the gallery."

Just outside the ballroom, the gallery was a long room dimly lit by candles with many small windows along one wall. The entire opposite wall was covered by a large painting of a battle scene. Chairs were placed between the narrow windows. Odette sat in one and Jorgen sat down beside her.

"I was not actually tired." Odette glanced at Jorgen out of the corner of her eye. "I just did not feel like dancing with Mathis."

"Then you will not have to dance with him. I will tell him myself, if you want me to."

"It isn't that I do not want to dance with him. It's more that I do not want to dance . . . at this moment."

Jorgen stared at the battle scene on the wall in front of them, a pensive look on his face. "A good painting, is it not? So lifelike."

Odette turned in her chair to study it. "Yes, except for the ladies there at the edge. I do not think ladies would be at a battle."

"No, probably the artist wanted an excuse to paint something more beautiful than a battle."

"They do bring more color to the scene."

Loud laughter drifted through the doorway leading to the ballroom. She watched to see if others would intrude on them.

"Perhaps we could take a walk," Odette said without thinking first. "Oh, that is probably not possible. Where would we go, after all?"

"There is a balcony at the end of this gallery. You could get some air."

"That sounds lovely."

They both stood, and Odette placed her hand on his arm. What would he think if she slipped her arm through his? The mask was making her bold—and foolish. But she slipped her arm through his anyway.

They wandered through the deserted gallery. At the end, Jorgen opened the door to a balcony. They walked to the stone half wall and gazed down at the deep ravine at the bottom of the rocky hill that lifted the castle out of the landscape. In the distance, beyond the ravine, the town of Thornbeck winked its tiny lights, while the moon looked down over them with a peaceful white glow.

"The air is perfect tonight," Odette murmured. "Not too hot or too cool."

Jorgen turned to look at her. "Are you sure you do not want to be inside meeting all the countesses and duchesses?"

"We can go back inside in a little while. It is pleasant here." *Alone with you.* She could stay here with him all night, allowing herself to imagine what it would be like if he kissed her, if they were free to fall in love. If only she were truly a swan princess and he were truly a prince.

# 20

JORGEN COULD NOT take his eyes off Odette. The mask somehow made her even more mysterious . . . and desirable. The white feathers were oddly appropriate, hovering around her perfect face. The memory of her pressing her cheek against his chest after he had taken her and Kathryn out of The Red House was never far from his thoughts tonight.

She turned her back on the scene below the balcony and faced him. "I know your parents died in the Great Pestilence, just as mine did. But how long did you live on the streets before you went to live with the forester and his wife?"

The question jarred him from his pleasant ruminations. He ran his hand through the back of his hair and cleared his throat. "It must have been about a year, or a little less."

When he didn't say anything else, Odette's hand moved down his arm, and she slipped her hand inside his. His heart beat like a thundering of horses' hooves as she gently squeezed.

"What happened when you were on the streets? Where did you live?" she whispered.

He had to swallow before he could answer. "My sister was much younger than me. I had to take care of her. We slept in people's courtyards and gardens behind their houses when the weather was good. When it was cold or rainy, we slept in the wealthier people's stables. After Helena died, my father, the gamekeeper, found me one day, sick and lying in a little shelter I had made in the woods." He didn't like thinking about that time, how helpless he had felt. He had never told anyone any of this except his adoptive parents. But somehow it felt good to tell her.

Odette took his other hand in hers, and now she was holding both of his hands. After a short pause, she said, "When my father and mother died, the neighbors took me in. I was only five, but they made me empty chamber pots and scrub floors. They only fed me twice a day, and they gave me only pea pottage and black bread."

Odette stared down at their joined hands while she talked. "I sometimes went through people's garbage. Once I stole a meat pie from a nearby house. I shared it with another orphan I knew. And I sometimes asked other neighbors for food. The way they looked at me made me feel lowly and despised."

He hated that she had felt those feelings, and yet it bonded them together. She understood what he had been through because she had experienced the same things. For the first time in his life, he could see that the pain he felt could have a purpose.

Already very near to him, she moved a bit closer. He disengaged his hand and touched her face. Her skin was like silk, and he let his fingers glide along her jawline. Her lips parted, and he noticed the rise and fall of her chest as she breathed more rapidly. His own breath felt shallow and raspy. He leaned down. Before he could let his reason take over, he pressed his lips against hers.

A tiny sound escaped her throat, and his mind seemed to leave him entirely. He cupped her cheek in his hand and pulled her mouth full against his.

Even though her hands slipped around his neck, she had not

responded to his kiss. He pulled back. The sight of her closed eyelids and parted lips was too much for his weak restraint, and he kissed her again.

She put her hands on both sides of his face and started to kiss him back. He let urgency overtake him. Was this happening? If not, it was the best dream he'd ever had. So sweet . . . so sweet.

Wait. What would she think of him? He had no right to kiss her.

He pulled away. She laid her head against his shoulder. *Dear, sweet saints.* If the feathers in her mask and headdress hadn't been tickling his cheek, it would have been a perfect moment.

"Odette. I have been looking for you."

She stepped away from him, pressing her hands against her face.

He turned to see Rutger standing at the other end of the balcony, and Jorgen blinked to clear his thoughts. Would her uncle be furious? He had every right to be.

"Jorgen. Odette. The ball is inside."

"Yes, of course, Herr Menkels," Jorgen said.

"Odette, I have some people I want you to meet."

But instead of going with her uncle, she took hold of Jorgen's arm. "We are coming."

She held on with both hands, and Rutger waited for them to catch up. "I want you to meet the Duchess of Peisterberg," he said to Odette, not including Jorgen, "and Lady Augenhalt, as well as Lady Keiperdorf."

Jorgen might not be able to speak to her again the rest of the night, now that Rutger was taking her over.

Instead of responding to Rutger's conversation, she looked up at Jorgen, her eyes startlingly blue and luminous, as if there were tears in them. *O Father God, have I made her cry?*

But perhaps he was imagining it, for when Rutger was not

looking, she pressed her cheek against his arm before moving away and joining Rutger. As they passed from the gallery into the ball-room, she looked back at him, her eyes wide and a tender smile on her perfect lips.

Jorgen stopped in the doorway and whispered, "How can I ever win her? What must I do? What must I do to ever be worthy of her?"

⁓

Odette felt as if she were floating. She could still feel Jorgen's lips on hers, could still see the vulnerability in his eyes. He had been reluctant to speak of his past, but his trust had touched her heart. And he understood. He had the same painful memories of child-hood that she had. And unlike the children she taught, he had been saved by the gamekeeper and his wife, just as she had been saved by Rutger. And now, in just the same way as she felt driven to save the orphaned and poor children from going hungry, he felt driven to save others, like Kathryn, from the cruelties of oppression.

Her heart swelled with an emotion she had never felt before. Did she dare call it love? For the second time tonight, she suspected her heart had ignored all her warnings that falling in love with the forester was imprudent and impossible. *Oh, dear heaven, what am I to do now?*

Her hand came up and touched her lips. Would the memory of his kiss fade? Would she forget the feelings he had created inside her? *Let it never be.* She wanted to remember them forever.

Rutger had led her to a handsome woman and her equally handsome daughter. Odette blinked, trying to concentrate on what Rutger was saying. He had just presented her to them, and they were staring at her. She quickly sank into a curtsy.

She had to stop thinking about Jorgen and his kiss, at least while Rutger was having her meet all these distinguished people. Her thoughts were in a fog, but she managed to mumble appropriate responses to what they were saying to her, if their languid smiles were any indication.

Rutger took her to meet several more people, and to speak to prominent people she had met before, like Mathis Papendorp's father and mother. Several of them commented on how beautiful her mask and dress were, and she was grateful to Rutger for them. She could remember as a child wearing old, stained, and ill-fitting clothing, of people wrinkling their noses at her or otherwise making her feel like an outcast.

An earl's son asked her to dance. She almost felt as if she were being disloyal to Jorgen as she joined the young man on the floor. She tried to behave in her most elegant manner, but her heart was not in the dance, and she found herself looking around for Jorgen.

When it was over, Rutger appeared by her side. "Let me take you to get something to drink. You must be thirsty."

"I am thirsty, thank you." She followed Rutger to the opposite end of the room where a table was spread with food and drink.

"Try this, my dear. I think it will revive you." Rutger placed a goblet in her hand.

"What is it?"

"Fruit compote, I think."

It was the same red color as the drink Odette liked so much, made from the juice of boiled cherries and other fruit. As she swallowed, she took a second gulp into her mouth, then choked. The liquid burned her throat like a fire. She coughed and sputtered, trying not to spew the drink out of her mouth, with no choice but to swallow the second gulp.

"Ugh! What is that?"

"Is it not fruit compote?"

"No, indeed. I believe it is some kind of strong spirits."

"Oh dear. Is there some water?" Rutger addressed the servants waiting on the table.

A servant handed her another goblet. Odette took a sip. Tasting water, she drank several large gulps. The cool water took a bit of the sting out of her throat.

Already a warmth was spreading over her forehead. She drank some more water, hoping it would make her feel better. She had never drunk anything stronger than watered wine.

"I hope no one can smell that on my breath."

"I would not worry," Rutger said. "Perhaps you would like to lie down for a bit."

"No, I am well. I just need to eat something and then I shall feel better." She chose a gooseberry tart and took a bite, hoping it would take the taste of the strong drink out of her mouth, and the smell as well.

"Very well, but I think you should at least sit for a few moments." Rutger placed his hand under her elbow, so she let him steer her through the doorway and into a small chamber with cushioned benches.

A lady was lying down on one of the couches while a servant fanned her face. Odette sat on another one.

"Go on and lie down," Rutger said. "I shall come and make sure you are well in a few moments. And why don't you take off your mask so you won't get too warm."

Since she wanted to do as he asked and had no desire to meet any more of the aristocratic people he had been introducing her to, she pulled off the mask, lay down, and closed her eyes.

After a few moments of taking deep breaths and feeling the air on her unmasked face, she sat up. She didn't want to ruin the feathers in her hair.

She took another bite of her gooseberry tart, which she still held in her hand. The tart was rich with cream and was the best she had ever tasted. Unfortunately, Rutger had placed her goblet of water on the table out in the ballroom, but she managed to swallow the rest of the tart.

She began to feel restless. Perhaps she should go back into the ballroom. But when she looked around for her mask, she didn't see it. Where had she placed it? Had she not put it on the floor beside her? She must have, but it was not there. She bent and looked under the bench she had been lying on, but it was not there either.

Now what was she to do? She would look strange without her mask, since all the other women were wearing theirs. After looking all around the room, she still did not see it. How strange. She had no wish to stay in this room all night, and since she was feeling better, she determined to go and find Rutger and ask him if he knew what had happened to her mask.

Jorgen talked with various men as he waited for Rutger to tire of introducing Odette to everyone at the ball. When she began dancing with a young man, he tried not to feel jealous or wonder if she found him handsome or interesting. Her uncle probably wanted her to dance with someone—anyone—besides Jorgen.

After dancing with the man, Odette joined Rutger and walked over to the table set up at the end of the room with drinks and food.

"Jorgen, are you enjoying yourself?" The margrave stood beside him, leaning on his cane.

"Yes, of course, Lord Thornbeck."

The margrave frowned, with scowling brows and hardened jaw. Was that what he had looked like in battle when he was a knight and the captain of the guard? "I cannot say the same," he growled.

"You do not enjoy the music, my lord?"

"I just don't like smiling and listening to everyone say how delighted they are with everything. People at parties are insincere, and we all just stand around talking."

Jorgen couldn't help smiling. "I understand that sentiment, my lord."

"Fighting men say whatever they want, and it is never anything about being *delighted.*" He shifted his weight a bit and tapped his stick on the floor. "I came over here to ask if you would accompany us on a hunt tomorrow afternoon. At least that will give us something to do, and no one can go on and on about how delighted they are. They will be too busy chasing a stag or hind."

Jorgen suppressed another smile and nodded. "Yes, my lord." But then his heart sank at the possibility that they might not be able to find a deer to chase. The mysterious night poacher had killed so many that they were becoming harder to find. Such a thing would not sit well with the margrave, especially in the mood he was in.

"You should dance, Jorgen. You are young and able." A flash of sorrow seemed to cross his face, then disappear. "I believe that beautiful white swan wishes to dance with you."

Jorgen turned to his left to see whom the margrave was speaking of, and Odette was coming toward him, her white feathers swaying with her movements. As she drew near, the margrave was drawn away by his chancellor, and Jorgen focused all his attention on her.

"Shall we dance?" he asked.

She reached out and grasped his hand in answer, and he led her to the middle of the ballroom where another dance was about to begin.

She held on to his hand and caressed his arm. Was she trying to tell him that she did not regret their kiss?

They faced each other just as the dance began. They stepped toward each other—and she stepped quite close, lifting her face to his, making him wonder if she would kiss him right there in front of everyone.

His heart beat hard at the way her lips curved seductively. What was she trying to do to him? He had never seen her so . . . uninhibited. She almost seemed like a different person. Was it because of his kiss? What else could it be?

As she turned all the way around in the steps of the dance, her hips swayed—something he should *not* be noticing. All through the dance she continued to get closer to him than was necessary, hold his hand longer than normal, and behave in a way that made his heart beat faster.

When the dance was over, Odette clasped his hands between hers and leaned against him.

"Odette," he whispered. "I . . . I do not know if you should let your uncle see you like this."

She stared up at him, as if she was hanging on his next word.

He swallowed. "Do you want to walk out to the balcony again?"

She nodded and hugged his arm against her side.

Perhaps Odette felt his kiss was a proposal of marriage. But of course a maiden like her would not let him kiss her if she wasn't willing to marry him. His heart pounded harder as they moved toward the doorway to the gallery and slipped into the darker, deserted room.

As his eyes adjusted to the lack of light, Odette turned to him and kissed him. The kiss was over before he could respond, and she turned around and ran toward the balcony, holding up her skirt as she went.

He followed after her. He had never seen this side of her, and it felt strange. Had Odette been drinking too much wine? Even her hair looked slightly different, less full and less wavy. But it must be Odette, since she was wearing the same swan mask and headdress.

Once he reached the balcony, Odette stood at the far end, staring out at the night. As he walked toward her, she turned her head and smiled that seductive smile again. Then she turned all the way around to face him, leaning back against the railing.

"Odette." He swallowed again as he gathered his courage. "I think you must have noticed how I take every chance to be with you, even though I know your uncle doesn't think a forester is good enough for you. But I love you, Odette, and I will do anything to make you my wife."

She stepped closer to him, grasped his shoulders, pressing close, tilting her lips up to his. How could he resist bending down to kiss her?

Just as he was about to do just that, she whispered in a strange, hoarse voice, "What did you say?"

"I said, I love you. I want to marry you. Please marry me."

# 21

ODETTE STAYED CLOSE to the wall as she made her way through the ballroom. A few people noticed her and stared, no doubt wondering why she was not wearing a mask. She kept moving, thinking she saw Rutger up ahead.

The man turned. It was Rutger. She went toward him, hoping to catch his eye. But Mathis approached him and said something close to his ear, and then they both moved toward the gallery where she and Jorgen had gone before. They disappeared through the doorway.

Odette hurried toward the gallery and slipped inside. Softly she called, "Rutger." But as her eyes became accustomed to the lower light, she saw him at the other end of the gallery, slipping out onto the balcony.

How frustrating. He probably didn't even know where her mask was, but she didn't know who else to ask or what else to do, so she kept going.

Someone was speaking out on the balcony. The closer she got, the more convinced she was that it was Jorgen. Was he asking Rutger for permission to marry her? Her heart beat out of rhythm, stealing her breath. What would she do if Rutger refused him? Her thoughts were in a tangle, like a patch of thorny vines.

Odette stepped out onto the balcony, but Jorgen was not with Rutger. He was standing with a woman, standing extremely close to her, and she was wearing Odette's mask!

Jorgen leaned down to kiss her. Odette felt ill, her stomach twisting. Then Jorgen said, "I love you. I want to marry you. Please marry me."

Who was he saying these things to? Who was this woman? As soon as Jorgen said the words, the woman threw her arms around him and kissed him on the lips. And Jorgen was kissing her back most enthusiastically.

A strangled noise left her lips as she forced herself not to scream. Then she saw Rutger and Mathis standing a few feet away. Rutger must have heard her because he turned and looked at her.

Jorgen must have heard her as well. He broke away from the woman and his eyes met Odette's.

His eyes widened. "Odette?" he gasped and turned back to the girl he had been kissing. "Who are you?"

Was he pretending? Did he truly not know that the woman he had been kissing was not Odette? Had the woman tricked him by wearing her mask? And where had she found a dress so similar to her own? None of it made sense.

Suddenly the woman started running toward Odette, laughing in a high-pitched voice. She ran past Odette, through the doorway, and to the gallery. As she passed by, something touched Odette on the shoulder, then clattered to the floor. Her mask. She bent and picked it up.

"Odette." Jorgen took a few unsteady steps toward her. "I . . . I thought she was you."

But all Odette could see as she looked at him was him kissing that other woman. "Do you expect me to believe that you could not tell she was not me?" Perhaps she was being unfair to him, but . . . Her stomach twisted again.

"Come, my dear." Rutger stood before her and took her by the arm. "This man and his love affairs are not our concern. We will leave him to his folly."

She followed Rutger to the gallery, letting him place her hand on his arm.

"Wait, Odette, please."

The anguish in Jorgen's voice made her turn and look at him.

"The woman tricked me. I did not know. I thought she was you."

The lost look in his eyes made her stomach sink even lower. Her eyes burned with tears, and a searing pain stabbed her like a knife, but Rutger urged her on, through the gallery.

"Odette." Jorgen was following them.

"Who was she?" Odette turned and faced him, in spite of Rutger urging her to keep going forward. "Why would she do such a thing?"

"It is a complete mystery to me. Please believe me. I could never love anyone but you." His voice was strained.

Odette's heart stopped. He loved her? But how could he not know that other woman was not her? It hurt that he could mistake someone else for her and actually kiss that other person.

"I hope you do not believe this, Odette." Rutger again pulled gently on her arm. "Let us go."

"Odette . . ." He held his hand toward her, palm up, in a gesture of supplication. "Please."

She still could not rid herself of the image of him kissing the other woman. It rose up every time she blinked. "I do not wish to speak of it anymore."

"We shall go at once," Rutger said as they continued down the long gallery toward the ballroom. "I shall send for the carriage."

Odette said nothing, feeling numb all over except for the ache in her heart and the burning sensation in her nose as she struggled to hold back tears.

She heard no more from Jorgen as she passed through the rest of the gallery, through the ballroom, and into the front hall to wait for Rutger's carriage.

"God, why?" she whispered. Why must she be in love with a man she could not marry? And now she had this painful memory of him kissing another woman and declaring his love for her. A flood of pain washed over her.

⁓

The despair in Jorgen's heart turned to anger. Someone had deliberately tricked him. But why? He rushed out the door and into the ballroom.

He glanced around. Where was that woman, the one who had so brazenly pretended to be Odette? He must find her. He must force her to admit the truth of who she was, of what she had done. He must force her to confess in front of Odette before she left.

He started through the crowds of people, searching everywhere. She had been wearing a dress like Odette's, but he couldn't see her anywhere. He went from one end of the ballroom to the other. He looked everywhere he could, but she obviously didn't wish to be found.

It seemed there would be no outlet for his anger. But didn't Odette understand that he had been tricked? He never would have knowingly kissed another woman. But the truth was, he *had* kissed another woman, and in front of Odette.

The thought of it made him sick. The memory would forever

be in Odette's mind. And the pain in her eyes would forever be ingrained in his.

He stared out at the joyful dancers and the people talking to each other as if Jorgen's hopes had not just been crushed. And what of Odette? What must she think of him? First he'd kissed her, and then he'd kissed someone else, like some unbridled cur.

Somehow he had to show her that he did not go around kissing women indiscriminately. He just had no idea how.

The carriage was dark as pitch, even with the lamp attached just outside. Odette could cry, as long as she was quiet, and Rutger wouldn't know. She propped her elbow against the side of the carriage, her hand resting against her cheek, so she could wipe the tears away without drawing attention.

"Odette, I am sorry you had to see Jorgen kissing that other woman, but perhaps it is for the best."

Odette took a deep breath to dispel the tears enough so he would not hear them in her voice. When she trusted herself to speak, she said, "I believe Jorgen was telling the truth when he said the woman deliberately tricked him. She must have stolen my mask when I was lying down. Why else would she steal my mask? And her dress was similar to mine. It is understandable that Jorgen would think she was me." But it still made tears return to her eyes that he had.

Rutger did not say anything for several moments. "I have always thought you wise beyond your years, and I never wanted you to throw yourself away on someone who did not deserve you. But Jorgen Hartman . . . He is only the forester. You could marry any unmarried man in Thornbeck. Think of Mathis Papendorp.

He is a good sort of man. Do you not think so? He would never treat you viciously or deny you anything your heart desired."

She fought back the tears again to say, "Do you want me to marry Mathis?"

He sighed. "I do not want to tell you who to marry, Odette. But I do believe you would have a good life with Mathis."

No other guardian—no other father, for that matter—would ever give so much freedom of choice to their ward or daughter. Rutger had been so good to her, and now that she was one and twenty, of course he wanted her to be married and settled.

Why didn't she marry Mathis? Rutger was right that Mathis would give her whatever her heart desired, to the best of his ability. Besides, people didn't normally fall in love until after they were married anyway. But Jorgen . . . How could she forget his kiss? How could she ignore the longing, deep in her heart, for him to love her and to love him in return?

But wasn't that foolish? Once he found out she was the poacher . . . Was she not being childish in wanting something she could never have? Wouldn't it be kinder to marry Mathis and let Jorgen find someone else?

Another tear flowed down her cheek, and she didn't bother wiping it away.

~~~

Jorgen and the gamekeeper rode just behind the margrave on the hunt the next day, in order to advise him of the best hunting spots. All of his highborn guests who were staying a few days at the castle were along for the hunt. Unfortunately, they were having difficulty finding any deer at all. The margrave was scowling.

Jorgen sat on the brown gelding, searching the undergrowth

for signs of a deer and praying that a deer would jump out of the bushes. If not, he might lose everything.

He had already lost Odette.

A heaviness filled his chest, the same heaviness that had settled there when Odette saw him kissing another girl. If only he could go back. If only he had realized the woman was not Odette. If only he had not kissed her and declared his love for that imposter.

There had to be some sinister reason that woman had stolen Odette's mask. What it was, he could not fathom, but he had a strange suspicion that Rutger had something to do with it. Could he so object to Odette falling in love with and marrying Jorgen that he would send a woman to trick him? Rutger was the person who had led Odette into that small room near the food and drink. That must have been where Odette had taken off her mask and it had been stolen. That was the last time he had seen her with it.

Rutger must be behind it.

Jorgen was *not* sorry he had kissed Odette. But he supposed it was that kiss that had led him to kiss the other girl. His mind had been clouded by his desire to make Odette love him the way he loved her . . . by desire for Odette. It was at least partially—mostly—his own fault. How could she ever love him now?

*I will not give up, God. So do not let her fall in love with anyone else. And raise me up, somehow, in her eyes.*

One of the men in the party lifted a bow and aimed it at the ground, then shot. "Got it!"

"What was it?" someone asked.

"A hare. If we cannot find deer, we can at least kill something."

Jorgen's neck burned. He felt responsible for everyone's dissatisfaction. *I pray, O Lord, let me catch that poacher. Please.*

# 22

THE WIDE-EYED FACES of the children outside the town wall as they listened to her teach her lesson lifted Odette's heart a bit from where it had sunk. She kept glancing up, looking for Jorgen, as the lesson progressed. But when the lesson was over and he still had not come, her heart sank to the pit of her stomach again.

She could still close her eyes and feel his lips on hers. But remembering him kissing that other girl dispelled the pleasant sensations and sent a jolt of pain through her chest.

What had she been thinking to allow him to kiss her? But what she really longed to know was, would he ever kiss her again?

Odette gave out the usual hugs to those children who always seemed to crave her attention and affection. But her thoughts were on Jorgen. Would he avoid her now?

"You sent for me, Lord Thornbeck?" Jorgen joined the margrave in the banqueting hall of Thornbeck Castle.

"Sit down, Jorgen." The margrave had a tense look on his face, which made the boulder in Jorgen's chest even heavier. "I am sure you remember how disastrous our hunt was yesterday. Even the dogs were unable to scent a deer." He leaned forward. "I need you to find out who is poaching the king's deer. If you cannot do this one task, I will be forced to find someone who can."

The margrave sank back in his chair. "I have sent for someone who is excellent at tracking. He should arrive next week. In the meantime . . ." He fixed him with a hard stare. "This poacher would shoot you if he thought he could get away with it, I have no doubt. It is time to put him and his black market out of business. I want you to find this poacher, and I want you to have no qualms about shooting him."

"Yes, my lord."

The next morning Odette was awakened by Heinke coming into her room. "Mistress Odette. There is a little boy named Hanns here to see you."

"Hanns?" Odette raised herself to sitting, forcing her eyes open.

"Yes. He is crying and begging to see you."

Odette grabbed a roomy underdress, pulled it over her head, and scrambled out of bed. She hurried down to find little Hanns standing at the back door and wiping his face on his ragged sleeve.

"Hanns, what is wrong?"

"Mama is sick. She says she thinks she's dying." Another tear slipped down his dirty face. "She has not gotten out of bed in two days, not even to go to the privy." His hands were trembling, and his cheeks were pale and sunken.

"When was the last time you ate? Come to the kitchen and I will get you something." She led him into the stone room and picked him up and sat him on a stool at Cook's counter.

Cook brought him some bread and butter, cheese, and cold

pork. He started stuffing the food in his mouth faster than he could chew it.

"Not too fast or you'll choke." Odette brought him a cup of water, but he ignored it as he continued to pick up the food and push more into his already overstuffed cheeks.

Tears pricked her eyes. "When was the last time you ate some of my deer meat, Hanns?"

He chewed and chewed and finally swallowed. "The last time you brought it to our house."

"But that was weeks ago!"

He looked at her with wide eyes, stuffing his mouth again.

"Have the boys been bringing anyone else any meat?"

Hanns shook his head. "We thought you ceased hunting."

Her heart stopped.

"I came to ask," Hanns said, after swallowing noisily, "if you could give me some money to get the doctor to come and save my mother." Tears welled up in his eyes again.

"Of course I will." Odette asked Cook to pack up some food for Hanns to take with him while she ran upstairs to fetch some money. As she hurried, she noticed the fine tapestry that hung at the top of the stairs was no longer there. When had it been taken down?

Heinke was passing through the corridor, and Odette stopped her. "Heinke, what happened to the tapestry that was here?"

Her eyes grew round as fear flickered across her face. She shrugged. "I do not know."

"And what about the Oriental vase that was always downstairs?"

Heinke shook her head. "Perhaps Master Rutger knows." She dropped a tiny curtsy and hastened down the corridor.

A feeling of dread ripped through Odette as she hurried the rest of the way to her room. She fetched the small purse of coins that she kept hidden in a secret compartment in her trunk. Thank goodness it was still there. She poured out enough money for a doctor and a little extra, put her purse back in its hiding place, and ran back down the stairs. Next she called their servant Sigfried and asked him to go with Hanns to fetch the doctor.

Odette hugged Hanns tightly, then sent him on his way with a promise to check on him and bring some venison as soon as she was able.

As she watched him hurry off, she whispered, "Oh, God, what is happening here?" Was someone stealing valuable items from their home? The venison she was shooting? She had to find out what was going on.

⁓

As Jorgen stood beside the fountain in the town square, his friend, Dieter, walked toward him with a big smile on his face.

"Jorgen! So good to see you." Dieter clapped him on the shoulder.

They talked and asked about the health of their families. "I have a request to make of you, Dieter. You were always a shrewd ally when we were boys, and I have need of a pair of shrewd eyes."

Dieter and Jorgen sat on the side of the fountain while people milled all around them, buying and selling in the *Marktplatz*.

"Someone has been selling poached meat at the back of The Red House. And there is a poacher who has been taking so many of the deer from Thornbeck Forest that they are becoming scarce. I must find this poacher and capture him."

"What can I do, Jorgen?"

"I want you to help me catch who is selling the poached meat. If you can discover who is behind this black market, I believe he will lead us to the poacher."

Jorgen discussed with him the days the black market was operating. "I also need you to track Rutger Menkels and find out what he does every day. Follow him when he leaves his house early every morning, and tell me where he goes and who he sees."

Dieter readily accepted the quest, and they agreed to meet again the next day at the same time and place.

Jorgen felt a little stab of guilt when he asked Dieter to follow Odette's uncle, but if Rutger had schemed to have someone steal Odette's mask and trick Jorgen into making a fool of himself with the imposter, then he and Odette both needed to know. And if he was not responsible, Jorgen hoped Odette would never find out that he had asked Dieter to follow him.

# 23

ODETTE WAS RUNNING. *Behind her she could hear a large stag crashing toward her, getting closer and closer. Over her shoulder she could see it was the stag she had injured weeks ago. Her arrow was sticking out of his haunch.*

*She kept running. He let out a loud snort, so close she could feel his hot breath on the back of her neck. She tried to make her legs move faster, but they were weighed down by something thick and sticky around her ankles.*

*Suddenly she tripped. She fell on her hands and chin, and her teeth snapped together. She covered her head with her arms, but the stag slammed his antlers into her back.*

Odette awoke with a gasp, pushing herself up with her hands. It was only a dream . . . only a dream.

It had seemed so real. Her jaw ached as if her teeth really had slammed together. But it was not real. The stag she had injured—and which Jorgen had been forced to put out of his misery—he was not still alive. He was not goring her in the back. It was only a dream.

"O Father God," Odette whispered, "I do not want to do this anymore." It was getting harder and harder to find deer to kill, and she simply was tired of it. "God, what am I to do? Help me."

She saw the pinched face of Hanns and the rest of the children, hungry and unsmiling. She couldn't let them down, could she?

She forced herself to get out of bed and put on her hunting clothes. She had wanted to stay awake and talk to Rutger, to confront him about what was happening to the deer she had been killing and also about the missing vase and tapestry, but he had not come home at his usual time, and she had fallen asleep. But it was dark now, and she had to go see if she could find a deer. For Hanns.

Half an hour later, she was stalking through the trees. She kept an arrow nocked and ready, for she had seen a deer only a moment before, barely visible between the leaves of a tree. She wanted to get a good shot at it since she couldn't afford to lose any more arrows and didn't want to wound any more deer.

She crept quite close, her feet soundless as she moved carefully. The deer also moved forward, bending toward the ground, then lifting its slender head. It stood motionless while Odette took careful aim. She was so close she aimed for the spot on its head that would kill it instantly. She let the arrow fly, and it found its mark. The deer fell to the ground.

As the boys swarmed to prepare it to be taken out of the forest, she heard one of them murmur, "Amazing shot," and shake his head.

Few people would ever know of her skill with a bow and arrow. But the food she was providing for the poor was what she was most proud of, and now she wasn't sure if the deer she had been killing were even going to feed the poor. What was happening to her kills? She would make sure part of this meat went to Hanns. She had the boys wrap up a big share of it and help her sling it over her shoulder as she trudged toward the little hovel Hanns shared with his mother.

⌒

"What did you discover?" Jorgen approached Dieter at the fountain the next day.

"Rutger is an interesting person." Dieter's lips twisted in a wry frown as he remained standing. "He went to the corner of Roemer and Butcher's Guild Strasse and waited for several minutes, as if he was looking for someone. Mathis Papendorp walked up and they talked for a few minutes. Then they went their separate ways."

"Mathis Papendorp?" Now that he thought about it, Mathis had been at the ball as well, lurking in the shadows with Rutger. Why hadn't he thought of that before? Maybe they had schemed together to have another woman trick him into kissing her, and they made sure Odette was there to see it. Of course Rutger would rather his niece marry Mathis, who was wealthy and influential, than marry Jorgen, who was merely a forester. But even though he had never thought of Rutger as the sort of man to do something so underhanded, Jorgen could easily imagine Mathis working to persuade Rutger to help him undermine Jorgen's character in Odette's eyes.

"Did he go anywhere else?"

"Yes. It was still very early in the morning, and he went to The Red House."

Jorgen blinked. "The Red House?"

"He went in the back door by way of the alley. I was afraid to try to follow him in. He would see me if I did. So I waited outside."

"Did he leave with anything, like a bundle?"

"No. He stayed for several minutes, then came back out."

"But today was not a black-market day," Jorgen said. "Where did he go after that?"

"He went to the storehouse near the north gate. Everyone there was bowing and showing deference to him so I assumed he owned it."

"Yes, I believe he does."

"But he also met three young men, just boys around thirteen or fourteen, and spoke to them for several minutes. He gave them each some money."

"Did you hear anything he said to them?"

"I tried to get close enough, but he was speaking too quietly."

"What did the boys look like?"

"Ordinary, their clothing rather poor, and they were all rather thin. After he gave them money, they left and Rutger went inside the storehouse. When I left to come here, he was still there."

Could the boys be the ones who had accompanied the poacher? Could Rutger be behind the poaching? It seemed strange but possible, especially if he was involved with the black market at The Red House. Of course, Odette's uncle could have been at The Red House for other reasons . . .

Jorgen sat on the side of the fountain and rubbed his forehead. He had never suspected Rutger of having anything to do with the poaching problem or the black market. Could he be the mysterious poacher? Possibly, but it seemed more likely that he was the one selling the poached meat at the black market. Could Rutger even be the owner of The Red House?

Poor Odette! If her uncle was involved with such reprehensible deeds, she would be devastated. He had to be sure before he said anything to her about it.

"Do you wish me to follow him again tomorrow?" Dieter looked eager to continue his spying, especially when Jorgen handed him two coins.

"No. Tomorrow I want you to follow our old friend Mathis

Papendorp. Find out whatever you can. Then meet me the day after tomorrow here at the fountain."

⁓

Heinke helped Odette get properly dressed, then Odette set out for the storehouse where Rutger conducted his business affairs. When she reached it, she asked the nearest man where her uncle was, and he pointed him out, talking with a man at the other end of the building.

Odette walked to him. "I need to speak with you."

Rutger took one look at her and his expression changed. "Very well. There is an office where we can speak in private."

They walked across the large building, only partially filled by bundles and trunks and stacks of crude wooden boxes. He took her to a narrow little room in one corner of the building, led her inside, and closed the door.

There were a couple of stools and a table with an inkwell and writing implements and some paper. Tiny shelves covering one wall were stuffed with papers. Neither Odette nor Rutger sat.

As she faced him, her breath started to come fast, her chest rising and falling. "What is happening?"

"What do you mean?" His eyes were shadowy and distant.

"What are you doing with the meat I have been providing? That meat was supposed to go to the children. What have you done, Rutger?" Tears of anger pricked her eyes.

"I do not understand."

"Do not pretend you don't understand! The children have not been receiving any meat. You told me you would deliver it."

"Please lower your voice, Odette. I don't want any—"

"What are you doing with the deer meat?" Odette spoke

slowly, pausing after each word. "You are selling it, aren't you?" Her voice rose dangerously high as the tears continued to well up. "How could you?"

"Odette, I am sorry." Now tears were swimming in Rutger's eyes. She'd never seen him cry. He cleared his throat, looking away from her, staring at the wall. He cleared his throat again and looked down at the floor. "I . . . I am in debt."

Her stomach twisted and the breath left her lungs in a rush.

"I did not intend to do it. My last two ships sank with all the goods I had paid to bring here. And then bandits stole the goods on the last caravan from the Orient. I was desperate, so I sold some of the meat. I only meant to do it once, but things went from bad to worse. The demand for the meat was so great and my debts were so pressing . . . I kept selling it."

Her chest ached and her face felt hot. "That is despicable." The pain in his expression softened her. "Why didn't you tell me you were in trouble? I never would have let you pay for that elaborate gown and mask for the margrave's masquerade ball."

"I didn't. Mathis Papendorp paid for it."

"What?" Odette stared at him. Had everything she'd believed about her uncle been a lie? Did she even know him at all? But how much money Rutger did or didn't have wasn't what she was most concerned about.

"How could you do it? How could you take their meat? What about the children? How long have you been selling the meat that was intended for them?"

Rutger turned aside from her so she couldn't see his face. He reached up to wipe his eyes. "Five or six months. I told myself it was only for a little while, but . . . I know there is nothing I can say that will make you not hate me."

Odette closed her eyes and covered her face with her hands.

All that work, all those nights of hunting . . . And it had not been for the children at all. She felt betrayed, as if a knife had been plunged into her back.

"This . . . This is something I never would have imagined you were capable of. You must have been desperate"—Odette chose her words carefully, trying to keep any bitterness out of her voice but failing—"to do such a thing." What could she say? That she was disappointed in him? That was far from adequate.

"I know. I am sorry, Odette. I never imagined . . . that I would . . . I'm sorry."

"How much money do you owe?" Her voice was hoarse as she held back tears, held back rage and despair at what he had stolen from the children—and from her. "Do you have any shipments or caravans on their way here that you could sell and pay your debt?"

He shook his head. "It is as if heaven conspired against me. I've never known such bad fortune. The two ships that were lost were new and very seaworthy. The caravan that was attacked had been well guarded and armed. I cannot understand how it could have happened." Rutger still was not facing her. "There is only one thing that can save our house."

Odette's stomach sank. It must be something truly terrible. Finally she asked, "What is it?"

"If you marry Mathis, he says he will pay all my debts and buy new ships."

She should have known. Heat seemed to rise into the top of her head like the steam in a covered kettle. She turned and walked out of his office.

Odette walked down the street, her head down, her vision blurred. She bumped into several people, but she didn't care. The walk home had never seemed so long before. She hadn't felt this alone since Rutger came for her, all those years ago.

She climbed the stairs to her bed and lay across it, too exhausted to even cry.

⁓

Jorgen left Dieter to walk to Peter and Anna's home. Since Odette said Kathryn was living and working with the servants, and it was just after midday, he hoped to catch her in the kitchen.

Jorgen knocked on the back door of the Vorekens' kitchen, which was behind the house in a detached stone building. The door opened and Kathryn stood staring at him.

"May I talk to you, Kathryn?"

She opened the door wider. She appeared to be alone in the large one-room kitchen. Jorgen stepped inside.

The heat of the room raised perspiration on his forehead almost immediately. It was a warm summer day, but live coals smoldered in the kitchen hearth as a large piece of meat slowly roasted on the spit and a pot bubbled beside it, hanging from a hook over the red-hot embers.

Kathryn pointed to a stool as she sat on another one, wiping her hands on her apron.

"I wanted to speak with you for a moment. Kathryn . . ." How would he ask her about her time at The Red House when he would not wish to upset her or drive her back there? "I know Peter and Anna are pleased, as we all are, that you are here with them instead of at The Red House. But I need you to tell me something." He hesitated for a moment. "Do you remember ever seeing Rutger at The Red House? Or did Agnes mention his name, ever?"

Kathryn looked aside, staring at the fire in the large hearth. She shook her head. "Rutger has been good to me. He made sure my little brothers had a good place to live, and he tried to help me. I do not wish to cause him any trouble."

"Of course not. I understand. But I need to know for Odette's sake. Please, tell me the truth. It is very important."

Her jaw clenched, flexing. He waited for her to speak again. Finally she said, "Rutger did come to The Red House, but not through the front door where the other men came in. I remember one of the maids coming to fetch Agnes a few times and saying, 'Rutger is in the back room.' Agnes would always go directly to meet him."

"Do you know why he went there?"

Kathryn shook her head.

"Thank you, Kathryn."

She just stared at him and he left.

Jorgen walked the short distance down the street to Odette's house and knocked on the door. A servant let him in, and as he waited for the servant to tell Odette he was there, he stood, trying to prepare himself for her anger and scorn. After all, the last time he'd seen her had been just after she witnessed him kissing another woman. Would she be angry? Would she throw him out?

The servant returned. "I am sorry, Herr Hartman, but Fräulein Odette says she cannot see you now. She is very tired and is sleeping."

"She said that?" The air went out of him, as if someone had punched him in the gut. "Is she sick?"

"No."

Jorgen nodded his thanks to the servant and walked out.

Why would she still be asleep if she was not sick? She was avoiding him, but how could he blame her? Perhaps it was best that he not yet mention what he was learning about her beloved uncle, who did not appear to be the man they all thought him to be. It would certainly hurt Odette even more.

When Rutger came home that night, Odette was waiting for him. "Are you responsible for the woman who stole my mask and tricked Jorgen into kissing her?"

He sat at the table, where the servants were beginning to serve the evening meal. He still looked humble, but not as much as when she had confronted him at his storehouse.

"That was not my idea," he said.

"Then it was Mathis's."

He hesitated. "He only did it because he loves you and was desperate to make you forget about Jorgen."

Odette imagined herself slamming her fist on the table and accusing her uncle of lying. Of course he knew it was Mathis. But she restrained herself. After all, he was her uncle. Even now, he wasn't demanding she marry Mathis, even though it would solve all his problems, and he would be well within his rights as her guardian to ask that she do so.

The servants brought in the bread and the main dish of fish and eel stew and then left the room. Even though she normally liked the dish, tonight she ignored the food. "Why have you not asked me to marry Mathis? Why allow him to carry out some elaborate scheme to make me dislike Jorgen? You could at least be honest now that I know everything."

Rutger only met her gaze for a moment before looking down at his food. "As I said, that was Mathis's idea. I had hoped you would see that he could solve all our problems and give you what you wanted—food for the children."

"I thought *I* was providing food for the children." The undercurrent of bitterness was in her voice again. "Besides that, Mathis cannot give me what I want." *Because I don't love him.*

"Do you think the forester can give you beautiful clothes and tutors and books? Mathis can. I understand Jorgen Hartman is a well-built, handsome man, but do not allow lust to rule your thinking."

"Lust? You accuse me of lust?" Odette hoped he could see the revulsion on her face. "You may accuse me of many things rightfully—I am sometimes reckless and unthinking, and I am a lawbreaker, as you well know—but do you dare call me lustful?"

"Perhaps I overstated. But you fancy you are in love with him, do you not? For a man, it would be lust. For an inexperienced young woman like you, Odette, it is only infatuation. But please, for your sake, take care that you do not allow your infatuation and supposed love for this man to overcome your good sense. He is only a forester, after all, and he did kiss another girl. Whether he believed she was you or was only doing what men naturally do, I do not know, and neither do you."

Odette felt her breath coming fast and heat rising into her cheeks. "After what you have done, do you dare try to cast Jorgen in a bad light?"

"I am only trying to help you see everything more objectively. Think of what is best for you *and* the children, Odette. Think of how you would feel if you threw yourself away on a man of low stature and then found out he was not the man you had thought he was."

Odette kept her lips tightly sealed.

Rutger lifted his hands toward her, palms up. "I know you are angry. And I have probably lost all credibility with you, after what I did by taking the meat and selling it. You were right. It was and is despicable. But as your uncle, I have always cared about you and tried to take care of you. If you cannot bring yourself to marry Mathis, even though he is quite in love with you and is capable of giving you everything you could desire, I will try to understand. And if you truly have considered the cost of marrying Jorgen and still want to marry him, then I will not stop you."

The cost of marrying Jorgen. He meant that the children would go hungry—as they had been for the last six months, thanks to him. And that Rutger would lose everything and be destitute. And that Odette would suddenly have a lifestyle far below what she had known for the past twelve years.

Odette stood up from the table. "I am not hungry. I think I will go up to my room now."

Rutger's face looked downcast. "Of course, my dear. Will you go out hunting tonight?"

"Yes. And I will deliver any meat I kill myself."

There would be a full moon tonight, which would make her more visible to Jorgen if he was out looking for the poacher.

As she made her way up the steps, her mind flashed back to the dream she'd had the night before, of the angry stag wanting to rip her apart, no doubt for all the suffering she had caused him and the other deer in the forest.

She had to remember who she was hunting for. She must not be squeamish, must not allow herself to become weak now. She would not let them down.

The person she had depended on for twelve years had betrayed her. And yet, after all he had done for her, she couldn't hate him. And now he needed her to marry Mathis.

Marrying Mathis made sense. It would solve all their problems. Except her problem of wanting Jorgen.

But it hurt too much to think about that.

Odette stalked through the trees, her arrow nocked and ready. With every step she took she reminded herself that for the last six months, the poor children had not gotten the meat she had hunted and killed for them. They had gone hungry. But tonight she would find and kill a deer for them. And she would take it to them herself. Tomorrow at least some of them would eat well.

She had no patience to sit and wait at a clearing tonight. With the full moon shining overhead, she would find a trail, she would stalk her prey, and she would not fail to bring down a deer.

She thought she heard a sound, a slight rustling. She studied the leaves to her right. All seemed peaceful and still. There. Something shook the leaves, a bit of movement. Odette stared harder. Was it her imagination? No, there it was again. Silently, she turned her body to face that direction, lifting her bow and arrow. Another movement, the flash of an eye through the leaves, and there was the partial outline of the deer's head. Odette aimed and let the arrow fly.

The deer jumped, but the arrow had found its mark. The animal made two quick leaps, then moved to the side and fell.

The boys ran forward to finish it off and dress it. Odette no longer trusted them, however. She knelt beside them and helped them cut up the venison for easier travel. When they had slung the pieces over their shoulders, Odette led them out of the woods to the small area just outside the town gate where the poor had built their makeshift houses. Odette knocked on doors, or what passed for doors, on four different shacks, waking the occupants and giving them a portion of the meat. Then she and her men went back into the forest for more.

Before the night was over, Odette had shot three deer, helped dress them, and delivered them.

By the time she got home, she could barely put one foot in front of the other. She practically crawled up the stairs to her room. Peeling off the bloodstained leather leggings and tunic, she collapsed in bed and fell asleep.

# 24

The next morning Jorgen was walking through Thornbeck Forest, looking for signs of deer tracks and other evidence of deer in that section of the forest. He often created stories or rhymes in his head as he went about his work. But today he couldn't seem to stop replaying the scenes of the last few days.

He had to remember that Rutger was Odette's uncle and she thought highly of him. He was the man who had taken care of her, but was he also the man who was behind the poaching and the black market?

Jorgen wanted to tell her, to warn her that her uncle may not be the man she had thought he was. If and when he did manage to tell her, would she believe him? He should not feel offended if she trusted her uncle more, especially after Jorgen had kissed another woman.

He longed to make her trust him again. Knowing she thought badly of him made him feel desperate but helpless—not a good feeling.

Forcing himself to focus on his job, he bent to examine some deer feces on the ground, trying to determine how fresh it was. He looked around more closely now. More was nearby, even more recent. Standing up straight, he spied some branches where the leaves had been nipped off. Deer had been here, more than one and probably less than an hour ago, which was an encouraging sign. But what he was hoping to find was a sign of the poacher. He didn't have much time to capture him. It was only a matter of days before the tracker the margrave had sent for would arrive.

As he started to lean down again, a shrill whistle pierced the air just as something sliced across the top of his left shoulder. An arrow struck the tree behind him.

Jorgen sank to the ground, lying flat. Someone was shooting at him.

He raised himself to a squat and searched the trees. "Who is there? Who dares shoot at the margrave's forester?" Anger lent a hard edge to his voice. He reached over his shoulder and took his bow and an arrow, and in a moment, he was ready to shoot. "Who is there?"

His shoulder was burning, but he didn't take time to assess the wound. "Identify yourself now or I'll shoot!"

A noise came from the same direction as the arrow, like someone crashing through the brush. Jorgen raised his bow but he could make out nothing. Soon the noise died away.

Jorgen went after him. He ran as fast as he could. Dodging tree trunks and getting slapped and snatched at by the vines and branches and thorns, he tried to catch a glimpse of the archer. After several minutes, he was near the edge of the forest. There was a clearing between the forest and the town wall. But when he reached the clearing, no one was there. He stood still, trying to slow his breathing so he could listen. Where had the archer gone?

Jorgen looked all around. His breathing and heartbeat slowed to normal, but he still could neither see nor hear anyone. Even the birds were silent.

He became aware again of the burning sensation in his

shoulder. He turned his head to see the torn leather and the blood oozing out, creating a dark patch on his mantle. Had the poacher been trying to frighten him? Or was he trying to kill him and missed his mark? The wound didn't appear to be very deep, but it filled him with rage.

He didn't care if the poacher was Rutger himself. Jorgen would do whatever he needed to do to stop this poacher once and for all. The moon would be full again tonight, and Jorgen would stay out all night looking for him. And he would not hesitate to shoot him.

~⌒~

Odette let her mind wander as she stared at her favorite tapestry, which hung on the wall next to her bed. The woman in the tapestry was obviously wealthy, as she held a falcon on her wrist and rode a sidesaddle on a beautiful white horse with a gray mane. Her head was tilted to the side, a tiny, secretive smile on her lips. Noblemen rode all around her, and dogs ran beside the horses' legs.

Odette had often imagined what it would be like to be that lady. She must hold a high position, as she was allowed to go hunting with the men. She had her own falcon and her own horse, so she was wealthy. Confidence flowed from her posture and her expression. That lady never woke in the night worrying that someday she would be poor and would have to rummage through other people's garbage to find food. That lady never felt betrayed by the one person she had depended on. That lady never worried that some helpless, innocent child would go hungry because of her incompetence. That lady was loved and protected and admired, and because she was married to someone with lots of wealth, her future was secure.

Heinke's slippers came swishing up the stairs and she peeked inside Odette's open door. "Fräulein, someone is here to see you. Mathis Papendorp."

Odette stood and smoothed out her skirt. "Thank you, Heinke. I'll be there in a moment." She rinsed her mouth out with water and chewed on a mint leaf for a few seconds before spitting it out and hurrying down the stairs.

Mathis stood, fumbling with his large sleeves, which were all the fashion now among the wealthier townspeople. "Odette," he said, smiling. "You look beautiful this afternoon."

"Thank you, Mathis. You look . . . fashionable."

"My dear." Apparently her greeting had set him at ease because his smile grew larger and less wavering. He took her hand and kissed it. "Thank you for seeing me."

"I want to know why you had a woman dress like me, steal my mask, and trick Jorgen into kissing her." She hadn't intended to blurt it out quite so bluntly, but she was glad to get it out in the open.

"Why, I . . ." He looked sheepish. "I don't—"

"Do not tell me you don't know what I am talking about. I know you did it. And Rutger probably helped you."

"Odette, please forgive me." He got down on one knee and gazed up at her. "I was so desperate. I wanted to marry you, but I was afraid you were in love with Jorgen. I know it was wrong, but I love you so completely, so madly."

"You had no right to deceive Jorgen in that way. He is a good man."

"You are right. If you can think of any way for me to make it up to him, I will do it. Only please end my suffering by saying you will marry me. You shall be my own pampered darling for the rest of your life if only you will say yes."

Staring down at his pleading face, she had an unaccountable

urge to laugh. She stopped herself. Would it be so bad to marry Mathis? She would at least have the joy of knowing she was able to feed the children, and she could do it lawfully, without risking her life. She would also have the comfort of knowing she had saved her uncle from losing everything.

With her skin prickling all over and a dreamlike fog around her, she asked, "Would you be willing to help the poor?"

"Would I be willing to what?"

"If I marry you, you will help my uncle recover his fortune?"

"*Ja, ja*, of course."

"Would you also be willing to feed the poor, especially the poor children of Thornbeck, and make sure they do not starve?"

"My darling, if you wish it, I will. You have my word."

"Then, yes, I will marry you."

Mathis sprang to his feet and clasped her hand with both of his, kissing it passionately. "I shall have the banns cried this Sunday. We can be married in three weeks."

Her face was still prickling like a thousand tiny blades of grass were touching her skin. She watched, as if she were still in a dream, as Mathis hurried from the room, bouncing and crying, "Hurrah!"

Odette merely stared after him, overwhelmed with numbness.

⁓

Jorgen had bandaged his shoulder himself, not wishing to alarm his mother. Now he prepared himself for a hunt. After donning a new tunic and leather shoulder cape, he placed extra arrows in his quiver. He kissed his mother on the cheek and went out just as twilight was beginning to fall.

Jorgen had met Dieter earlier in the day at the fountain. He had followed Mathis this time and had met him at his place of business. By flattering him, he convinced Mathis to show him around his own storehouse, which was not far from Rutger's.

"He showed me various goods—spices, fabrics, carpets—stored there, but there was one section of the goods that was covered with tarps. When I asked him about those, he said he was holding those until later. I asked, 'Holding them for what? For whom?' He would not tell me, but I think if I keep at it, he will eventually. He dearly loves to boast, and he is very proud of whatever he has under those tarps."

Now Jorgen used his walking staff to slash at a bush in his path.

Jorgen was fairly certain Rutger was behind the poaching and the black market, but he couldn't prove it yet. When the truth was known—and truth always had a way of making itself known—Odette would be hurt. What would she do if Rutger was found guilty of these crimes? He would no doubt be severely punished, be stripped of his wealth, and Odette might have nothing and nowhere to go. And that would be where Mathis would come in. Mathis could give her every material luxury, and he might even be able to prevent her uncle from suffering the most severe punishment.

She would be foolish not to marry him.

Regardless of whether she married Mathis, Odette had suffered enough in her childhood. Her kindness and goodness to the poor must make her worthy of God's special care. And yet, how could she be saved from this inevitable pain and grief? For Jorgen was determined to capture this poacher who was involved with Rutger and employed by him. Then both Rutger and his poacher would have to pay dearly. And if either of them had killed Jorgen's father, the margrave would have them executed.

Jorgen moved more quietly through the trees, pausing every few steps to listen for any man-made noise.

After a few hours, he had not heard or seen anything out of place. There was the occasional rustle of leaves from a small animal, a hare or squirrel or nesting pheasant. He yawned, then pinched his arms to wake himself up. He wanted to catch this poacher much more than he wanted to sleep.

As he stood listening to the still night air, he heard a sound. He peered through the trees and saw a young hart with his head held high, also listening and perhaps sniffing the air for predators.

He was a sleek, healthy yearling, and he soon stretched his neck down to feed on the grass. A moment later, he lifted his graceful head again, then bounded away. That was when Jorgen caught sight of a shadowy, leather-clad figure holding a bow and arrow ready but pointed to the ground.

Jorgen did not hesitate. He nocked an arrow, pulled it back, and aimed for the poacher's left arm. He sent it shooting through the night toward its target. Jorgen grabbed another arrow as he heard the poacher gasp. His first arrow had found its mark.

The poacher seemed too stunned to run. Pulling back on the string, Jorgen let his second arrow fly toward the poacher's left leg.

The poacher cried out and reached for his leg. "Run!" the miscreant grunted before turning and starting to run himself.

Jorgen was already running after him, determined not to lose the culprit, even as the poacher's companions ran away, crashing through the trees.

He lost sight of him for a moment. When he came back into view, he was crumpling to the ground, unable to run anymore on his injured leg.

Within moments, Jorgen stood over the poacher, who was curled on his side in the leaves. The poacher was gasping, clutching his leg with his right hand and letting out tiny grunts of pain.

Jorgen froze. Something was wrong. This poacher sounded like . . . a woman.

His face began to tingle and his stomach sank to his toes. *O God. It couldn't be.* But the poacher's hair was spilling out of her hood, blond curls covering her shoulders, and Jorgen could see half of her face.

He sank to his knees, his hands shaking. "Odette. What have I done?"

She turned her face toward the ground, but her hood had fallen back to reveal her unmistakable profile.

She groaned. Her features were twisted in pain, her eyes clenched shut.

Odette was bleeding, with two arrows sticking out of her body. Jorgen's arrows.

He pushed her good shoulder back so he could see her left arm. His arrow was sticking out, but it had not gone all the way through her arm. Then he checked her thigh where another arrow protruded, dark blood oozing out and wetting her brown hose.

Jorgen unclasped her cloak and left it lying on the ground. He scooped her up in his arms and started walking toward the game-keeper's cottage.

Odette pressed her face against his shoulder, her hand limp against his chest.

⟋⟍

Odette saw the arrows sticking out of her, but she somehow didn't feel the pain until she fell to the ground and saw Jorgen coming toward her.

Jorgen had shot her.

It hardly seemed real, even though the pain was real enough.

He had gazed down at her, his hands limp at his sides, his eyes wide and mouth open.

She tried not to writhe or cry out when he slid his arms underneath her and lifted her off the ground. He carried her so her left arm and leg were not touching his body, but the jostling of his footsteps sent sharp, aching pains shooting through her arm and leg.

What would Jorgen do to her? Her dream would come true now. He would lock her in the dungeon and hate her.

How hurt Jorgen must feel at how she had fooled him. How sickened he must be that the girl he had claimed to love had betrayed him. She had gotten him in trouble with the margrave by poaching so many deer. She had broken the law it was his duty to uphold. And now his expression was pained, crushed, shocked. *O God, I am sorry for hurting him. Please do not let him hate me.*

She tried to muffle the sounds of her groaning against the soft leather of his shoulder cape, but she could no more control her gasps and moans than she could control the pains shooting through her body.

Jorgen had really shot her.

He walked quickly, carrying her as if she weighed little. She wished he would say something, anything. He should rebuke her, demand to know why she was poaching, express his anger at her betrayal. The silence was like a wall of pain separating them.

After many minutes, he began to slow his pace and his breathing became more labored. She was not small, being rather taller and broader than most women. But Jorgen was obviously very strong. Still, even he would have a hard time carrying her so far.

To distract herself from the pain, and from worrying about Jorgen's suffering, her mind conjured up his broad shoulders and rock-hard arms, his muscled back and leather-encased thighs. He would not like her to think him incapable, but she couldn't help wanting to save him from carrying her the whole way.

Odette made an effort to choke back her tears. "You do not have to carry me. I think I can walk."

He kept up his pace and did not answer her.

Somehow his refusal to answer, which she assumed meant resentment, helped her dry up her tears. She bit her lip to stop herself from moaning and let her head lie against his shoulder.

After what was probably only a few more minutes, they reached the gamekeeper's cottage. He pushed open the door with his foot and carried her inside.

It was dark and Odette was feeling light-headed. She closed her eyes and didn't try to see where they were going.

Jorgen moved carefully through the house before lowering her to a soft surface. When he did, he brushed against the arrow protruding from her arm, and she gasped in pain.

"I am sorry."

"Jorgen?" His mother's voice came from deeper in the cottage. "Is that you?"

"Mother, can you bring a lantern and some candles?" he called, his voice strained.

Odette felt his breath on her cheek as he leaned close.

"Odette?"

"Yes?"

A sound like a choked sob escaped him. She couldn't see him, but she felt his hand on her hair. "I am sorry," he whispered.

"Please forgive me," Odette whispered back. "I want to explain." Her own voice sounded strained, too, as she failed to bite back another gasp of pain.

"Do not talk."

Did she detect a note of bitterness in his voice? She didn't have a chance to say more because his mother shuffled into the room carrying a lantern.

"Oh, saints among us!" she cried as she held the lantern over Odette's bloody arm and leg.

"Mother, I need to go fetch the healer at the edge of the forest. Can you stay with Odette until I get back?"

"Of course. Oh, my dear, you poor thing. What happened?"

Jorgen's face was a hard mask as he turned away. "I will return as fast as I can." And he was gone.

~⁓

Jorgen ran all the way to the healer's cottage. Thankfully, she did not object to leaving her bed in the middle of the night and going with him to tend a wounded person. She pulled on a cloak, picked up her bag of supplies and her own lantern, and followed him back to the gamekeeper's cottage.

When he returned, Odette lay on his bed, shaking from head to toe. Jorgen's mother stood from where she was sitting beside Odette.

The healer, a woman nearly as old as Jorgen's mother, stepped forward. "Hester," she said, addressing his mother, "bring me some hot water for her to drink."

His mother hurried away.

The healer set her bag on the table next to the bed and drew out some shears and started cutting away Odette's sleeve. The arrow protruded from her snow-white skin, with blood oozing out around the wound.

She moved to Odette's leg and started cutting a circle around the place where the arrow pierced her thigh.

Jorgen's stomach flipped queasily, and he looked away from the bare skin.

His mother came back in the room with a steaming mug. The healer took a small pouch out of her bag and dumped it into the mug. She stirred it with a small stick, then carried it to Odette.

"Drink this." She helped Odette sit up, causing her to wince and turn pale. After several sips, the healer said, "That's enough," and let her lie back. She set down the cup.

"Come here." The healer beckoned to him with a claw-like hand. "I need you to pull out the arrows."

Odette made a strangled sound.

Of course the arrows had to come out. Jorgen braced himself.

"The quicker, the better. Just pull straight out, as straight as possible," the hardened old woman said.

Jorgen stood over Odette, staring down at his arrow protruding from her soft, pale arm. *God, can I truly do this?* He had to.

Ignoring his sick stomach, he bent and took hold of the arrow while the healer held her arm down on the bed, and Jorgen yanked it straight out.

Odette screamed, panting and writhing while the healer pressed clean cloths against her bleeding arm. Then she became still, apparently losing consciousness.

He grabbed the arrow in her thigh and yanked it out too. He dropped it on the floor and left the room without looking back.

Once outside, Jorgen heaved the contents of his stomach on the ground. He threw up until he forced himself to stop thinking of what he had done to Odette. Then he walked a little farther on and sank to his knees. He leaned forward until his forehead was touching the cool grass.

Questions and truths swirled through his head, but none of them were comforting. Tears squeezed from his tightly clenched eyes. Odette was the poacher. *Odette.*

He should go back inside and see if they needed his help. Now that the arrows were removed, she would be bleeding profusely, but the thought of her blood flowing from her body made his stomach threaten to heave again.

He pushed himself up from the ground, breathing deeply through his nose. His mother's geese were honking nearby. He had come too close to their nesting area. He concentrated on the noise they were making while he took more deep breaths. He could do this.

He must face the truth—Odette had betrayed him, had pushed him to tell her what he knew, had pretended to know nothing about the poacher threatening his position, his livelihood, his relationship with the margrave, and even his home and all hope for the future.

Odette was the poacher, and he had shot her. Twice.

He had to do whatever he could to help make sure Odette didn't die. His stomach clenched again. *O Father God, please do not let her die.*

# 25

ODETTE WAS AWAKENED by a groan, and then she realized the sound had come from her own throat.

Two intense centers of pain commanded her attention as she tried not to move—one in her thigh and the other in her upper arm. The night was hazy after Jorgen had carried her to his home. There was the nightmarish pain of him pulling the arrow out of her arm. She had blacked out, and when she opened her eyes again, the arrow was out of her leg, too, and Jorgen, his mother, and the other woman were pressing cloths against her arm and leg to stop the blood.

The pain was so bad, and the smell of blood so strong, she had floated away again, unable to stay conscious. Then, for what seemed like days, but was probably only a few hours, she kept waking up to horrendous pain and the strange woman giving orders to Jorgen and his mother as they tried to get her to drink something or changed her bandages.

Now she was almost afraid to open her eyes. Even though the pain was still there, at least no one was pressing on her wounds, making them hurt worse. Perhaps she was still asleep and could go on sleeping. But finally, she had to open her eyes.

Jorgen's head was near hers, his face buried in his arms resting on the bed beside her. He appeared to be the only other person in the room.

Her arm was wrapped tight with some white bandages. Her leg was covered with a sheet, but it also felt tightly wrapped. Was Jorgen asleep? If he was, she didn't want to wake him. His hair looked soft and boyish the way it curled in disarray on his head and by his ears. How long had he been sitting there, his head on his arms?

The sun was streaming through the window, and it appeared to be late morning. The healer had probably given her something to make her sleep since it was difficult to imagine sleeping through all the pain.

Jorgen suddenly lifted his head, and his blue-green eyes locked on hers. His eyes were bloodshot and his lashes were wet.

Her stomach clenched at the hurt in his eyes.

"Can I get you anything?" His gaze flicked from her face to the bed, as if he didn't want to look her in the eye.

"No, I thank you."

"The healer wants you to eat something as soon as you awaken. I'll go get—"

"Wait. Please." Odette touched his hand. She wasn't sure what to say to him, but she couldn't bear for him to leave. "Stay with me."

He stared down at her hand and bowed his head over it. She couldn't resist lifting her other hand to touch his hair. It was as soft as she thought it would be. When he didn't move, she slowly wrapped a lock of it around her fingertip.

There was sadness in the way his shoulders and head were bowed. He must be so angry to discover that she was the poacher. Was he feeling bad that he had shot her? Or was he sad that he would have to take her to the margrave's dungeon?

"I will not be angry with you if you take me to the margrave and tell him what I have done."

His hand tensed beneath hers, but his head stayed bowed. Finally he said quietly, "You betrayed me. You deceived me." His voice was hard. "Why did you do it?"

"For the children. I did it for the children."

He lifted his head. "For the children?" His brows lowered as he gazed at her, his mouth open.

"We were giving the meat to the poor." At least in the beginning. But she didn't want him to know that Rutger was involved because then he would be in trouble too. "I mean to say . . . I was giving the meat to the poor."

He narrowed his eyes at her. "Who? Who was helping you?"

"I cannot tell you."

"It was Rutger, was it not? But he was not giving the meat to the poor, Odette."

She closed her eyes as a sharp pain streaked through her leg. "I know." Her voice broke and a tear ran down her face.

"What do you mean, you know? I thought you said it was for the children, but Rutger was selling it. He was selling the deer you were shooting and making money off it." He leaned forward. Intensity made his eyes seem greener and his jaw twitch. "He had a black market set up in the back of The Red House."

Odette's stomach twisted at the words. "He confessed it to me yesterday. I confronted him when I found out the meat was not going to the children. Please believe me. I did not know he was selling it before." Tears ran from the corners of her eyes over her temples and into her hair.

"Are you saying he was using you?"

"Yes, but it was because he was in debt. I didn't know, but I had noticed some things were missing in the house. Rutger hadn't intended to keep selling the meat, but he kept losing his shipments and . . . He said he was sorry."

Jorgen's jaw tensed, twitching as he clenched his teeth. "How could you break the law, Odette? How could you poach deer, knowing it was wrong? How could you ask me about the poacher, listening to me talk about my struggle to catch him?" He lowered his head again. He slid his hand away from hers and covered his eyes with his hand, as if he couldn't bear to look at her any longer.

She yearned to touch him, to comfort him. "I am sorry. Perhaps I shouldn't have done it. I thought I was doing it for the poor, that I was doing the right thing, until I met you. Then I wasn't so sure. I did not want to hurt you. Please, please forgive me. I never should have deceived you."

Rutger had deceived her, and she'd been furious with him. But she had done the same thing to Jorgen. "You must hate me for betraying you." *Please don't hate me.*

He slipped his hand under hers and bowed his head over it. His breath touched her skin and sent a tingling sensation up her arm. "I believe you thought you were doing it for the children." He shook his head. "But how could you break the law, and at such great risk? How?"

How could she tell him she didn't know? Now it seemed so obvious that it was wrong, when seen through his eyes.

Another wave of sleepiness came over her, and the next thing she knew, she was opening her eyes to see Jorgen's mother beside her. Jorgen was gone.

Frau Hartman helped Odette up so she could use the chamber pot. Even though her leg hurt horribly when she put her weight on it, she was grateful it would still hold her up and grateful for Frau Hartman's help.

In spite of her age, Frau Hartman was a sturdy woman with a no-nonsense look on her face. Did she know that Odette was the poacher? Surely Jorgen had told her, or she had figured it out herself at seeing a woman wearing a man's hunting clothes. But she said nothing and gently helped Odette back into bed, then propped up some pillows so she could sit up.

Odette noticed she was wearing an unfamiliar nightdress. "Did you and the healer help me put this on?" She vaguely remembered the process, of the two women stripping her of her leather tunic and hose and pulling the nightdress over her head.

"Yes, my dear. Susanna, the healer, gave you some herbs that made you sleepy so you wouldn't feel as much pain. How are you feeling today? Well enough to eat something, I hope?"

"Yes, thank you. I believe I could eat something."

A tray was sitting on the table beside her with a bowl of something that smelled like warm apples.

"I brought you my apple pasty." She picked up the bowl and handed it to Odette.

"Thank you."

Frau Hartman stood and straightened the room while Odette ate. The room must have belonged to Jorgen. No wonder he had looked so tired; she had taken his bed.

When Odette considered the situation from Jorgen's mother's perspective, Frau Hartman had every reason to dislike Odette. Her son had loved a woman who thought him beneath her, and she had been poaching secretly, which had caused problems for Jorgen for many weeks. And now she lay in Jorgen's bed while he looked sad and broken.

Odette seemed like a wicked person from Frau Hartman's point of view.

She wanted to ask where Jorgen was, but she didn't dare. Instead, she ate the rest of the apple pasty, which tasted wonderful, and drank the water by her bedside, humbled by the woman's kindness.

"Susanna says you have no broken bones. The arrows went through the muscles. You should heal, in time."

Odette nodded. "Thank you for telling me. And thank you for taking care of me last night. I remember almost nothing of it." What she did remember was clouded by a haze of pain.

"Susanna left you some herbs in case you need them."

She was still in a lot of pain but didn't want to complain. "It does not hurt so much as long as I stay still. Not that I plan to stay here a long time," she quickly added. "I'm sure I will be well enough to leave soon. I could probably leave today."

"Nonsense. You will stay right here until you are healed."

Odette could sneak away tonight. But if Jorgen wanted to take her to the margrave's dungeon to be punished for her crimes, he could easily find her at home and seize her. No doubt he would take Rutger to the dungeon as well.

"Are you in much pain, my dear?" Jorgen's mother looked down at her in such a motherly way, it made her breath hitch.

"No. Thank you for asking. I was only thinking of something . . . unpleasant."

She shook her head and clicked her tongue against her teeth. "Why don't you take some of Susanna's herbs? They cannot do you any harm, after all, and they might help."

"Will they make me sleepy?"

"Probably." Frau Hartman found the tiny pouch the healer had left. "I shall go get some hot water. Wait here for me."

"I will." Odette nearly laughed. She couldn't get far, even if she felt well enough to try to leave.

Frau Hartman returned and gave her the steaming mug with the dried herb leaves lying on the bottom. She took a sip.

"Tastes like honey."

"It has honey in it. Honey is good for all kinds of ailments."

Frau Hartman smiled. She had brought some mending and sat down to sew a rip in an apron.

As she sipped the drink, Odette tried to think of what she might ask Jorgen's mother about him. "Jorgen must be a wonderful blessing to you, now that your husband is gone."

"Yes, Jorgen is the best son. My only wish for him is to find a good wife." She did not meet Odette's eye.

"It was very kind of you and your husband to take him in. I know he is grateful."

"He was ten when my husband brought him home. He had been living on the streets since his mother and father died. Poor thing, he was so thin and ragged the first time I saw him. And he was small—you would not know it to look at him now. He was so small I thought he was only about seven or eight. But I never talk about those days when he is around. He does not like to be reminded." She sighed. "I don't think he will ever stop grieving over his sister. He tried to be tough, even as a little boy, but the pain of her death and suffering went very deep."

The lines on her face suddenly looked more pronounced as she shook her head. "Sometimes children who have lived on the street for a long time are unable to accept love and a home. We had tried a couple of times before Jorgen to take in orphaned boys, but they always ran away, sometimes getting in trouble for stealing, and then . . . We usually never heard from them again. But Jorgen was extraordinary. I could see that right from the start." A wistful smile transformed her features.

"For a while Jorgen had trouble trusting people, but he was always kind to anyone he thought needed help, and he never stopped being so. And he trusts you." She glanced at Odette without lifting her head.

Odette had seen the pain in his eyes when he asked her why

she had deceived him. After all he had been through as an orphan, now the woman he had thought he loved had cruelly violated his trust. "You mean, he *trusted* me. He could not trust me, not after . . . what he knows about me now." She might as well mention what Frau Hartman surely knew.

"He knows what was in your heart."

Had she spoken to Jorgen this morning? Could he still love Odette after what she had done? Could he forgive her?

Even if he forgave her, he would still have to tell the margrave that she was the poacher.

She felt as if she had swallowed a bag of rocks. At least her worries about what would happen when the margrave found out took her mind off the pain in her arm and leg.

Frau Hartman sat placidly sewing, a slight smile on her lips.

Odette closed her eyes to rest them and immediately started drifting. Blessedly, the herbs were making her fall asleep again.

# 26

WHAT SORT OF torture was this, having Odette in his house, in his *bed*, but knowing she was there because he had *shot* her?

Jorgen continued his job of checking the forest for signs of deer. He would have to report his findings the next day. What would he say when the margrave asked him about the poacher? And what would the margrave do to him if he knew he was harboring the poacher in his own home?

Jorgen still had a lot of questions to ask Odette. Perhaps he was foolish to believe that she had thought she was poaching for the children. How could an intelligent woman like her be so fooled? Surely she had seen clues of Rutger's deceit and lawbreaking. And there was the small matter of her grazing his shoulder with her arrow. After he had told her, more than once, about the poacher, about his fear that the margrave would hire someone else to take his place as forester . . . And all the time she must have been laughing at him.

Soon he headed toward home again. He was so tired he could barely keep his eyes open, but he also wanted to see how Odette was feeling. She had seemed so weak that morning.

Truly, he was a fool.

Jorgen went inside his bedchamber. His mother was sewing

near Odette's bedside. Odette lay still, her eyes closed, her blond hair spread across the pillow. She took his breath away, lying there asleep, looking so vulnerable.

His mother looked up and smiled at him. She stood and left quietly. She knew Odette was the poacher he had been searching for. After her husband was killed by a poacher, she must feel at least some resentment toward Odette. She also knew, at least in part, how Jorgen felt about Odette. What was going through his mother's mind? Did she think him as a big a fool as he thought himself?

He desperately needed sleep. If he were wise, he wouldn't try to talk to Odette without it, but he wasn't feeling particularly wise.

Jorgen walked to the side of the bed and her eyes fluttered open.

"These herbs are making me sleep." She covered a yawn with her hand.

"Odette"—he sat on the stool beside her—"did you shoot at me yesterday?"

After a moment of staring up at him and blinking, she shook her head. "I would not shoot at you."

"You were not in the forest yesterday morning?"

"In the morning? Do you mean, after the sun was up?"

"Yes."

"I never hunt in the daytime. I went to Rutger's warehouse to confront him, then I was sleeping in my bed the rest of the morning."

"Someone shot at me."

"Were you hurt?" Her brow creased.

"The arrow only grazed the top of my shoulder."

"I have no idea who that might have been. But it does prove that someone is trying to harm you."

"Perhaps."

"Is that why you shot me? Because you thought I shot at you?"

"Not *you*, but I did think the *poacher* may have been trying to kill me."

"But you wanted only to wound me?"

Jorgen rubbed a hand over his eyes and down his face, then heaved a sigh. "Odette, I never would have hurt *you* at all. If I had known it was you, I would not have shot a single arrow. But yes, I was trying to wound the poacher, not kill him." Thinking how he might have killed Odette if his arrow had gone a few inches to the left made a cold sweat break out at his temples and on the back of his neck.

Odette nodded, looking contrite as she stared down at her hands. After a few moments, she said, "I have been away from home all night and nearly all day today. My uncle will be worried about me. Would it be possible for you to send word to him that I am well?"

Jorgen shook his head. Could she honestly be worried about her uncle? But she would be a cold person indeed not to care about her guardian and only living family member.

"I will go myself and tell him where you are. Odette? Do you think Rutger might harm you, thinking you might tell me or the margrave that he was behind the poaching and the black market?"

She inhaled a noisy breath of air, sitting up straighter. "No. No, my uncle would never harm me. But I know you must tell the margrave what we have done, and I don't want you to feel bad about it. Go ahead and tell him. I do not want you to get in trouble because of me."

A stab of pain went through his chest. He wanted to protect her, but it just wasn't feasible. "I don't have any choice but to tell him."

She nodded.

He suddenly wanted to take her and run away, to go where the margrave would never find her. "I have to go." He practically ran from the room.

He had to get away from her. He had to think without having her so near that she made him lose all perspective. The walk to her uncle's house would give him time to clear his thoughts.

⌒

As soon as she heard Jorgen leave the house through the front door, Odette allowed the tears to slip down her cheeks. Of course he had to tell the margrave. Lord Thornbeck would be furious with him if he found out Jorgen had been hiding her at his own home when she was the poacher.

But the hurt look on his face had reminded her so much of her recurring dream. It was the same expression he'd had then—hurt and anger.

Odette wished Brother Philip were there so she could ask him what she should do. How could she get absolution for her sin? Even though she had justified her poaching by saying that God would want her to feed the poor, she knew what she had done was wrong. Seeing the pain in Jorgen's face brought on her the full force of that truth. And since Rutger had been selling the meat instead of giving it to the children, the margrave would never believe she had been poaching to help the poor. Who would believe it? Did Jorgen even believe it? It seemed the height of folly that she had trusted Rutger so completely. She had been blindly loyal to him. Was she any different from Kathryn, blindly loyal to Agnes because she had helped Kathryn and her little brothers when no one else had?

Rutger had betrayed her, Agnes had betrayed Kathryn . . . And she had betrayed Jorgen.

⌐~⌐

Even though he was exhausted and had slept very little, Jorgen walked to Thornbeck and down the main street that led to the *Marktplatz* and Rutger Menkels's house. Besides carrying Odette's message to him, he had something he wanted to say to her uncle.

Rutger met him in the first-floor room. "Have you seen Odette?"

"My mother is taking care of her." He said the words wryly, but he might not have answered him at all if he had not seen true concern in his eyes.

"What has happened? Is she ill?"

"No, she is injured."

"Injured?"

"Odette wanted me to let you know she is safe and well. But I came here also to ask you why you would allow her to poach the margrave's deer. How could you, her guardian, condone such a thing?"

His face went white. "So you have captured her." He rubbed a hand over his eyes and blew out a breath. "She was doing it for the children. You do not know how determined she was to help them."

"And then you sold the meat instead of letting her give it to the poor."

"Did she tell you . . . ? I never intended to do it. I was helping her by distributing it to the poor. But then everything went wrong. My ships and all their cargo were destroyed, and my caravan was beset by robbers. I lost everything. I was in debt and desperate. I know I shouldn't have done it, but—"

"So Odette knew nothing about what you were doing?"

"Not until a few days ago. And she had no idea I was in debt. I did not want her to know."

"Until Mathis offered to help you if you would convince Odette to marry him."

"But he loves her, and I believe he will treat her well. If you truly cared for her, you would want her to marry Mathis." His jaw hardened as he said the words that were a death knell to Jorgen's hopes.

For a moment, Jorgen wanted to slam his fist into Rutger's face. But that would not help. "You would sell Odette to the wealthiest suitor, then. I had thought you better than that. But I also never would have thought you would use Odette so shamefully as to let her go out poaching, believing she was helping the children, when you—" Jorgen halted his tirade and ran a hand through his hair. Ranting would not serve any good purpose either.

Rutger took a step toward the door, then stopped and stared at Jorgen. "Even if I did not need help from Mathis, he would still be her best choice of husband, the choice that makes sense for her. And she has made that choice. She told Mathis yesterday that she would marry him. He's having the banns published on Sunday."

Jorgen seemed to go numb all over. Even his mind was numb. But Rutger was right. She was wise to choose Mathis. And he would be wise to let her.

Odette slept fitfully that night. In addition to the occasional sharp pains in her arm and leg, she had stayed awake wishing Jorgen would come back to talk to her. She couldn't stop wondering if he had gone to tell the margrave he had caught the poacher. All night she kept waking up, her mind going over and over what he must think of her. She also kept thinking of how worried Rutger must be that she had not come home, even if Jorgen did go and tell him she was safe.

As the sun finally came up, she prayed for wisdom and mercy.

Jorgen's mother came to her bedside to bring her some food. She rearranged Odette's pillows for her, even though she could get up, although painfully, and fluff her pillows for herself.

"I made you some pheasant and stewed fruit. I remember you said you liked pheasant more than pork."

"You don't have to cook special things for me." Odette wished she hadn't admitted to the woman the foods she liked and disliked when she had asked her. "I will eat whatever you make. I am in no position to be picky." She gave Frau Hartman what she hoped was a meek expression.

She only smiled and briefly touched Odette's cheek after placing the tray of food across her lap.

Was this how mothers treated their daughters when they were sick in bed? She could not remember her own mother. Odette was rarely sick, and since moving with Rutger to Thornbeck, she had been tended by servants. But to be treated like a cherished daughter . . . It warmed her and made her sad at the same time.

Frau Hartman sat beside her with her sewing again as Odette began to eat. She couldn't stop thinking about how many reasons Jorgen's mother had to dislike her.

"Why are you so kind to me?" Odette asked, afraid to hear the answer and bracing herself for it.

"I would think, for the same reason you are kind to those poor children. And for other reasons as well." She tucked her chin to her chest and continued sewing.

Odette didn't ask the other reasons.

She suddenly remembered something Jorgen had told her. "I

wonder if I could read Jorgen's Psalter. He also said he has two Gospel books."

"Of course, my dear." She set her sewing aside and stood.

"Do you think he would mind?"

"He would be pleased to let you read them. I know just where they are." She bustled out of the room and came back a few moments later with the books in her arms.

"Thank you so much." Odette held them reverently and then opened one. "Shall I read aloud?"

"That would be lovely."

Odette began to read some of the gospel of John. After a while, Frau Hartman said, "Would you read a few psalms now?"

"Of course." Odette randomly opened the Psalter to Psalm 91. As she read, she thought about Jorgen. He was out in the forest, alone, and someone was possibly trying to harm him. They had already shot at him.

> You will not fear the terror of night,
> nor the arrow that flies by day,
> nor the pestilence that stalks in the darkness,
> nor the plague that destroys at midday.
> A thousand may fall at your side,
> ten thousand at your right hand,
> but it will not come near you.
> You will only observe with your eyes
>   and see the punishment of the wicked.

*God, please, please keep Jorgen safe from whoever wants to harm him.*

She read on, finishing Psalm 91, still praying in her mind for the psalm to come true on Jorgen's behalf. Didn't he love God and follow God's commands? Surely God would not allow anything bad to happen to him.

After Odette read a few more psalms, Frau Hartman laid her sewing aside. "Would you like me to braid your hair?"

"Oh, that is very kind, thank you." It must look a hideous mess.

Odette had finished her food, so Frau Hartman fetched a comb and started combing her hair. It felt so good Odette closed her eyes.

"I always wanted a girl so I could fix her hair." Frau Hartman sounded wistful, but not sad.

"Were you hoping Kathryn would stay here and be your daughter?"

"Yes, but she was at the age and had been through so much that . . . She did not know how to think of Jorgen as a brother. I was grateful when I learned she was staying at your friend's house."

"She seems content to work for Anna. I think Anna's cook has been very motherly toward her, which I am sure she needed." Odette sighed at how good it felt to have a woman braid her hair. Perhaps Kathryn wasn't the only one who needed someone to be motherly toward her.

"You have beautiful hair." She worked it in and out and between her fingers with gentle tugs. "I always thought Jorgen's hair was thick and beautiful. It was a bit of a shame that he was not a girl."

Odette laughed. "He would have been a beautiful girl." But as a man, he made her want to study him, to know him, and to memorize each hard angle and plane of his chin, jaw, cheek, and brow.

What a scandalous thought. Her cheeks heated. Had she forgotten she had promised to marry Mathis? She'd hardly thought of him the last two days and nights. Was it not wrong to marry someone she thought so little of?

When she finished braiding her hair, Frau Hartman unwrapped the bandages around Odette's arm and leg. "Susanna says it is best to let the wound ooze, to let the bad humors out since it has stopped bleeding." She placed a cloth under Odette's leg and left the bandages off her arm and leg.

The wounds looked raw and disgusting.

"If anyone comes in the house, you can cover yourself with the sheet. I am going out to tend the geese and the garden."

"Is there anything I can do to help you? I can sew something or shell some peas or beans."

"I will bring you some peas to shell."

Odette was thankful she would be able to do at least this little thing to try to repay Frau Hartman for all her kindness.

A couple of minutes went by before the front door opened and shut. Hoping it was Jorgen, Odette quickly covered herself with the sheet so he wouldn't see her uncovered leg and the open wound.

A moment later, Rutger entered the bedchamber and Odette felt a prickling on the back of her neck.

# 27

"I DID NOT expect to see you. How did you know I was here? You haven't been worrying, have you?"

Rutger walked toward Odette's bed. "I was worried, but Jorgen came last night to tell me you were safe."

"Oh. That was very kind of him." Considering how exhausted he must have been—and how much Odette had hurt him.

Rutger did not look pleased. "What happened to you? He said you were injured."

"I was shot in the arm and the leg, but no bones are broken."

"Who shot you? Jorgen shot you, didn't he? Now I suppose you will give up your girlish idea of him."

"I do wish you would stop insulting me over Jorgen."

"Mathis told me you accepted his offer of marriage."

Odette's stomach did a queasy flip. "I have not married him yet." She didn't care if she sounded defiant.

"Do you think Jorgen has told the margrave anything?"

"I don't know, but he will have to tell him what we have done."

"He has no proof. I shall speak to the magistrate, the margrave's bailiff, and the margrave himself. You shall not be punished for this. Who would ever believe that a beautiful, wealthy merchant's niece could be a poacher? It is preposterous. We shall make this forester a laughingstock and the butt of jokes. No one will believe him when I am done."

"No, Rutger . . . I think I must pay for my crime."

His face hardened into an expression Odette had never seen before. "And you intend for me to pay too?"

"I do not see how we can get away with it now."

"You are not to tell anyone anything, do you understand?" He pointed his finger at her nose. "Stay silent and do not implicate yourself or anyone else. Just stay silent." Rutger lowered his finger but continued to give Odette that hard look.

Odette clamped her bottom lip between her teeth to stop it from trembling. Rutger had never spoken to her this way before. She never imagined she would ever feel frightened of him. "I do not intend to tell the margrave anything about your involvement." She made an effort to breathe more normally and calm her heart. "I will be careful to say that I was the one who poached, and I will refuse to implicate anyone else."

"It may all turn out well." Rutger was no longer looking at her but was pacing in a tight line by her bed, tapping his chin with a finger. "After all, you shall be married to the Burgomeister's son, and Mathis will no doubt have a lot of influence. But the marriage must take place soon. Very soon."

Her stomach did that sickening flip again.

"My dear"—he turned to face her—"I am so thankful to see that you are not near death. Still, it must be painful for you to walk. I would not be surprised if you hated Jorgen." He eyed her.

"I do not hate him. He had to shoot me. It was his duty as the forester."

"I brought some peas," Frau Hartman called as the back door opened and shut.

Her uncle squeezed her hand. "I am sorry. I must go." He

turned and ran out of the room, down the corridor, and out the front door, letting it slam behind him.

Frau Hartman stood in the doorway with a basket of peas. "Who was that? Was someone here?"

"It was Rutger."

"Oh. He did not have to run away like that."

No doubt he was frightened. Guilt would do that to a person. "I see you have some peas for me."

While Odette shelled peas, which she had learned how to do as a little girl when she worked for her neighbors—popping the pod, then pushing the little round peas out with her thumb—her mind was left to go over and over the visit from Rutger.

She had felt real fear at the way Rutger had spoken to her. Surely her uncle would not harm her. But what would he do to avoid punishment by the margrave? Would Mathis be able to bribe Lord Thornbeck to spare both her and Rutger? Would her marriage to Mathis save her and her uncle from punishment?

And what about the poor children? They had not starved, even though for six months the food she thought was going to them was actually being sold by Rutger. God *must* have been providing for them. And if she had not decided to go out hunting one last night, thinking she had to provide meat for them one last time, Jorgen would not have shot her.

While Jorgen's mother was out of the room, she whispered, "God, I know Rutger and I do not deserve it, but would You provide for us too? I want to do the right thing, and I don't want to be punished for poaching, but I do not want to marry Mathis."

She couldn't imagine how God could get her out of it.

Jorgen arrived at Thornbeck Castle in the morning to report to Lord Thornbeck. His hands were cold and sweaty, and he still was not certain what he would tell the margrave. *God, give me wisdom and the words to say.*

Ulrich met him as soon as he was inside the castle and walked him to the margrave's library. For once, Ulrich smiled and talked about the weather. His friendliness made the hair on Jorgen's arms rise. What was he scheming?

"Good morning, Jorgen." The margrave stood and leaned on his cane when Jorgen walked in.

"Good morning, Lord Thornbeck." If only he could meet with the margrave without his chancellor there. The shrewd look in Ulrich's eyes made him seem even more suspicious. He would do his best to turn the margrave against him.

"What news do you have for me about the notorious poacher of Thornbeck Forest?"

"My lord, I now know who is responsible for the poaching, as well as the black market."

"That is excellent, Jorgen." The margrave's eyes grew wider and a wisp of a smile crossed his lips. "Excellent work."

Ulrich looked as if he had just swallowed an eel whole, as his face turned ashy green.

"Who is this poacher? I will send my bailiff at once to capture him and all his helpers and bring him here."

"My lord, I . . . I can tell you that the poacher will no longer be poaching."

The margrave's smile disappeared. "He is dead, then?"

"No, my lord. The poacher is not dead, but the poacher is . . . unable to do any more poaching."

"You are speaking nonsense, Jorgen. What are you saying?"

As the margrave's expression grew harder, the chancellor's eager gaze darted back and forth from the margrave to Jorgen.

"I am saying that I shot and injured the poacher, but I will be trying to find more evidence against the person who is responsible for coercing the poacher into killing the king's deer."

"Coercing?" The margrave frowned.

"This is a travesty of justice," Ulrich announced. "Your forester is defying you, my lord, and refusing to respect your orders. This man should be thrown into the dungeon until he reveals the identity of the poacher."

"Jorgen," the margrave growled, "what reason can you give for not telling me who this poacher is?"

A trickle of sweat slid down the center of Jorgen's back. "My lord, I . . . I can give you no satisfactory answer, except to say that this poacher thought she was doing the right thing, that the deer she was killing were going to feed poor people who were starving."

"That is no excuse," Ulrich sputtered. "No excuse for breaking the law and killing the king's deer."

The margrave lifted his hand to silence his chancellor. His brows lowered and came together in a crease. "You said 'she.' Do you mean that the poacher is . . . a woman?"

"Yes, my lord. She did not know that the meat was being sold in the black market."

Ulrich let out a snort.

"Jorgen," the margrave said, "is the poacher someone you know? Someone you want to protect because you have tender feelings for her?"

He bit the inside of his mouth. Finally he said, "Yes, my lord."

"Am I to believe that you feel more loyalty to this poacher than you do to me?"

The air seemed to thicken as no one made a sound. "No, of course not." But even he didn't think he sounded convincing.

"Tell me who is responsible for selling the meat to the black market. You must at least tell me that much, Jorgen, or I shall wonder if you are not telling me the truth at all."

"I would rather wait until I have more evidence. But whether I can give you the irrefutable evidence or not, I will tell you soon, in the next few days."

The margrave did not look pleased. His eyelids hung low as he said, "You have two days. I am not a patient man, and I want to know who has been breaking the law. Two days, Jorgen."

"Yes, my lord."

⁓

Jorgen had managed to avoid her all day, staying busy with his work after meeting with the margrave, taking his midday meal in the castle kitchen with the servants so he wouldn't have to come home. But when his mother met him at the front door with a worried look on her face, he was seized with fear.

"Did something happen to Odette?"

"She is well, but you need to let her tell you about her uncle's visit earlier today."

He forced himself not to run toward his bedchamber.

"I will have supper ready soon," his mother called after him as he reached the doorway.

Odette sat propped in bed, sewing up a seam in a pair of Jorgen's hose.

"You should not be doing that." He closed the distance between them.

She pulled the fabric close to her chest, as if she thought he might snatch it away. "I need something to do all day while you are out doing your work and your mother is doing hers. Besides, she ran out of peas for me to shell."

She was so beautiful when she smiled, but now was not the time to tell her so. "Tell me what happened when Rutger came to see you."

"Yes, of course. But sit first. You look tired. You have been working all day. Please."

He sat down, his eyes locked on hers. Although his gaze did stray to her lips, if he was honest with himself, and he did think about kissing her. But then he locked on to her eyes again.

She laid the mending in her lap. "Rutger came in the front door after your mother went out to tend the garden and the geese." She proceeded to tell him what Rutger had said. "I tried to tell him I didn't think we could avoid punishment, but to be honest, I was a bit frightened by his response. I've never known my uncle to look at me or speak to me that way."

"He might try to harm you, Odette. He is obviously afraid you will tell the margrave about his role in the poaching and the black market."

She hesitated, then shook her head. "He is my uncle. He would not do that. He believes he will probably not be punished because . . ." Odette looked as if she might cry.

"What is it? What do you not want to tell me?" When she still seemed to be fighting tears too much to speak, he said, "If it is about you marrying Mathis, I already know." He tried to sound cool and unaffected, but he had to stand and turn his back on her. He folded his arms across his chest. "I do not blame you, Odette. I know you have to marry him. You would be a fool not to marry him. His money will protect you and . . . give you all the things you want." *All the things I cannot.*

She didn't say anything.

When he had control of himself again, he turned back toward her. Tears were trembling on her lashes. She ducked her head and wiped her eyes. "I know it does not matter now, but I want to say again how much I regret kissing that other woman. I thought she was you, but I—"

"Please, you do not need to say it. She looked like me, and it was not your fault. Someone tricked you." She stared down at her folded hands in her lap, her lips parted in a way that made his heart pound against his chest at the thought of kissing them.

He shoved the thought away.

"Odette, you should consider that the person who is responsible for trying to trick me could possibly be your uncle."

"It was not Rutger," she said quietly, not looking up at him. "It was Mathis."

Heat spread through him and he turned away from her again. He tried to breathe, not to lash out in a rage. How dare that weasel? Knowing this, Odette was still willing to marry the little schemer? But he shouldn't be angry with her. She had little choice. Jorgen could not keep her out of the dungeon—at least, not for long—but Mathis probably could.

He would deal with Mathis later.

"I am sorry, Jorgen. I found out the day after I discovered Rutger was selling the deer I was poaching."

Mother walked in carrying a tray of food. "We shall eat in here with Odette tonight."

She stopped and looked from Jorgen to Odette and back again. The tension between them must have been obvious.

"You do not have to disrupt your mealtime for me." Odette pushed herself up, trying to sit higher, and winced.

"Nonsense. Jorgen and I want you to keep us company, and

you need to stay off your leg. Susanna said as much, and you must obey your healer."

It was sweet that Mother wanted to protect her. If only Odette didn't have to marry someone she didn't love to protect Rutger and herself.

⁓

Odette awoke to darkness—and to pain. Sharp pains were shooting through her leg from the wound, as they sometimes did.

She saw something on the floor in front of her doorway. Frau Hartman had offered to leave a candle burning, and Odette had accepted it after the fitful night she had had the night before. Perhaps a light would help chase away the painful, fearful thoughts. And now the pale light showed something large in the corridor.

Her heart thumped wildly. She would never be able to go back to sleep unless she found out what it was. "Who is there?" she whispered. The large mass did not move or respond, so she asked again, a bit louder, "Who is there?"

The large thing was a person that turned over and whispered back, "It's Jorgen. I am guarding your door. Go back to sleep."

Her heart slowed back to normal. "You are not lying on the floor, are you?"

"I have a pallet of blankets."

Warmth spread through her, much as it did when Frau Hartman was so attentive and kind to her, bringing her food and straightening her pillows. "*Danke*, Jorgen."

"*Bitte schön.*"

# 28

THE NEXT MORNING Jorgen was talking with his mother in another part of the house. At the sound of his deep, mellow voice, Odette's heart skipped a beat.

She got up on her own to take care of her morning needs. She determined not to lie in bed all day, no matter what Frau Hartman or the healer said. Even though she limped and putting weight on her leg made it throb, she could walk now and didn't want to be a burden on Jorgen's mother.

Odette managed to slip unseen out the front door and hobble to the well to get some water. It felt good to be outside in the fresh air, so she stood propped against the side of the well, drinking a ladle full of water and listening to the morning songs of the forest birds.

"Odette!" Jorgen called from inside the house. In a moment he stood at the front door. When he saw her, he grabbed at his chest.

Frau Hartman came out behind him. "My dear, you gave us a fright! We did not know where you were. You should not be walking around by yourself."

"I am sorry I frightened you. It does not hurt so much to walk now, and I am trying to do more things for myself."

Jorgen approached her. "Please, come inside." He stood close to her side and held out his arm to her.

Odette leaned on him as they made their way into the house. All the time, Jorgen was glancing one way, then another.

"Are you expecting someone to attack?" She tried to sound teasing and lighthearted.

At first Jorgen didn't answer. Then he said, "I don't want you to fall and get hurt."

"Thank you."

He handed her a cup of water his mother brought.

A knock sounded on the front door. Jorgen seemed to be listening as his mother answered it. There was a murmur of voices, then Frau Hartman came back into the room.

"It was a messenger from Thornbeck Castle. The margrave wants to speak to you, Jorgen, right away."

He nodded and turned to go.

"Jorgen?" Odette said, before she lost her courage.

He ducked through the doorway again. "What?"

"I . . . I know you will be in a lot of trouble if the margrave finds out you are hiding the poacher in your house. You should let me go with you, to confess to him."

"No, Odette." He frowned, then sighed. "There is no need. Besides, the margrave already knows that the poacher is here, injured." He seemed about to say more, then shook his head. "I will return soon."

He turned and left, his bow strapped over his shoulder next to his quiver of arrows.

Odette bit her lip. Was the margrave furious with Jorgen for protecting the notorious poacher who was killing all the king's deer? Jorgen didn't deserve to get in trouble because of her. As soon as her arm and leg were a little better healed, she would insist on turning herself in.

If she were able to walk that far, she would go now.

⁓

Jorgen arrived at Thornbeck Castle several minutes later and was greeted by a servant. "Lord Thornbeck is expecting me."

The servant had him wait in the entrance hall. A few minutes later, instead of the servant, Lord Thornbeck himself was walking toward him. "Jorgen. Do you have information for me?"

Jorgen cleared his throat. "No, my lord. You sent for me."

The margrave stared. "I did not send for you."

"The messenger, he came to my house and said you wanted to speak to me." A burst of light seemed to explode in his head.

"Which messenger?"

"It was a boy, about thirteen years old, with brown curly hair."

"That sounds like Ulrich's nephew, but I did not send him. Perhaps someone is playing a trick on you."

Someone who wanted to harm Odette? "Thank you, my lord. Forgive me—" Jorgen turned and began to run.

He ran as fast as he could down the steep winding road that led away from Thornbeck Castle. He took a shortcut through the forest, skidding down a deep ravine on his heels. In two more minutes, he would reach the clearing in front of his cottage.

Suddenly, something buzzed past his ear, so close he felt a tiny puff of air as it passed by. A soft *thunk* sounded just ahead as an arrow struck a tree.

For the second time in a few days, Jorgen hit the ground on his stomach because someone was shooting at him.

He raised himself to his knees, staring in the direction the arrow seemed to come from. The trees were so dense he could see very little here. His blood was pounding in his ears, but there seemed to be no movement at all. Jorgen drew out one of his own arrows and his bow. "Who is there? I will shoot if you do not tell me who you are!" Let him think Jorgen could see him.

Instead of staying where he was to get shot at again, he crawled on his hands and knees. If the archer came looking for him, Jorgen was confident he would see him before the archer could see Jorgen.

Then the person started running, crashing through the brush, heading toward the cottage where his mother and Odette were.

Jorgen leapt to his feet and ran after him. Within a minute, he was in the clearing around the house. All appeared quiet as he ran the last several feet and burst through the front door.

No one was in the front room, so he ran to Odette's bed-chamber. His mother sat in a chair beside the bed, and Odette was reading from his Gospels.

"Jorgen, what—?"

"Have you seen anyone? Did anyone come through here?"

"We haven't seen anyone. What is the matter?"

Jorgen turned and ran toward the door. "I'll be back soon."

⟨⟩

Something was wrong. Odette could see that Jorgen had been run-ning, and he had his bow and an arrow in his hands. Had someone shot at him again?

"Frau Hartman, would you help me up?"

"Of course, child. Do you need to use the chamber pot?"

"No, I want to . . . get some fresh air." She didn't want Jorgen's mother to realize he was in danger. "Can you hand me my bow and my arrows?"

"Your bow and arrows? Why, child, whatever for?"

Odette clenched her teeth and ignored her leg's screams of pain as she put her feet on the floor and stood. Frau Hartman grasped her arm.

"I do not think you should be doing this."

Odette reached out for her weapons, and Frau Hartman handed them to her. Odette hobbled as quickly as she could to the doorway.

"No, no, you should not be doing this. What are you and Jorgen hiding from me? What is happening?"

Odette unclenched her teeth to say, "Jorgen may be in danger. I want to see if he needs help."

"No disrespect to you, my dear, for I can see you are a very brave and capable woman, but I do not think you can help Jorgen in your injured condition."

"Perhaps not, but I have to try." Odette began to walk faster as her muscles seemed to loosen up. Even though her injured leg was throbbing, she kept moving toward the front door. When she reached it, she pushed it open and peered outside. Then she nocked an arrow to her bowstring, ignoring the twinges of pain in her arm, and walked out.

Frau Hartman was beside her but silent. They moved toward the small clearing on the right side of the house. Odette stood listening. She couldn't move fast so she didn't know what she thought she could do. She didn't even know which direction Jorgen had gone. She stepped out into the clearing, looking all around her as she walked. Frau Hartman stayed just behind her, no longer attempting to support her.

Then she saw him. Jorgen was walking toward the house. He still looked very alert. She knew when he saw her because he stared for a moment, then continued looking around.

Suddenly to Jorgen's left and just behind him, a man stood up. He had been hiding behind a bush. Now he drew back an arrow, aiming for Jorgen.

Odette lifted her bow and arrow and drew the bowstring back all in one swift movement and let the arrow go.

The man sent his own arrow flying toward Jorgen, who spun around when he saw Odette raise her bow. Frau Hartman screamed. The archer let out a little cry and clutched at his arm as Odette's arrow seemed to graze him. He turned and disappeared in the trees, crashing through the underbrush.

Jorgen, who was holding his own arrow aimed in the direction of the mysterious archer, lowered it as he focused on Odette.

"Did he get you?" She swayed where she stood.

Jorgen ran the rest of the way to her. "No, he missed. But I think you hit him."

"I only nicked his arm."

Odette's knees threatened to buckle beneath her, her vision spinning. Jorgen took the weapon from her trembling hands.

She whispered, "I think I need to sit down." Her vision started fading.

Jorgen slipped one arm behind her back. He bent and put his other arm under her knees and lifted her.

"I think I am all right. I just feel a bit . . . faint." She laid her head on his shoulder, and it was just like the last time Jorgen had carried her. Only this time his journey was much shorter.

"Who was that?" Jorgen's mother asked as he carried Odette into the house and laid her on the bed.

"I do not know." Jorgen smoothed Odette's hair back from her face.

She was so weak she wasn't sure she could have done it for herself.

"Thank you for saving my life." His voice was rough and thick, and his throat bobbed.

Her heart thumped against her chest. As he leaned over her, oh, how she wished he would kiss her.

But he couldn't. Of course he couldn't. She was marrying Mathis.

His face clouded. Was he also thinking about her marrying Mathis? He turned and walked out.

Odette opened her eyes as voices drifted to her from another room.

"You shot her!" someone said. It sounded like Mathis.

"She does not need to be moved. She nearly fainted this afternoon." That was Jorgen's strident voice.

"I brought a litter," Mathis answered.

"I do not care what you brought, she doesn't need to be moved."

Then several people seemed to be speaking at once, and one voice sounded like Rutger.

The voices got louder and three men—Jorgen, Mathis, and Rutger—spilled into her chamber.

Jorgen stood with his arms crossed, his brows lowered, and his jaw clenched.

Rutger and Mathis came toward her bed. Mathis smiled and cocked his head to one side. "Odette, please allow your uncle to take you home. It is not good for you to be staying here with Jorgen, in this small house."

"You don't have to go if you do not want to," Jorgen said.

"Odette," Rutger said, "I have a litter outside. You won't have to walk at all, and you do not want to trouble the forester and his mother any longer."

Trouble. It was true. Her presence there would get Jorgen in trouble with the margrave.

"Will you not let me take you home?"

Mathis hovered over Rutger's shoulder. Jorgen still looked like a dark thundercloud.

Odette said softly, "It is best if I go."

Mathis and Rutger chorused their agreement.

Frau Hartman gathered her things and handed them to Rutger—and handed him a harsh glare at the same time.

"Stand aside." Jorgen pushed past Mathis.

"What do you think you are—?" Mathis halted his objection as Jorgen threw back the sheet and slid his arms under her. He lifted her easily and carried her past Mathis and Rutger, who stood with their mouths open.

He carried her through the narrow corridor of their house and through the front door. He knelt beside the litter attached to Mathis's horse and laid her down so tenderly, something inside her chest seemed to break.

She gazed up into his eyes, searching . . . What for, she wasn't sure. His blue-green eyes gazed back at her. But with Mathis and Rutger bursting out of the door and striding toward them, Jorgen stood.

Mathis took his place. "Is there anything I can get you, my dear?" He looked nervous as he clasped his hands and smiled.

Frau Hartman nudged him out of the way and tucked the blanket around her and placed a bundle—her hunting clothes and bow and arrows—beside her on the litter.

"If you need anything, my dear, you send for me." She spared a glare over her shoulder before saying, "Men do not know how to take care of an injured woman. Humph."

Soon Rutger and Mathis were ready and the horse started forward, and she began her bumpy journey home.

~~~

Odette awoke in her own bedchamber the next morning. Everything looked normal and familiar. But . . . Odette blinked. Sunlight was streaming in her window. She shivered and tried to pull the blanket underneath her chin, which took more effort than she would have thought. Either the blanket was extraordinarily heavy, or she was very weak. Her body ached and her head was hot. She touched her face with her right hand. It was so hot it seemed to singe her fingers. Her throat burned and she was so thirsty.

She became aware of someone sweeping the floor nearby. "Who is there?"

The person seemed to be just outside the room in the corridor. "It is Heinke."

"Will you bring me some water? I do not know if I can stand." Her leg throbbed and it hurt to open her eyes.

Heinke brought her some water a few minutes later.

"Will you get my uncle?"

"He is not here." Heinke stared at her with wide eyes and her mouth open.

"Will you send for him? I think I need a doctor. Or better yet, can you send for Frau Hartman at the gamekeeper's cottage?"

Heinke hurried out the door. She was a timid girl, but Odette prayed she would do as she had asked.

Odette was barely able to swallow a few sips of water. It seemed a very long time that she lay in bed alone. Finally Rutger stood beside her, touching her forehead.

"I thought you only needed sleep, but now you have a fever."

He looked at her with much the same expression as Heinke—wide eyes and open mouth. "I shall send for a doctor."

⌒

When Odette awoke again, she heard humming and soft singing. Someone was touching Odette's leg. She opened her eyes with a groan. The healer, Susanna, was bending over her, dabbing something yellow and foul smelling on her wound.

Frau Hartman sat at Odette's side. She touched her cheek. "The healer is here." She wiped Odette's cheeks with a cool, wet cloth, then laid a damp cloth on her forehead. "And God will make you well. He hears our prayers for you."

"Thank you."

The healer called Frau Hartman to help her and to give her instructions. Odette's eyes watered from something pungent in the air. The smell of turpentine overwhelmed her. Her leg must have turned septic, and they were putting turpentine ointment on her wound.

If her wound was septic, she might die. The realization didn't bring fear, only resignation.

Frau Hartman resumed wiping Odette's face, dabbing her lips with the cool water, pushing her hair back from her temples. But Frau Hartman's voice came from the other side of the room as she talked with the healer. Who was wiping Odette's face?

She opened her eyes. Jorgen sat beside her, touching the cloth to her cheek.

"How are you feeling?"

"A little better, I think." But she wasn't sure that was true.

"I am so sorry, Odette." His eyes were luminous above her, his lashes dark and thick. Truly, his was a pleasant face.

"Sorry?"

"For shooting you." He swallowed, as if the words were painful to say.

"You do not have to be sorry for that. It was my fault."

He continued the task his mother had abandoned, and Odette closed her eyes, too weak to say more.

Soon Frau Hartman shooed him away, and Odette fell asleep, dreaming that Jorgen was carrying her through a hot, dry desert.

Jorgen made his way to Thornbeck Castle. It was time to tell Lord Thornbeck the whole truth about the poacher. His two days were up.

He entered the castle and followed the servant to the margrave's library. Ulrich was sitting at his own desk a few steps away from the margrave's. They both appeared to be writing something.

Lord Thornbeck motioned with his hand for him to come forward. "I hope you have information for me today."

"Yes, my lord."

"Before you tell me who the poacher and black-market seller are, tell me what happened yesterday. You said someone came to you, a messenger. What did he say?"

"He said you wanted to speak with me." Jorgen glanced at Ulrich. He was staring down at his paper, but from the look on his face, Jorgen was certain he was listening. "And after I left here and was nearly home, someone shot at me. The arrow just missed. Then, near my home, someone shot at me again."

"What did this person look like?"

"He was wearing dark clothing, and a hood covered most of his face."

"Were you able to shoot back at him?"

"No. He was aiming at me when someone else—Odette Menkels—shot at him. I think she nicked his arm . . . his right arm." Jorgen stared hard at Ulrich, whose face was red. Sweat ran down his cheeks, and he swiped at it with the back of his hand.

The margrave was also looking hard at Ulrich. "Do you have any idea who this person is who is trying to kill my forester?"

Suddenly Jorgen knew. He stepped to Ulrich's desk, forcing him to look up, and took hold of Ulrich's right arm.

Ulrich cried out, a mixture of fear and pain. "Let go of me!"

Jorgen squeezed harder, making Ulrich cry out again.

Lord Thornbeck was standing beside Jorgen now. The margrave took Ulrich's arm and, with a knife, split Ulrich's sleeve all the way to his shoulder. A white cloth was wrapped around his upper arm. Lord Thornbeck slashed it off as well, drawing a tiny line of blood with his knife point.

There, on Ulrich's arm, was a bloody cut, like someone might get from the tip of an arrow grazing his skin, nearly identical to the one on the top of Jorgen's shoulder.

"It is not true, my lord." Ulrich's voice was pleading. "Jorgen is lying. I never tried to kill him."

"Then where were you yesterday after your nephew delivered that message to Jorgen?"

Ulrich opened his mouth but nothing came out.

"Guards!" Lord Thornbeck's face was dark and dangerous.

Two men appeared in the room, swords drawn.

"Take this man to the dungeon."

"No, my lord, please!" Ulrich fell to his knees, putting his hands out in supplication. "Please!"

But Lord Thornbeck turned and stalked back to his desk, thumping his walking stick on the floor with every step. He sat down and folded his hands in front of him. "Now, Jorgen, I believe you were going to tell me something." He spoke as Ulrich's pleas for mercy were still ringing through the corridor outside the open door.

Jorgen's mind was reeling. "My lord, why? Why would Ulrich want to kill me? I know he never liked me. He always seemed to hate me when we were boys at school, but why now?"

Lord Thornbeck gave a little shrug. "I suspect he was jealous of you when you were boys and was still jealous of you, afraid you would somehow end up besting him. He saw the reports you wrote and gave to me every three months, which were very well done and showed intelligence, diligence, and organization that was lacking in Ulrich. And I complimented you on more than one occasion."

Lord Thornbeck pushed back from his desk a bit and stretched out his bad ankle, wincing slightly, before continuing. "I began to see a lot of weaknesses in my chancellor that I did not like. I was thinking of giving you Ulrich's position, before all this trouble came up with the poacher. Ulrich suspected as much. But I never imagined he would try to kill you until you came yesterday and told me his nephew had given you a false message. I could not find Ulrich anywhere, and now, of course, you have solved the mystery of where he was."

The margrave quirked a brow at Jorgen, then gave him a more piercing look. "And now, I believe you have something to tell me."

"Oh yes, my lord. You wish to know the identity of the poacher. I have discovered some very interesting information. But first, I will tell you—the poacher is Odette Menkels." Even as he said the words, his heart crashed against his ribs as he felt as if he was betraying her. But he had no choice. Lord Thornbeck could find out fairly easily who had been injured and staying at his cottage for two days, if he didn't know already.

"Yes. Go on." The margrave didn't seem surprised.

"Odette started poaching deer almost a year ago because she wanted to be able to feed the poor of Thornbeck. Her uncle, Rutger Menkels, provided her with three to five young men to help her dress the animals and take them from the forest. He also helped distribute the meat to the poor. But six months ago, he had just lost two shiploads of goods, as well as a caravan from the Orient, and, unbeknownst to Odette, he started selling the meat out of the back of The Red House."

Jorgen tried to read the margrave's reaction, but he wasn't sure if his expression was cold, hard, or something else.

"Odette is the young woman who was wearing the white swan costume at my ball, is she not?"

"Yes, my lord." No doubt he had seen Jorgen dancing with her.

"Mathis Papendorp seemed very interested in marrying her. I think I may have heard something about his having banns published."

"Yes, my lord." It made his heart sink just to acknowledge it. "But Mathis had a small part in all of this as well."

"Yes?"

"Rutger had not lost his land shipment to robbers after all. In fact, my friend Dieter Vogel discovered that Mathis was playing a trick on a fellow merchant. This fellow merchant thought a caravan of his goods had been stolen en route to Thornbeck, but Mathis had connived to have his own men steal them, after bribing the guards who were protecting the caravan. Mathis planned to hold the goods until this friend helped Mathis get something he wanted."

Lord Thornbeck was staring at him with a fierce look in his brown eyes. "I want names."

"The merchant Mathis had duped was Rutger Menkels. Once

Mathis got what he wanted, then he would miraculously recover the goods from the brigands who stole them and give them back to Rutger. He seemed to think it was a great jest."

"Very interesting. Go on."

"It turned out that Rutger was not rich anymore. Instead of being one of the wealthiest merchants in Thornbeck, he is in debt after losing his last few shipments of foreign goods. Mathis made sure Rutger thought he was completely ruined. Then he told Rutger that he would help him restore his fortune if Rutger would use his influence to convince Odette to marry him."

Lord Thornbeck nodded. "Thank you, Jorgen. You have been very helpful to me. You have rooted out a most unstable advisor in my chancellor and proven your loyalty to me by telling me that the woman you love was the notorious poacher."

Jorgen's face heated at the margrave's words. "I surmised that you would find out anyway, my lord."

"You surmised correctly. I had already found out the identity of the injured person you were harboring at your home. I merely wanted to see if you would tell me the truth yourself. And you also hoped that she would not be punished since she was marrying Mathis. Is that correct?"

"Ah . . . yes, my lord."

The margrave said nothing for several moments as he stared down at his desk. "Tell Odette that I shall wish her to answer for her crimes as soon as she is enough recovered to stand trial."

His throat clogged, and he had to swallow before he could speak. "Yes, my lord. At the moment, she is very ill. Her leg wound has turned septic."

"I am sorry to hear that. Is there anything I can do? The healer in the forest has a very good salve for septic wounds, I have heard."

"Susanna—and my mother—are tending her now. I thank you, my lord."

"She shall recover, then, I dare say. I shall expect her when she has. And her uncle I shall arrest today. And now . . ." Lord Thornbeck paused, staring at Jorgen for a long time. "I have need of a new chancellor to keep up with my letters and ledgers and other documents. I have been impressed with you, Jorgen, and I would like you to take over the position."

"My lord, I would be honored."

Another trace of a smile came over the margrave's face. "Good. I shall speak with you later about all your duties and the other details of the office. For now, you may go."

"Yes, my lord."

Suddenly, Jorgen was not sure he had done the right thing. Odette's uncle would be thrown in the dungeon, and with this new information, the margrave might not allow Mathis to protect Odette.

Jorgen would do what he could to protect her, but he would also be praying hard for God's mercy and power to save her.

# 29

ODETTE AWOKE THE next morning to the turpentine smell. This time Frau Hartman was spreading it on her leg.

"Good morning. How are you feeling?" Frau Hartman smiled at her. No one else appeared to be in the room.

Odette pushed herself up. "Much better." She no longer felt hot and feverish.

Jorgen's mother wiped her hand, then fetched Odette some water. It tasted wonderful.

"Are you hungry?"

"Famished."

"That is a good sign. I will go find you something to eat." She smiled and patted Odette's cheek before leaving the room.

Odette lifted the sheet to look at her leg. The wound was covered with a yellow salve that smelled of turpentine and beeswax. Her arm was covered with a bandage. It barely hurt but did itch. She reached up to scratch it, but it was still too sore, and anyway, the bandage prevented her from getting at it.

When Frau Hartman returned with a bowl of soup, Odette took it gratefully and ate it as quickly as she could keep getting the spoon to her mouth. She also ate the bread and stewed fruit she had brought her.

"Thank you, that was wonderful." Odette sank back into the pillows. "Is Rutger well? I know he must be worried."

Frau Hartman half smiled, half frowned. "Your uncle was taken away by Lord Thornbeck's men yesterday. It is a good thing one of your servants came and told me how sick you were so I could look after you."

Her stomach twisted at poor Uncle Rutger's fate. "I am so grateful to you. And how is Jorgen? Is he . . . Is he well?"

Frau Hartman winked. "He is well enough. Only worried about you. He fell asleep after I told him your fever had broken and your wound seemed better."

Odette nodded, her heart pounding extra fast. Perhaps Jorgen still cared for her. "He did not get in trouble with the margrave because of me, did he?"

"No, I expect not."

It was hard to imagine Rutger in the dungeon.

The margrave should know by now that Odette was the poacher. Soon she would be locked in the dungeon beside Rutger.

⁓

Odette did not see Jorgen that day. But Frau Hartman stayed and took care of her. Cook and Heinke also stayed and helped, but the other servants had abandoned them after hearing that Rutger was in the dungeon. No doubt they suspected Odette could not pay them without Rutger—which was true.

"I feel guilty," Odette said when Frau Hartman came in to bring her some food. "Letting you take care of me seems wrong."

"Child, don't say another word about it." Frau Hartman pointed her finger at Odette. "It has been so long since anyone let me take care of them. This is what I love, and I will not let you deny me the pleasure of seeing you get well." She gave her a smile before leaving the chamber.

Later that day, Mathis entered her room without any preamble. "My darling Odette." He came toward her bed. "I heard how sick you have been. I have sent for my own physician to come and tend you."

"That is not necessary. I have all the help I need."

"But I want to care for you. Are you sure?" His clothing was pretentious, and Odette found herself comparing him to Jorgen, who dressed sensibly in soft leather and linen. Mathis wore silk and fine wool and layers of clothing that were much too warm for late summer. The liripipe from his hat hung down past his waist, and the toes of his shoes curled over the top of his feet.

"Yes, I thank you. I am much better now anyway."

"I also heard that your uncle was taken to the dungeon, and I assure you I am working to get him released. I shall protect you, Odette, and I shall save your uncle. This I vow to you." He took her hand between both of his and bent to kiss it. "I shall use my influence—my money—to make sure your uncle shall be restored to his place in business and in society in Thornbeck. My wife shall be safe, and all her family as well."

Odette's stomach flipped, as it always did when thinking of marrying Mathis. She was grateful at the thought that he would save Rutger, but . . . She wished she didn't have to be in debt to him. Even Jorgen had said she would be foolish not to marry Mathis.

"Thank you," Odette said, hoping she sounded weak. "When I am fully recovered, please come back and talk with me some more."

Mathis took the hint and stood to go. "My dear." He kissed her hand again, then gazed into her eyes for a few moments before turning to leave.

Two days later, Odette was able to walk around her house with only mild pain. Her arm was better as well, and she felt much stronger. She had not seen Jorgen since the night she was so feverish and in pain, when he sat by her bed and bathed her face with water.

As she sat by the front window watching the people walking by below, she wondered when she had last done this. It felt strange just to sit and do nothing, not to go hunting, night after night, to know that the poor were going hungry, to miss teaching her class. Were the children sitting there outside the town wall waiting for her, wondering why she did not come, why she had abandoned them? Did they feel as alone as she had felt after her mother and father died?

A tear slipped down her cheek just as she heard footsteps coming up the stairs. She wiped it away before Jorgen called, "Odette, may I come in?"

"Please do." She smiled in anticipation.

Jorgen appeared in the doorway and came toward her. "My mother says you are well, and I can see that you are."

"I am much better. No fever."

"And your leg wound is no longer inflamed, I hear."

"Thanks to your mother's care, I am doing very well."

He came and sat in a chair near her. "I want to ask you about the children."

"I have been thinking about them too. I feel so sad that I haven't been able to teach their lessons. And now that I realize the meat I was poaching was not going to feed them . . ." Odette shook her head. "I feel like the last year of my life was wasted, stolen, blackened. I wronged you, I wronged the margrave, and I stole from the king. And I failed to help the ones who truly needed help."

"You were doing what you thought was right." Jorgen took her hand between his, but then he seemed to realize what he was doing, and he gently laid it back down and pulled his hands back.

"Odette." He cleared his throat and began to look and sound more businesslike. "I want you to think about what should be done. If you could do anything you wanted, what would you do for the poor children?"

"Well . . ." Odette had thought about this before. "I think there should be a home for orphaned children. The children should be provided food and clothing and be allowed to go to the town school. They should have kind people watching over them, people who love children and will make them feel loved. And for poor mothers there should be a place for them to go where their children are watched over while they learn a skill or learn how to create things to sell, like clothing or candles or something that will earn them enough money to live."

"Would you like to be in charge of a place like that?"

"Me?" Odette laughed. "Of course. I am a hard worker, you know."

"Yes, I do know."

"And even though I am good at hunting, I am good at other things as well."

Jorgen nodded. "I have no doubt of that."

"But I am sure the margrave will want to see me, and I am ready to confess my wrongs to him."

"Yes," Jorgen said with a sober expression. "He will send for you when you are feeling better. Perhaps even tomorrow."

She deserved punishment. Even she could admit that. She also quaked inside at the thought of that punishment, but she nodded so as not to reveal her fears to Jorgen.

He stood. "I must go, but I shall return when the margrave sends for you."

Odette's stomach sank a little. Must he go so soon? She had hardly spoken to him in days. But she merely nodded.

Jorgen had been gone for a few minutes when Odette looked out the window and saw Anna hurrying up the street. She seemed to stop at Odette's door. A few minutes later, she came into her room.

"Odette!" she cried in her breathiest voice, her hands cupping her cheeks. "I just heard you were hurt! And Rutger is in the dungeon! What happened?" She sank into the chair that Jorgen had just vacated.

Odette sighed. "What is the gossip?"

"That Rutger was selling poached meat out of The Red House and that you were the poacher." Her voice sounded shocked. "I heard you were hurt from someone who knows Susanna the healer and that Rutger is in the dungeon. What happened? Please tell me!"

"Jorgen saw me poaching and he shot me, once in the arm and in the leg."

Anna gasped and covered her mouth.

"He did not know it was me. His mother has been taking care of me. But, Anna"—tears filled her eyes—"Rutger was not giving the meat to the poor. For the past six months, all the good I thought I was doing . . . It was only for Rutger to try to pay off his debt."

Anna put her arms around Odette's shoulders as she couldn't hold back her tears any longer. She wiped at her eyes with her handkerchief, taking deep breaths to try to dispel the tears.

"Why didn't God stop me? Why didn't He let me find out what Rutger was doing?"

"I do not know, but you were doing what you thought was right. Rutger is the one who did wrong."

"I did wrong too. I wronged Jorgen. I wronged the margrave. I stole, and it was all for naught."

"God knows our hearts, Odette." Anna pulled away and looked into Odette's eyes. "He knows your heart and your love for the poor. God knows everything."

"Perhaps the worst part is that I told Mathis I would marry him. And Jorgen told me he thought I should marry Mathis. That I would be a fool not to." She put her face in her hands, her tears turning cold. Jorgen didn't care for her. How could God fix this? Did God even care about her, after what she had done?

"You must not cry so much. It will make you sick and cause an imbalance in your humors."

Odette made an effort to stop crying, and Anna sat back in the chair. "Tell me something about you," Odette told Anna. Odette needed to think about someone else for a change.

Anna sighed. "My two children have been sick. That is why I did not come here sooner. But they are better now."

"I am so sorry they've been sick! But very glad they are well again. Did anyone else get sick?"

They talked about which servants were also sick and for how long, and all about her children's sickness, plus several household matters. Anna took great pride in keeping her household running smoothly. And Odette told Anna all the reasons it was best if she married Mathis. Then Anna said she had to get back home.

She hugged Odette. "You do not think the margrave will put you in the dungeon? No, of course he won't," Anna answered her own question and shook her head. "Do not even think about such a thing. Since you are marrying Mathis, I'm sure nothing bad will happen. But if I can help with anything, please tell me."

"Thank you, Anna. I will." But the only person who could help her now was God Himself.

# 30

JORGEN ARRIVED AT Odette's home the next morning on horseback with a second horse in tow. He dismounted and tied the horses so they would not wander off. He knocked on the door and was allowed to go up to see Odette.

"I have been sent to bring you to face the margrave."

Odette sighed. "Let us get this over and done."

She wore a dark-purple underdress with a lighter purple surcoat. The cutaway sides draped in folds below her hips that she had to hold up with one hand when she walked. It was beautiful, and she was beautiful in it. Her blond hair hung down her back in large curls, with a simple circlet and ribbons at her temples. She was more breathtaking than usual.

He helped her down the steps, going in front of her and letting her lean on his shoulder.

When she saw the horses, she stopped and looked at him. "The margrave sent two horses? Was he not afraid I would break away from you and escape?"

Jorgen shook his head as he untied them. "I know you would not try to run away." He glanced at her. "I did get these horses from the margrave, but he is selling them to me."

"You own two horses now?" She smiled at him.

Was she impressed? He wrapped his hands around her waist and lifted her into the sidesaddle, careful of her injured leg and arm.

They set out for Thornbeck Castle. While walking the horses through town, they were both silent, but every time he glanced at her to make sure she was following him and not having any difficulties, she was looking at him.

Once they had gone out the town gate and started on the road to Thornbeck Castle, Odette's expression turned dejected, and she stared down at the horse's neck. No doubt she was dreading having to face the margrave.

After riding in silence for a few minutes, Odette asked, "What do you think the margrave will do?"

"I do not know." What if the margrave wanted to have her tried by a judge and executed? He would have to risk his new position as chancellor to save her. He would do anything, even lose the position he had always hoped for—even though Odette didn't love him enough to marry him. Even though she was marrying Mathis.

He shook off these morose thoughts, for Odette's face looked drawn and pale.

"Are you in pain?" he asked as they reached the front of the castle.

"No."

He went to help her dismount. Odette held on to him. She didn't meet his eyes, and she did not remove her hands from his shoulders. Instead, she seemed to be staring at his chest. Then her hands slipped around his neck and she pressed her face into his shoulder.

He wrapped his arms around her. Was she crying? She wasn't shaking or making any weeping sounds.

"I know I have no right," she whispered.

He stroked her hair and squeezed her shoulder. When she pulled away, he felt his heart wrench. But he let her go.

Odette took his arm, looking a little less pale as they went inside.

Odette and Jorgen were led into the margrave's library. Odette held her head high and tried to hide her limp. She greeted the margrave with a curtsy.

The margrave remained seated. He was scowling, but she thought that was probably his usual expression. Though he was handsome, it was not a warm and friendly handsome, like Jorgen's. It was a rugged, serious, intensely masculine handsome that made her shiver. He was the highest authority in Thornbeck and could do to her as he saw fit.

She and Jorgen stood in front of him. Her hands shook, so she clasped them together.

"Odette Menkels, I suppose you know why I have summoned you here."

"Yes, Lord Thornbeck."

"Do you deny that you poached scores of the king's deer from this forest?"

She calculated in her head. Yes, it was safe to say it was "scores."

"I do not deny it, my lord, but I am very repentant for what I did. I thought all the meat was going to feed the poor. I . . . I wanted to help the poor children whom I knew were going hungry."

The margrave's brows were still lowered. "So I have been told by Jorgen. But most of the meat was not going to the poor. Is that not true?"

"Yes, my lord."

"Can you prove that you did not know what Rutger was doing with the meat?"

Odette opened her mouth, not sure what to say. "I do not suppose I can prove it."

"You knew, did you not, that killing the deer in Thornbeck Forest is a crime against the king? And that the punishment for poaching is imprisonment, the loss of one's hand, or even execution?"

Her chest rose and fell, her face burning and her hands sweating. "Yes, my lord."

"The poaching of so many large animals was a grave loss to the king and may be the cause of wild boars, and therefore wolves, invading this area. Do you realize you are responsible for this?"

"N-no, my lord," she stammered. Jorgen had not told her that. "But I am very remorseful." Her lip trembled. She caught it between her teeth.

"Your actions were lawless and rebellious."

She glanced at Jorgen. She was ashamed that he had to hear his lord speak to her of all her sins. By the look on his face, perhaps Jorgen had thought the margrave would be lenient to her and he hadn't expected the margrave to berate her.

"You destroyed perhaps hundreds of the king's deer, and all to help pay your uncle's debt."

"That is true. I did." Her voice sounded breathy as she held back tears.

"You will leave your home by the end of the week, as it now belongs to me, in payment for the loss of these deer. In fact, all of your uncle's property is forfeit to me from this day onward."

"Yes, my lord."

"You will be available to help control the population of dangerous predatory animals, such as wolves and wild boar, should that become necessary, by virtue of your great skill with a longbow."

"Yes, my lord." The air rushed back into her lungs. At least he did not intend to execute her. And he couldn't mean to cut off her hand, since she could not stretch a bowstring if he did.

"For the sake of my forester, Jorgen Hartman, I will not punish you beyond the wounds you have already sustained by consequence of your poaching. However, I have one stipulation." The margrave paused, looking from her to Jorgen and back to her, as if to make sure he had their complete attention. "Since I cannot have a lawless woman running around with only a weak-willed uncle to restrain her . . ."

Again he paused while Odette's heart beat faster.

"You must marry—immediately."

"Oh."

"Mathis Papendorp has informed me that he is planning to marry you. However, I have another suggestion." He glowered at her from beneath thick black brows.

Odette's mouth had gone dry. She couldn't even swallow. What would he say next?

"I suggest you marry Jorgen Hartman. In fact, I strongly suggest it."

Odette looked at Jorgen. He looked back at her. By his wide eyes and open mouth, he had not expected the margrave to say that any more than she had.

She had heard of men avoiding execution if a woman, any woman, agreed to marry them.

Wait. Had he not said that he would not punish her? She could marry Jorgen and not have to worry about punishment? She didn't have to marry Mathis!

But what about the children? What about Rutger? Mathis would not use his money to help either one of them if she married

Jorgen. But God had provided for the children without her help for the past six months.

She gazed up at Jorgen, standing just beside her. His chest was rising and falling fast. He licked his lips. Was his mouth as dry as hers?

Jorgen turned to the margrave. "My lord, I do not wish you to force her. I—"

"No, Jorgen, let her decide," Lord Thornbeck cut him off. "You deserve to have the woman you want to marry."

Odette's face went hot. Yes, Jorgen deserved the woman he wanted to marry. But did he still want her? And he also deserved a woman who wanted to marry him. Would he protest to the point that the margrave would become enraged at him? She couldn't allow that.

"My lord," she said quickly, "I must first ask a question. Why would you have your forester marry me? Should you not allow him to choose?"

"He has already chosen." The margrave's voice was cool and expressionless. "He wishes to marry you. And I wish to grant him his desire—if you are as worthy as he thinks you are."

Jorgen was still red faced, but he was staring at her with that vulnerable look she could never resist, the look that was melting her heart. "Marry me, Odette."

Her heart stuttered. She swallowed and pushed back the longing to throw her arms around him. "I do want to marry Jorgen Hartman"—she wrenched her gaze from Jorgen and turned to the margrave—"with all my heart, but I do not accept him to escape punishment or to escape marrying someone I do not love. I accept him because he is the best man I have ever known. He is good and kind and honest. He is exactly the kind of man I would wish to marry. I may not be worthy of him, but I love him."

She was afraid to look at Jorgen, her insides trembling at the bold words she had just spoken.

"Very well. I see." Lord Thornbeck cleared his throat. He gave a half smile and picked up some papers off the desk behind him and gazed down at them a moment. "And now I have some other problems to discuss with you both."

Odette's stomach fluttered. Other problems? Would he tell her that he had been in jest, that she, a poacher, would not be allowed to marry Jorgen, the best and most noble man in Thornbeck?

"Your uncle, Rutger Menkels, whom I have locked in my dungeon and from whom I have confiscated his property for his crimes . . . I have become aware that he was also wronged. Mathis Papendorp stole a large shipment of his goods."

What? Mathis had stolen from Rutger?

"Mathis schemed to make him destitute in order to marry you. Although he planned to give Rutger his property back, this is not something I take lightly. I was not amused when I heard this story, and now I plan to free your uncle and force Mathis to give him back twice as much as he stole from him, with interest."

Rutger would be released! Her shoulders relaxed as she let out a breath. And he wouldn't be destitute. "I thank you, my lord."

"I want to know"—he fixed Odette with a severe look—"why you were so determined to help the poor. Is this such a problem in Thornbeck that you, a young woman, would be bent on feeding them?"

She stared at the margrave. "Yes, my lord." Odette blinked, trying to think how to answer the unexpected question. "There are orphaned children who live in rickety shelters they have built themselves just outside the town wall. They are forced to steal and beg and look through garbage heaps to keep themselves alive. I believe there are at least twenty or thirty of these children, besides the ones who live on the streets in town. They need our help. They are only children and unable to earn enough money to buy food or provide decent shelter for themselves. It is our Christian duty to help them, for anyone who is able to help them."

"Odette teaches them to read a few days a week," Jorgen said when she paused. "She also brings them food and helps them when they are sick."

The margrave frowned again, his smile gone. "Jorgen has devised a plan whereby the people of Thornbeck might look after the poor orphan children of the town. I believe it is a plan you helped him with." He glanced at Odette. "It is a feasible plan that might all but eliminate the problem of children stealing bread and other food from the vendors at the market, while the merchants exercise their Christian duty, as you say, to care for the poor widows and orphans. Jorgen has spoken to the Bishop of Thornbeck, and he has offered a certain portion of the church's assets to this effort."

Odette's heart was in her throat as the margrave stared down at the parchment in his hands.

"Jorgen has some donors already secured from among our wealthier citizens. You have done a good job with this proposal." He raised his brows approvingly at Jorgen. "I do believe that Rutger Menkels's house, which is not far from the city center, will serve well as a home for orphans. What do you say, Odette?"

"Y-yes, my lord. I believe it would."

"And as I have acquired Rutger's storehouse near the north gate, I believe it may serve as a place for young widows to learn to work and earn money while their children are being cared for. What do you think, Jorgen?"

"Yes, my lord, I think you are right."

The margrave cleared his throat and frowned. "Jorgen may have told you, Odette, that I discovered it was my chancellor, Ulrich, who had been trying to kill him. It is fortunate he is not as good with a longbow as you are." Again, he looked pointedly at Odette. "Therefore, I have sent Ulrich to the dungeon and am in need of a new chancellor. Jorgen has shown that he is a man capable of great organization. He is intelligent and hardworking, as well as honest and trustworthy. Welcome to your new position, Jorgen."

"Thank you, my lord."

Odette sucked in a breath. She reached out and squeezed Jorgen's hand, smiling up at him.

"Now that you will be my new chancellor, I shall wish to have you living nearer to me. And since I have taken back the chancellor's property, I would like to bestow upon you the manor house on Red Stag Hill, which you can see from this window."

"My lord, I am grateful." Jorgen bowed.

"A new husband and wife need a home. And now I insist you take to wife this lawless young woman as quickly as may be."

Odette and Jorgen replied, "Thank you, my lord."

Jorgen looked across at her, a glint in his eye.

How their fortunes had reversed. She had thought his position too far beneath hers a few days ago. Now she was poor, stripped of her home and her security, and Jorgen was the new chancellor of Thornbeck, the owner of a beautiful manor house, and the advisor to the margrave. Just minutes before, marrying Mathis seemed her only choice, and now she found herself being ordered to marry Jorgen. But somehow she didn't mind.

"Jorgen," the margrave said, "come back tomorrow when we can discuss your new duties, and think about who you might choose to replace you as forester. In the next few weeks we will have a lot of work to do to implement your plans for the orphanage and workhouse. Odette may also come and give her input, if she wishes. But for now, you both may go."

Jorgen clasped her hand and they walked out of the margrave's library. As soon as they were out of sight of the margrave, she turned to him in the dimly lit corridor, slipped her arms around his neck, and before she could close her eyes, he was kissing her.

# 31

Jorgen kissed her like a man dying of thirst and she was the only source of water. He took her breath away. Odette was transported to a place that was above the earth, above the clouds, floating higher and higher.

She was marrying Jorgen Hartman.

When he pulled away, he looked into her eyes, then kissed her again, as if he needed one more sip. But then he needed another, and another, his hands coming up to cradle her face. Soon she was quite dizzy. She held on tighter, choosing not to tell him she needed to sit down until her knees stopped shaking.

He eventually stopped kissing her and pulled her close, her cheek against his shoulder and his arms encircling her. There seemed to be so much to say, so much to take in, so much she could hardly believe. They stood still, their hearts beating close together, not speaking, waiting for their rapid breathing to slow.

As the dizziness subsided, she squeezed him tighter, breathing in the smell of pennyroyal mint coming from his freshly washed shirt, filling her senses with Jorgen. "Thank you for wanting to help the children, and for your plans to start an orphanage and to help the poor."

He buried his hand in her hair and bent until his forehead touched hers. "I hoped it would please you."

"It does. Very much." His nearness, his touch, his smell, and the lingering feeling of his lips on hers all combined to make her heart soar. How was it possible to feel so free when she was about to be married, to belong to someone forever?

"Odette," he breathed. The masculine rumble of his voice sent a shiver across her shoulders.

"Are you sure you want to marry me?" Odette asked.

He tilted her face up and kissed her again. "Yes."

Her heart was racing. Might someone be watching them from down the long corridor? The heat in her cheeks intensified and she whispered, "We should go before someone sees us."

He stared into her eyes before breaking away and helping her walk toward the front door of Thornbeck Castle. As she held on to him and leaned against his side, she couldn't seem to stop sighing. Or smiling. Or reliving his kisses.

He stopped her halfway down the corridor and kissed her again.

How had she not always known she loved Jorgen Hartman? And how had God worked everything out so she could marry him? After all she had done—poaching the deer that it was his job to protect, deceiving him, and after her uncle had spurned him because he was a forester—to be ordered by the margrave to marry Jorgen seemed the greatest of ironies . . . and miracles.

⁓

Jorgen helped Odette down from the horse. She was so focused on him that she was surprised to see Mathis standing just behind Jorgen.

"Odette," he said quickly, "I know your uncle is in the dungeon, but I assure you I am working to get him out as soon as possible."

"That is not necessary, Mathis. Lord Thornbeck has already agreed to set him free."

"Oh. That is very good." Mathis stepped closer to her, but so did Jorgen, putting himself between them. Mathis glanced up at Jorgen but then kept talking to Odette. "I still want to marry you, no matter what the margrave says or does—"

"The margrave has taken my uncle's house and will turn it into an orphanage. And he has ordered you to repay Uncle Rutger's goods that you stole, double, with interest."

Mathis blanched and clutched at his throat. "But I . . . It was only a joke. I was going to give it back to him."

"The margrave was not amused."

Mathis stammered, "I . . . I . . . but I—"

"And the margrave also knows about the little joke you played on Jorgen and me when you tricked him into thinking another woman was me."

Mathis, still pale, just stared at her with his mouth open.

"I will not marry you, Mathis. But Lord Thornbeck has approved my marriage to Jorgen Hartman. And now you may go. I do not wish to see you again."

Odette grabbed Jorgen's hand and led him inside her house— soon to be the orphanage—without saying another word.

⌇

Once inside Odette's former house, Jorgen said, "You certainly set Mathis Papendorp straight. I almost felt sorry for him."

She slipped her arms around his back. The invitation in her eyes was too much to resist. Pulling her closer, he kissed her.

Oh, but she was sweet and mysterious and almost too good to be earthly. He had to rein himself in and cut the kiss short. After all, they had a lot of planning to do, a lot of moving, and a lot of decisions to make. He couldn't spend all day kissing her, no matter how much he wanted to.

She nestled against his chest in the sweetest way, making his breath hitch in his throat. He hugged her close, brushing his cheek against her silky hair.

"When can we marry?" She sounded breathless.

Was she so eager? His breath hitched again. "The margrave said I should take my lawless young woman to wife as soon as possible."

He squeezed her tighter and she laughed, a soft sound.

"Are you sure you are able to keep me from being lawless?" She pulled away and looked up at him.

"I believe I am."

There was a dangerous glint in her eye. "I hope you do not start talking like the margrave now that you'll be working so closely with him. 'Take to wife this lawless woman,'" she mimicked in an approximation of Lord Thornbeck's gruff voice.

"No wife of mine is allowed to mock the lord of the land." Jorgen looked down at her, trying to feign a stern expression.

She grinned and pulled his head down for another long, satisfying kiss.

Marriage. Yes, how soon could they marry? "I suppose it will take three weeks to cry the banns."

"Three weeks," she breathed, then pushed him away. "You had better go see the priest, then."

He touched her cheek, then squeezed her shoulder. "I will leave one horse here, in case you need it."

He leaned down and kissed her, harder than he meant to, and when he pulled away, her eyes were still closed, as if she hadn't wanted the kiss to end. His heart skipped.

Three weeks. Just three more weeks.

# 32

AFTER TWO WEEKS, Jorgen was pleased to report to Lord Thornbeck that Odette already had a dozen children living in the former Menkels home. Their cook had stayed on, and Kathryn had also moved in to help and seemed to enjoy taking care of the younger children. His own mother was helping, and she had never seemed happier, as she now had many children to care for.

"Odette will be staying at the house for one more week, until our marriage, and she will help with managing the women's workhouse at Rutger's old storehouse. We are still trying to get that set up since the storehouse needed to be cleared out and made a bit more comfortable."

"Excellent," the margrave said. "I shall come and inspect it and the orphanage when all the work is complete. And I hear the townspeople are being generous, but I shall not allow anyone to outgive me." Lord Thornbeck gave a half smile.

"Yes, my lord."

And now that things were working out so well, Jorgen was more and more preoccupied with getting the chancellor's manse ready to bring Odette home as his bride.

But first . . . He and his mother had prepared a basket of food, and Jorgen left Thornbeck Castle, bound for the orphanage. He found Odette playing a game with several of the younger children. When she saw him, her eyes widened and she smiled. She left the children to play with Kathryn and walked toward him.

The children were making a lot of noise, so when she came near, he figured it would be safe to say quietly, "I wish I could kiss you. Would you think it improper if I did?"

"Yes, I would." Her cheeks turned a gratifying pink.

"Then will you go on a picnic with me? I have not been able to talk with you alone since the day you agreed to marry me."

Her lips curved deliciously, and she leaned toward him. "That sounds lovely."

He waited while she went to tell Kathryn that she was leaving, and after giving some instructions to those in the kitchen, they were on horseback and headed to his favorite spot by a small stream, deep in Thornbeck Forest.

"I don't think I have ever gone on a picnic." She smiled at him from atop her horse.

"Never?"

"Never alone with a handsome young man." She glanced at him out of the corner of her eye. If she was trying to be flirtatious, she was doing a worthy job.

They reached the spot, and she jumped down from her horse before he could help her. He unstrapped the basket from the back of his horse and carried it to where she stood with the blanket still folded under her arm.

"This is beautiful. Look at the blue flowers there, and the pink ones. And the stream sounds peaceful." She spoke in a hushed voice. "I have never seen this place . . . well, not in the daylight, leastways." She spread out the blanket on the ground and he set down the basket.

She was quiet as they set out the food, sat down, and began

to eat. Perhaps she was listening to the birds or the stream gurgle over the rocks, but he got the feeling that she was thinking, hard, about all the things that were still between them. Or maybe that was only because that was what he was thinking about.

When they had eaten their fill of the bread and cheese and drunk some water he had brought, she took a handful of walnuts and raisins and picked them up one by one with her fingertips and put them in her mouth. A strand of blond hair fell loose from her braid and waved against her cheek. He longed to brush it back, imagining how it would feel against his palm.

But that was not why he had brought her here.

"Odette?"

She turned to look at him, her eyes wide and innocent. Then her face sobered. "What is it?"

"I want to know, honestly, how you feel about marrying me. I would have asked you to marry me anyway if Lord Thornbeck had not practically ordered you to. That is not the way I would have wished to have done things."

She gave him a half smile. "I meant what I said to the margrave. You are the best man I have ever known, and I love you." Her tone sent a shot of warmth through him.

They were seated a little too far apart for him to touch her. He should have brought a smaller blanket.

"But I keep wondering, what must you think of me?" She looked away, then down at her hands. "I know you were very angry with me, and rightfully so, when you realized you had been telling me about your struggles to find the poacher, and all along I knew exactly who the poacher was. You cannot deny you were furious with me. Why would you want to marry me?"

Jorgen stood and held his hand out to her. She took it and he pulled her to her feet. The pained-but-hopeful look in her blue eyes made his heart expand and fill his chest. "I wanted to avenge my father's death so much that I wanted to shoot the poacher. But I only wanted to wound him, not because I had mercy on him, but so he could suffer execution for what he had done to my father."

He closed his eyes a moment. When he was able to speak again, he went on, determined to say it. "When you were bleeding, and then again when your leg turned septic, I thought it was my fault . . . because of my hatred for the man who had killed my father."

He brushed back the strand of hair that had escaped her braid, letting his fingers linger on her soft cheek. "And then when you saved my life by shooting Ulrich . . ." He looked into her eyes to convey the truth of his words. "It was not difficult to forgive you."

Odette's warm smile sent an ache through his chest. "And I forgive you. You did not know you were shooting me, and you were only doing your job." She placed her hand on his shoulder.

"You could have died. And you almost did."

"But I didn't die. And it was my own fault, anyway." After a pause, she said, "I am glad we found out that it was Ulrich trying to kill you, but I'm sorry you still have not captured the poacher who killed your father."

"Perhaps someday we will. Even though I do still want to capture him, it no longer seems to matter as much." He thought for a moment. "You know, I would not be marrying you if you weren't such a good archer."

"How is that?"

"Because if you had not been so good at poaching, Rutger might have convinced you to marry Mathis months ago."

"Very amusing."

"I love you, Odette." In case she was still wondering, he made it very clear. "Even though I did feel hurt when I realized you were the poacher, it was not difficult to forgive you. I love you too much to stay angry with you for long."

"Good." She nestled her face against his neck. "I do not think I was able to forgive Rutger that quickly. But he has suffered too. I am thankful the margrave allowed him out of the dungeon after three days. He found a small house near the south gate. Did you know?"

"Yes."

She sighed, her breath warm against the base of his throat. "I keep thinking how everything has turned out, how everything is the reverse of how it began . . . the opposite of what I thought would happen."

He rubbed the back of her shoulder, wondering when he might kiss her again. "I know."

They stood like that for several moments. Then Odette lifted her head and looked him in the eye. "I am so overjoyed to be marrying you. I hope you don't change your mind."

She was looking at his lips. He kissed her but purposely kept it brief.

One more week. Just one more week.

⁓

Odette awakened with a sense of anticipation, a bit of crispness in the late-summer air.

Her sleepy eyes flew wide. No wonder she felt a sense of anticipation. Today was her wedding day!

She jumped out of bed as Anna came into her room, bearing a tray of food.

"I was astonished at you sleeping late on your wedding day!" Anna said. "I did not sleep at all the night before my wedding."

While they ate breakfast together, Odette was thinking that

she would never wake up in this room again. Already she shared it with two other girls. With Odette married and gone, more girls could come and have a home here. It felt so good and so fitting. Odette sighed.

When they were finished, Anna helped Odette on with her dress. A shade of blue green, the dress was made from Flemish fabric Rutger had brought home eight or nine months ago. The fabric itself was decorated with a repeating pattern of silver and green stitching, with a matching border around the neck and a belt that settled below her waist on her hips.

The style of the gown was simple and fitted, with sleeves that hung down to the floor. When she had first tried it on, Anna said, "It brings out the color in your eyes."

"I will go see if the children are getting ready to go to the church." Anna hurried out of the room while a servant finished preparing Odette's hair.

A few minutes later, her hair was ready and Anna was running up the stairs. "Jorgen is here! And he is impatient to see you. He sent me to hurry you down. Odette, you look beautiful." Anna stood staring at her from head to toe. "That dress is perfect."

"Thank you." Odette gathered her skirt to go.

"No, don't go yet!" Anna held up a hand to stop her.

"Why not?"

"You should make him wait."

"But you said he was impatient."

"That is why you should make him wait." Anna winked. "Husbands need to know right away that we will not be rushed. And they like it when we stand up to them and do not let them order us around."

"And you know this how?" Odette couldn't decide whether to laugh or look shocked.

"Because Peter and I have been married four years." Anna winked. "And my mother and father have been married for thirty years and they are still in love. I used to hear them laughing together every night, and I don't have ten brothers and sisters for nothing." She gave Odette a knowing look. "My mother never lets my father tell her what to do without telling him what she thinks."

"Does she do what he tells her?"

Anna shrugged. "Usually. But he is never left to wonder what she thinks about it."

Odette laughed. "It sounds like it works for them. But I see no reason to keep Jorgen waiting. I am ready."

Odette made her way down the steps, holding up her skirt so she wouldn't tread on the hem. As she neared the bottom, Jorgen stared up at her. He brought his lips together as if he were about to whistle, then put his hands behind his head. "You take the breath from my chest, you are so beautiful."

"Thank you."

The look in his eyes was everything she could have wanted. He didn't even blink. But while he couldn't take his eyes off her, he seemed reluctant to touch her. So she stood on the tips of her toes and kissed him on the lips.

He gazed into her eyes while lifting her hand to his chest. He pressed her palm over his heart and she felt it pounding. She smiled as she took his other hand and placed it over her heart.

"I am ready to marry you," she whispered.

"Are you marrying me because you want to or because the margrave ordered you to?" There was a twinkle in his eye because he already knew the answer to that question.

"Neither."

He raised an eyebrow at her.

"I'm marrying you because . . ." She frowned and looked up at the ceiling, as though she were trying to think of a reason. "Because you are the only person I know who is as good with a longbow as I am."

He snorted, grinned, then kissed her.

"Can you not wait until after the wedding?" Anna was standing behind Odette, frowning and shaking her head at them.

When everyone had gathered on the ground floor of the now-lively house, including all the orphans living there, they set out for the church.

Thornbeck Cathedral had never looked more radiant, its stained glass windows sparkling in the midday sun and its turrets rising into the blue sky. Odette squeezed Jorgen's hand and didn't let go as the priest met them on the steps. Soon she would be the wife of the Margrave of Thornbeck's chancellor, the wife of the former forester, the wife of Jorgen Hartman.

As they said their vows, she couldn't stop glancing at him, with his thick brows low over his eyes, his perfect face serious and even reverent. When she had met him at the Midsummer festival, she could never have imagined everything that would happen. Now she was marrying the right man at the right time for the right reasons.

Because love was the best reason of all.

# ACKNOWLEDGMENTS

I WANT TO thank everyone who has helped me with this book, starting with my wonderful agent, Natasha Kern. Thanks for pushing me to come up with the best possible stories with plots that hold together, and for always being willing to give advice and help. Besides helping me with proposals and so many other things, you are simply the most savvy and courageous defibrillator of stalled-out dreams I know.

I owe so much to Becky Monds for helping me whip this book into shape! You saw exactly what needed to be fixed, tweaked, and changed in the characters and the plot, and I am more grateful to you for that than I can say. I am happier with this book than I could have ever been without your expert insight! Thank you.

I want to thank Julee Schwarzburg for her meticulous line-editing expertise. Thanks so much for all the help! It is much stronger for all your work, and I learned a lot from you.

I want to thank my first readers and critiquers: Carol Moncado and Katie Clark, who made me feel good about the early draft. And thanks to Carol, Suzy, Regina, Grace, Faith, and Joe for being willing to let me bounce plot ideas off you. You guys are the best!

I want to thank those who are always willing to pray for me and encourage me, especially Regina Carbulon, Suzy Parish, Jessica Bates, Karma Malone, and Ken and Dene Finley. Thank you so much! I don't know how I would do this without your prayers.

I want to thank Daisy Hutton and Jason Short for seeing potential in me and being the impetus for this series of medieval fairy tales for adults, and Daisy for making it happen so quickly. I thank God for you and all the people at Thomas Nelson who do the work to make sure my book is well received. May God bless you for it!

Lastly, I want to thank my awesome readers who write me the sweetest messages through Facebook, Twitter, and e-mail. You are my inspiration! I love you all.

# DISCUSSION QUESTIONS

1. Do you think Odette is justified in shooting the margrave's deer illegally in order to feed the poor? Why or why not? What about her background has led her to become a poacher?

2. What do you think of Odette's criteria for the man she should marry? What about Rutger's criteria for the man Odette should marry? Did you understand why she felt obligated to marry someone who could help feed the children?

3. What do you think of hunting animals for food? If you had lived in the 1300s, do you think your ideas about hunting would have been different? How has a modern lifestyle influenced people's thoughts about hunting?

4. How did the fact that Odette and Jorgen were both orphans and had gone hungry as children influence how they felt about the poor? What was Anna's point when she said to Odette, "You're not responsible for every single person in Thornbeck"? Was it healthy or unhealthy for Odette to feel so responsible for feeding the poor and to go about it the way she did?

5. What do you think of Odette's and Jorgen's efforts to help Kathryn when she was working at the brothel? What caused her to go back to The Red House?

6. Is it possible to be too loyal or to be loyal to the wrong people? Who or what were Jorgen and Odette loyal to? How did their loyalties influence their behaviors?

7. Did you blame Jorgen for kissing the look-alike woman at the ball? How would you have felt if you were Odette?

8. What was Jorgen's reaction to shooting Odette? How would you have felt if you were Jorgen? If you were Odette? Would you have found it easy to forgive?

9. What was Brother Philip's attitude toward women? How do you think men's attitudes toward women have changed over the centuries?

10. What were Jorgen's and Odette's attitudes toward the Bible? Do you think Odette treasured the Bible more because it was scarce and she could only read it when she could borrow portions of it from someone else? Does this change the way you think about owning a Bible?

11. Do you think the margrave's judgments and punishments against Odette and Rutger were just? What was your favorite action taken by the margrave?

12. Did you like the parallels in this story to the *Swan Lake* story? What were the similarities to "Robin Hood"?

13. If not for Jorgen, do you think Odette would have married Mathis? Would Mathis have made a good husband? Why or why not?

14. How did this verse come true for Odette: "In all things God works for the good of those who love him and are called according to his purpose"?

# The
# GOLDEN
# BRAID

## The one who needs rescuing isn't always the one in the tower.

Rapunzel can throw a knife better than any man around. And her skills as an artist rival those of any artist she's met. But for a woman in medieval times, the one skill she most desires is the hardest one to obtain: the ability to read.

Available in print and e-book
November 2015

THOMAS NELSON
*Since 1798*

# ABOUT THE AUTHOR

MELANIE DICKERSON is a two-time Christy Award finalist and author of *The Healer's Apprentice*, winner of the National Readers Choice Award for Best First Book in 2010, and *The Merchant's Daughter*, winner of the 2012 Carol Award. She spends her time writing romantic medieval stories at her home near Huntsville, Alabama, where she lives with her husband and two daughters.

Website: www.MelanieDickerson.com
Twitter: @melanieauthor
Facebook: MelanieDickersonBooks

# About the Author

Jodie Westfall Photography

MELANIE DICKERSON IS a two-time Christy Award finalist and author of *The Healer's Apprentice*, winner of the National Readers Choice Award for Best First Book in 2010, and *The Merchant's Daughter*, winner of the 2012 Carol Award. She spends her time writing romantic medieval stories at her home near Huntsville, Alabama, where she lives with her husband and two daughters.

Website: www.MelanieDickerson.com
Twitter: @melanieauthor
Facebook: MelanieDickersonBooks